# JADE DRAGON

## Andy Phillips

ACTION
GIRL
BOOKS

*For Shakti Chen, the actress who played China / Scarlet Leader in the 1986 action movie "Unmasking the Idol." Many years later, I created my own female ninja in this work. But she played the character who first got me interested in heroines and villainesses.*

# CHAPTER ONE

## *A Woman in the Crowd*

Jade arrived at the Moscone Convention Center just before eight o'clock. Unlike other, more historic buildings in downtown San Francisco, the conference venue was a modern structure fit for the twenty-first century. Its top-notch facilities, central location, and proximity to the bay attracted companies from all over the world. Admittance to most meetings was by invitation only, and tonight was no different.

As usual, Dragonsoft had spared no expense on presentation. Laser beacons shone on a banner draped above the main entrance. On black sheeting, the company logo was displayed prominently: a scaled, fire-breathing dragon straight out of medieval legend. And superimposed over the creature's belly in silvery, old style English lettering: *Annual Conference XII.*

Jade had never been to the Moscone Center, but a quick

browse through the official website had given her an idea what to expect. Within the glass and steel walls were three floors of presentation rooms, meeting areas, restaurants, and Internet connections for a thousand laptop computers. Just as well, since the crowd outside was at least two hundred strong.

Other than a few homeless people squatting along Fourth Street, everyone present was here for the big event. The male to female ratio was approximately four to one. The few women wore thick coats to ward off the effects of the wintry night. All except for Jade.

Her bright green evening dress flapped against her knees as she strode purposefully towards the entrance, unfazed by the chilly December breeze. Three brute-faced Neanderthals in tuxedos manned the front doors. One man checked tickets while the others lingered in the background, ready to leap into action at the first sign of trouble. Jade's name—real or assumed—wasn't on the official guest list, but she'd devised a plan to get past the gatekeepers. All she needed was an unsuspecting victim.

Twenty feet from the entrance, she chose her target. Acting the dumb blonde, Jade tripped over a raised manhole cover and stumbled into the path of an Asian businessman. Despite being handicapped by high heels, she ably regained her balance.

The man was not so agile or fortunate. He tried in vain to recover from his fall, but only succeeded in landing chest down on the sidewalk. As he wiped his bloodied nose, Jade turned, kneeled beside him, and extended a silk-gloved hand.

"Ever so sorry," she said, greeting him with a warm smile. "I really should watch where I'm going."

When he noticed he'd become the center of attention, the Asian reluctantly accepted Jade's offer of help. Whatever anger he'd suppressed resurfaced once he saw oily smears all over his five hundred dollar suit. Without so much as a word, he pushed her hands away, and stormed off to join his partner: a shapely Oriental who looked less than half his age.

While the couple engaged in heated conversation, the cause of their grief turned her back and allowed herself a faint smirk of triumph. Several minutes later, the Asian would realize his ticket was missing, but by then it was too late. The thief had disappeared into the crowd.

The conference center's lobby was packed. Even amongst their business associates, high-ranking executives stood out like proverbial sore thumbs, drinking vintage wine and munching fine chocolate whilst those lower down the corporate ladder looked on with envy. Elsewhere in the room, groups of guys (and the occasional girl) gathered by fifty-inch plasma TVs, cordless video game controllers clenched tight in their palms. These hardcore gamers seemed oblivious to those around them, lost in a fantasy world of sleek cars, alien hunters, and scantily clad heroines. One bearded, spiky-haired geek noticed Jade and beckoned her across, but she ignored him and proceeded directly to the big event.

Inside the auditorium where the president's speech was to take place, luxury chairs were arranged in curved rows around a central, curtained off stage. Attendees filed down the aisles with decreasing frequency, while those already seated talked amongst themselves as they waited for the presentation. Jade was among the last to enter. She chose an aisle seat in the back row, dug her heeled shoes into the cushion ahead, and stowed her purse beneath the chair.

At eight o'clock precisely, the lights dimmed, and the stage curtains parted to reveal two suited men behind a lectern. The speaker nearest the stand stepped forward.

Randall Forbes was the company's legal consultant, a middle-aged man dressed in a glossy gray suit with matching trousers, a spotless white shirt, and a checkered necktie. His short, pale brown hair was neatly combed. He approached the podium with a confident, self-appreciative swagger.

Randall held his arms out wide with his palms facing outwards, like a car salesman pressurizing a customer to go over budget. He waited for the guests to fall silent, then addressed them over the microphone.

"Ladies and gentlemen, it is my pleasure to welcome you to Dragonsoft's twelfth annual meeting. I won't bore you with the trivial details of why we're here. These lavish ceremonies are quite familiar to us."

His joke went down well with the business-orientated crowd, but the uninvited blonde guest was far from amused. In stern silence, Jade reached into her purse and pulled out a digital camera. Not for a single moment did her eyes leave the stage.

"And now, without further ado, let me introduce the individual who made all this possible. The man, whom one might say, is the epitome of the American dream. Please welcome Dragonsoft's president and founder, Toshigi Tasoto."

Deafening applause echoed round the room as Randall stepped aside. Toshigi was a white-haired Japanese man in his mid-fifties, dressed in traditional black tie. As he took his place behind the lectern, Jade switched on her camera and adjusted the focus. The wonders of modern technology countered effects of glare and distance, and Toshigi's facial features appeared crystal clear in the viewfinder.

Toshigi acknowledged the crowd with a brief wave, then began his address.

"Thank you," he said in eloquent English. "The American media prefer me to avoid technical jargon, so I'll put things in simple, everyday terms. In twelve years, under my personal guidance, Dragonsoft has matured from a humble dream into one kickass video game company."

He yelled the final four words out loud, almost demanding a round of applause. The assembled guests responded in kind, even throwing in the occasional whistle or cheer amidst their synchronized claps.

While Toshigi bathed in the limelight, Jade took several pictures of his face. "Happy anniversary, f—" she muttered under her breath, but Toshigi spoke again before she could finish.

"Thanks to generous contributions from the directors, our latest masterpiece hit the streets last week and has received rave reviews across the board. Well, with the usual exceptions from human rights anonymous and the worried parent collective."

Jade voiced her thoughts over the ensuing laughter. "You mean *my* masterpiece, don't you? That's right, Toshigi. Why not bathe in the glory? I don't see too many people from the design office with invitations to your little party."

She snapped one last image for her collection.

"Your lies are almost as pathetic as your jokes."

Jade uttered her comments so loud the man beside her took offense and poked her in the shoulder. The lady photographer returned his gaze, her expression cold as she stared him down. It wasn't long before he became unsettled by her unblinking, bright green eyes and turned his attention back to events onstage.

Toshigi's humor was getting worse with every paragraph.

"Apparently, there are certain liberal groups who

believe our company's logo is inappropriate. They think a fire-breathing dragon sends out the wrong message to impressionable young children, and that it might turn them into arsonists. Who knows? Perhaps they could burn down some of our rivals and make the world a much better place."

Jade had heard enough. She put away the camera, vacated her seat, and headed towards the exit. Nobody in the audience noticed her premature departure. They were too busy following their host's unspoken requests for laughter and applause. The blonde woman left the conference center through a side door, walked half a block down the street, and turned into a narrow alleyway. Unlike the major downtown routes, this rarely visited section of San Francisco was poorly illuminated. Heaps of trash lay against graffiti-tagged walls, and discarded soda cans rolled back and forth in the wind. Except for Jade, there wasn't a single pedestrian in sight.

She paused by her parked motorcycle, a high-powered sports model painted dark as the night sky. A tanker truck passed by on the intersecting street. For a split second, its headlight beams silhouetted the woman's tall, athletic figure. Then darkness descended once more. Jade took off her evening dress, exchanging it for biker leathers hung from the handlebars. She slipped into the jumpsuit and fastened its zipper up to her neck. The shiny black jacket and leggings fitted loosely around Jade's body, disguising her femininity.

After swapping her high heels and silk gloves for the motorcyclist's unisex equivalents, Jade tucked her blonde hair inside a crash helmet and lowered the dark, opaque visor over her face. Her transformation complete, she mounted her bike, started the engine, and rode off into the moonlight.

* * *

Toshigi's personal chauffeur applied another polish to his master's company car. Kenji was so absorbed in completing his task that he hadn't looked at Jade since her arrival, or even wondered why she'd kept her motorcycle engine running. They were alone in the third sub-level of an underground parking garage, and the only ambient sounds were dripping water and the low-pitched buzz of fluorescent strip lights.

Jade had stopped her motorbike in a damp, shadowy corner at the opposite end of the exit ramp. From there, she observed her target fold his cleaning cloth neatly down the middle.

Kenji had done a commendable job. The limousine's creamy white paintwork gleamed like a million dollars, and the silver Dragonsoft crest sparkled on the hood. The only dark spots that remained were the vehicle's tinted windscreens. Toshigi valued his privacy and only invited a select few into his mobile headquarters.

In terms of appearance, Kenji and Toshigi were very much alike. Both were white-haired natives of Japan and, like his boss, Kenji was in his fifties. When it came to their working lives, the two men shared little in common. While Toshigi spent a typical day attending celebrity dinners and negotiating business contracts, it was Kenji's job to ensure the Dragonsoft president's ride was smooth and comfortable.

Jade had spent enough time profiling Toshigi's staff to know Kenji only performed his thankless duties out of respect for a man he'd once admired. Twelve years earlier, when they'd traveled together to the United States, the two countrymen were close friends. Over the years, their relationship had grown increasingly distant as prominent Californians displaced the loyal servant down the importance scale. Wealth and media influence mattered a great deal to the new Toshigi, and Kenji failed on both counts. These days, the president rode to his meetings in silence, hidden behind an opaque privacy screen.

Kenji probably knew his days were numbered, but couldn't bring himself to abandon his childhood companion. Jade had considered involving the driver in her plan, but she couldn't trust someone so blindly loyal to the company with her secrets. Kenji might not have committed any sins against her, but a man so forgiving deserved no reprieve.

"I appreciate your long service," said Jade, choosing words Toshigi might use before firing an employee. "But it's over."

She revved her bike's engine while applying the handbrake, causing abrasive pads to screech against the tires. Her actions had the intended effect. The spooked Kenji glanced nervously over his shoulder.

The lamp nearest Jade flickered on and off, giving away her position. Jade sat still, watching the frightened little man through her helmet visor. There were a dozen potential hiding places in the garage. It was a veritable maze of cars and concrete pillars. If Kenji fled now, he might prolong his worthless life, but Jade knew he'd no intention of leaving the limousine unattended. Faced with an unknown stalker and no visible means to defend himself, the servant remained predictably faithful to his master.

Jade released the brake and sped towards her target. She transferred control of the bike to one hand, then used her other to remove a Japanese-style katana she'd placed between her knees. The woman in black gripped the weapon's hilt tight and swung the sword to one side. Fittingly, its handle was carved from pure jade, shaped like a dragon's head. The chauffeur saw his face reflected on the steel blade, interspersed between blurry images of lights and cars.

The faceless, leather clad huntress pressed her accelerator pedal down and closed in on her prey. Kenji backed into the limo. As Jade came within striking distance, he dived for cover, but even a world-class athlete wouldn't have escaped her swing.

The biker entered a tight spin and slashed her sword in a perfectly executed, arcing motion. Its razor-sharp blade sliced clean through Kenji's neck, separating his head from his body. Blood sprayed off the Katana's edge, tracing a red line across the car's rear door.

The killer spun to a stop on the tarmac. She switched off her motorcycle engine, stepped down, and pried the cloth from Kenji's twitching fingers. A single rub was enough to clean the blood from her blade. Jade placed the sword in a storage box fastened to her bike, then used the cloth's reverse side to wipe down the limousine. Satisfied that all traces of blood had been removed, the killer threw the blood-soaked rag into a nearby trash receptacle.

A loud beeping noise attracted Jade's attention. She turned and scanned the garage. Within a split second, she traced the sound to its source: a pager clipped to Kenji's belt. A message scrolled along the liquid crystal screen: *Meet me out front. Toshigi.*

The killer deactivated the pager and grabbed Kenji's corpse by his legs. Although the average woman wouldn't have been strong enough to lift a grown man's body by herself, Jade was far from average. She had little difficulty moving Kenji's torso out of sight, and no qualms about collecting his severed head and depositing it in the same trashcan as the cloth.

"Okay, Mister President," Jade said. "It's time to play."

* * *

Shortly after ten, Toshigi bade the last attendee farewell. The petite, auburn-haired lady was certainly a lot more attractive than the usual stockbroker. She had the looks of a supermodel and, more importantly, the shrewd instinct required to succeed in a cutthroat business environment. While a short skirt would have suited her better than trousers, she'd make a useful addition to Dragonsoft's pool of financiers.

As the woman's executive cab drove her away, Toshigi made a mental note to invite her for a private discussion. She was likely to refuse an alliance at first, but he was certain he could persuade her to join his team.

The president glanced at his gold Rolex wristwatch. Kenji was already fifteen minutes late. The driver was becoming forgetful and complacent in his old age. Toshigi was about to reach for his cellphone when his company car screeched to a halt beside the curb.

Barely able to control his anger, he yanked open the rear door. The handle felt sticky, and a globule of dried red fluid glistened underneath. Now Kenji was getting unreliable, not to mention reckless. It was time to hire a new chauffeur, perhaps a bodyguard or a young girl easy on the eyes. Toshigi made a snap, on-the-spot decision. Once he found a suitable replacement, he would relieve the aging servant of his duties.

Toshigi stepped inside his limo and slammed the door shut. The car's rear compartment was outfitted with everything he needed to conduct business on the move. Leather seats afforded him the highest level of comfort, and the one-way windscreens allowed him to enjoy the scenery whilst ensuring his privacy. For security reasons, a scrambler routed all calls made from his videophone.

Toshigi pressed a button on his seat's armrest and spoke into the limousine's intercom.

"Let's go home," he ordered his chauffeur.

"Let's not," a female voice replied.

The tone was ice cold, enough to send a tingle down Toshigi's spine. He glanced at the darkened glass partition that separated him from the driver's cabin, but the person seated up front was shrouded in shadow. Toshigi reached for the switch that lowered the divider, then thought better of it and withdrew his hand.

"Who are you? Where's Kenji?"

"So you care about him after all," the woman said in the same icy tone. "I had the impression he was low down on your list of priorities."

She paused for a moment before continuing.

"Your precious driver's probably in a black bag by now. They'll need another one for his head."

Toshigi hoped for a follow up remark to show the flatly delivered statement had been a sick joke, but the insane chuckle that came across the intercom implied she was deadly serious.

Trembling with fear, Toshigi grabbed the door release handle, but the kidnapper anticipated his move well in advance. She stabbed a button on the dashboard. Almost immediately, unseen locks clunked into place, trapping the president inside the limousine. Toshigi pressed the window switch, but nothing happened. The woman had evidently tampered with the mechanism. Running out of options, Toshigi operated the videophone. It was no use. The power supply was disconnected, and the screen remained dark.

"I thought you enjoyed conducting your business in private, Toshigi, especially with the ladies. Or does that only apply when you're the one in control? Relax. Listen to some music."

Not that she gave him any choice. The kidnapper selected a compact disc from a rack, inserted it into the player's tray, and ramped up the volume. A modern rendition of a classical symphony blared over the limousine's internal speakers.

The woman started the car and drove away from the conference center. Traffic was relatively light now rush hour was over, and it only took her a couple of minutes to reach Union Square. Locals and tourists mingled on the streets. Some stopped to watch mime artists, but most were doing late night Christmas shopping in department stores around San Francisco's famous plaza.

Toshigi thumped the car windows and screamed at the top of his voice, but the soundproofed, tinted glass thwarted his efforts. Nobody could see the imperiled president, nor hear his pleas for help.

"What do you want? Money?"

"Who do you think I am?" The kidnapper's swift response suggested she was offended. "Some game reviewer you can simply buy off?"

"What are you insinuating?"

Toshigi's feigned innocence was more of a natural reaction than anything.

"I know all of your secrets."

During his tenure as Dragonsoft president, Toshigi had weaseled his way out of tricky situations many times, but this was different. No amount of smooth talking would help here. He composed himself and tried to impose some authority.

"Listen to me, you crazy bitch," Toshigi stated firmly.

"Now, that wasn't a very nice thing to say," the woman said. "I suggest you sit back and drink some of that expensive champagne you keep in the beverage cooler. You know, the stuff you and Randall like to share when you toast other people's successes. This is the last day of your life. You may as well make the most of it."

Her speech left Toshigi shaken. When it came to verbal intimidation, his abductor had him totally outmatched, and she seemed to know everything. Worse, there was no room for negotiation. The kidnapper had already decided Toshigi's fate. He was about to die by her hand. It was simply a matter of where, when, and how.

The president wiped his sweaty forehead with a handkerchief. "What do you mean?" he asked.

The woman chose not to reply. In any event, the answer was obvious. Toshigi glanced through the side window. They had entered one of San Francisco's industrial districts. It was a no-go zone at this time of night, a run-down part of town home to dilapidated warehouses, steel shipping containers, and chain-link fences.

"Where are you taking me?"

"It's a surprise," the driver said. "Wait and see."

Toshigi suspected he would find out soon enough. The president racked his brain, trying to think of a way out. Then he remembered the mobile phone in his suit pocket. As stealthily as he could, Toshigi groped for his only lifeline. He felt the buttons through his jacket's lining, but before he could even switch on the phone, it was too late.

The driver brought the car to an abrupt stop. She lowered the divider screen and turned to confront her prisoner. The woman wore a black balaclava mask. From the parts of her face he could see, Toshigi guessed she was a Caucasian in her twenties, with bright green eyes and crimson red lipstick. The rest was a mystery.

"I'll take that if you don't mind," she said, holding out

her gloved palm. The pistol she aimed between Toshigi's eyes made it quite clear that wasn't a request.

Seeing no other option, Toshigi handed over his cellphone.

"Please don't do this. I have a daughter who just turned eighteen."

"So you do," the masked driver said. "Pretty little thing she is as well. Not that she'll mourn your passing. You were too busy counting your easily earned Yen to care about being a good father to Nicole. I hope you're feeling comfortable. It's hot where you're going."

Her hand tightened around the pistol grip.

"Who are you? What do you want?"

He'd asked both questions already, but the woman had kept him in the dark.

The kidnapper squeezed the trigger. Her weapon was silenced. Instead of a loud bang, Toshigi heard a muffled thud. He looked down, expecting to see a bullet wound circled with blood. Then he realized the gun was a tranquilizer, and his attacker had fired a sedative tipped dart into his chest.

"You can call me Jade."

Before Toshigi could make sense of her answer, everything faded to black.

# CHAPTER TWO

## *Ninety Minutes to Live*

When Toshigi opened his eyes, the first image that shimmered into focus was the towering Amazonian figure standing over him, one boot on either side of his waist. The woman called Jade looked down at him through the narrow eye slits of her balaclava. In the early morning light, she was nothing more than a shadowy outline. Although he couldn't make out her mouth, Toshigi knew she was smiling. For some twisted purpose known only to her, the kidnapper had kept him alive.

Toshigi's initial reaction was to crawl out from underneath her, but his legs refused to move. A loud metallic clank alerted him to the chains Jade had secured to his ankles. Even through his socks, Toshigi felt the bite of cold steel. Each chain looped twice around his lower knees and through a concrete brick. The links were industrial strength, a quarter of an inch thick, and held in place with combination padlocks. Toshigi's wrists and neck were similarly bound. He attempted to break free, but it was hopeless. There was no way to escape.

Jade chuckled as she watched his futile efforts. With no forewarning, she grabbed his shirt collar and leaned in his face. The woman was so close he smelled a faint whiff of perfume from under her leather jumpsuit.

"It's not very pleasant being someone else's plaything. Is it Toshigi?"

The woman's voice sounded oddly familiar, but he couldn't place it.

"If you're going to kill me, then get it over with."

"Well, if that's the way you want it."

On that ominous note, Jade retreated into the darkness. Toshigi had been awake for several minutes now, and his eyes were growing accustomed to the gloom.

The prisoner took in his surroundings. He was being held captive in an abandoned warehouse, or so he presumed. Apart from puddles of murky water and rotten pallets, the storage space was vacant. The windows were dirty and obscured by cobwebs, and it was so quiet Toshigi heard rats scurrying across the stone floor. One of the unseen rodents screeched so loud he almost wished Jade hadn't left him alone.

That thought vanished the second he saw her wielding a katana. The masked woman stepped into the light, sword drawn and at the ready.

"No!" Toshigi screamed as she advanced towards him. "I'll do anything you want. Please. Wait!"

Despite his pleas, Jade's stride never faltered once. She stopped by Toshigi's side, raised her weapon two handed, and swung down at his neck. Sharpened steel flashed before his eyes. Toshigi was certain he would die, but Jade halted her attack the instant her katana touched his skin. A lesser swordswoman would have drawn blood, but this girl was a master of the blade.

"Anything? How about a game?"

Still in shock, Toshigi only managed a stuttered reply. "Game? I... I don't understand."

"Oh, that's right. I forgot. You're not really a games designer, are you? You're an uncharitable businessman who enjoys taking credit for everybody else's hard work. A common thief. Which reminds me. I'm feeling generous."

Jade tossed her katana on the floor and unzipped her suit. She only exposed a narrow section of her body, but Toshigi could see she wasn't wearing anything underneath her jacket. Not wanting to offend this dangerous woman, he closed his eyes. He sensed her gloved fingertips brush his cheek.

"What's wrong? You've had sex with me before. You gave me special treatment. Don't you remember?"

Something told him it wasn't a lie. He recalled the many girls he'd employed—secretaries, personal assistants, call takers—and tried to connect a face to the voice, but his mind came up blank.

"Come now. Don't be shy," Jade said. "There's nothing under my jacket you haven't seen already. Except this, perhaps."

Something long, round and heavy landed on his chest. He opened his eyes to look. The object was a black cloth bundle tied with string. Jade carefully undid the knot and rolled open the pouch. Inside were tools that might conceivably belong to a thief: lock picks, wire cutters, and several others Toshigi couldn't identify.

"While I do think you're a miserable, conceited bastard, I'm not completely without heart," Jade told her captive. "If you're able to free yourself, you can go running off to the boys and girls in blue. You might even live to say something original at next year's annual meeting."

Toshigi tried to wrestle his arms free of the restraints. One concrete brick toppled, then returned to its former position.

"Is this your idea of a joke?" he asked. "How am I supposed to reach those things?"

"How indeed? I suggest you hurry, though. There is a time limit."

Jade zipped her jumpsuit and stepped out of sight behind him. Toshigi resisted the temptation to ask her to elaborate. It was clear she enjoyed toying with him.

A minute later, his tormentor returned with three items. Toshigi couldn't see two of them, but the other was unmistakably a fuel can. He watched in horror as the psycho woman unscrewed the cap and doused him in petroleum. Jade emptied the liquid over his shoes, trousers, and suit, deliberately taking her time.

When she eventually got around to soaking Toshigi's face, he'd already shut his eyelids. The anchored restraints prevented him from turning his head. Jade took full advantage, shaking the can until she'd exhausted every drop of fuel.

The kidnapper wound up a brass alarm clock and placed it between his legs. Chuckling to herself, she fired up a cigarette lighter and balanced it precariously on top of the bell.

Toshigi saw the clock's face clearly in the flickering orange light. Now he understood what Jade meant by a time limit. The timer was set to go off in approximately ninety minutes, and when it did, the dislodged lighter would ignite the spilled gasoline. Toshigi was literally watching his life tick away.

Jade pulled Toshigi's handkerchief from his suit pocket and laid it flat on the ground. She waited for the material to soak up enough fluid, then rolled the rag into a narrow strip.

"Why are you doing this?" Toshigi screamed. "What do you want from me? What did I—"

Before he could complete his third question, Jade shoved the handkerchief between his teeth. She tied the silk into a knot behind his head. Toshigi was forced to swallow the droplets that dripped down his throat. He coughed, choking on petroleum fumes.

"Chew on that. Just imagine. If you fail, Mister Dragonsoft truly will breathe fire."

She kneeled down and stared straight into Toshigi's eyes.

"Oh. And since you're playing the thief, you'll need this."

Jade smiled, pulled off the balaclava, and tossed back her blonde hair. At first, the young woman seemed like a complete stranger. Then Toshigi saw through the disguise, and a look of recognition crossed his face. The gag muffled his exclamation of surprise.

"All this time, and you never even guessed. I hope the police are smarter than you."

She lifted Toshigi's head, pulled the balaclava over his head, and turned it back to front. He felt powerless, unable to see, speak, or move. Although his nose and ears were covered, he could smell the surrounding petrol and hear his kidnapper walk away.

"You were wondering why I'm doing this," Jade said. "Well, you've got eighty-five minutes to figure it out."

Footsteps echoed through the warehouse. Somewhere nearby, a sliding metal door opened and closed. Jade had left Toshigi alone, with only rats, spiders, and a ticking clock for company.

* * *

The sun dawned behind Jade as she left the hustle of downtown San Francisco for the more scenic environs of Twin Peaks. After dealing with Toshigi, she dumped the limousine and reclaimed her motorcycle before heading west. The city by the bay, a picturesque landscape of hills and skyscrapers, was visible from her present location in all its morning glory. It was the perfect vantage point for a holiday season tourist, but Jade was here on business.

Traffic had stopped on the opposite side of the road. Agitated commuters beeped their horns, but there was no immediately foreseeable end to their frustration. Few paid attention to the hell's angel who zoomed past in the other direction. The female biker weaved in between the occasional cars or trucks that obstructed her path. She was happy to avoid the congestion. She was racing against the clock, and didn't want to be late for her appointment.

Jade arrived at her destination five minutes early. The Dragonsoft development labs were housed in a tower block modeled after a Japanese pagoda. The oriental architecture and slanted roofs would have pleased most visitors, but she knew it was just for show. Behind the fancy exterior, the offices did not differ from any other game production company. Employees worked long shifts in mediocre conditions, while the greatest share of the profits went to the men who deserved them least.

"Well," Jade thought. "Toshigi won't be getting paid today."

It was time to set her plan in motion. She left her motorcycle in the rear parking lot and entered via the delivery door.

This near to Christmas, the mail room was busy with temporary staff sifting through greeting cards besides the usual Dragonsoft fan letters. Jade showed the duty manager a manila envelope. The guy gave the helmeted woman a curious glance, but relaxed when he saw the name she'd printed on the label.

"Nicole Tasoto. Assistant Designer. Makes a change from all the mail we get for her old man. Not that the Lord Almighty ever reads them, mind you. Private courier service, eh? What you got in there? Design secrets or somethin'?"

"Private means private," Jade said bluntly.

While she wouldn't have minded sharing her negative opinions, she was in a hurry and couldn't risk a lengthy, drawn out conversation.

Jade left the stunned manager to sort his mail and rode an elevator to the top floor, the office space reserved for Dragonsoft's assistant game developers. The job title was an insult, considering Toshigi only played a token role in the actual design process.

Marble tiled backdrops and tiered fountains were a step up from the featureless cubicles given to low-level programmers, but Jade knew from personal experience the reality was a lot grimmer than people outside the development community perceived.

The elevator opened into a long, narrow passageway decorated with framed posters. Jade's game designs were all featured, including *Pirate of Trinidad, Ghost in the Night, Space Mercenaries,* and many more. Her favorite, the martial arts themed adventure *Jade Dragon,* was there too. In effect, the displays chronicled her entire life's work, but Jade wasn't interested in the past. Her name only appeared in small print near the bottom, if at all.

She hastened to the reception desk at the end of the corridor. The curly haired brunette sat behind was no stranger to her. Rebecca Masters had worked as a secretary at Dragonsoft for five years now and, like most women on Toshigi's payroll, she was in her twenties, attractive and subject to the president's strict dress code. Being encouraged to wear a skirt had always made Jade feel uncomfortable, but Rebecca didn't seem to care.

"Is this the office of Nicole Tasoto?"

Jade disguised her voice, just as she'd done with Toshigi. Rebecca was the inquisitive type, and the courier wanted to avoid being recognized.

"That's what it says on the wall, isn't it?"

She didn't bother to look up, and simply pointed her thumb at the brass plaque behind her. As if anybody would have trouble deducing which wall she meant, or seeing Nicole's name engraved there in large print. The receptionist had lost none of her irritating sarcasm.

Jade decided to change the dynamics. She slammed her manila envelope on the desk, rested her elbow on top, and waited in silence. The secretary glanced up from her computer terminal. She shifted uncomfortably in her seat, clearly unnerved by her visitor's stance.

"You want something?" Rebecca asked, with no trace of the steely wit that had been present earlier.

Jade smiled to herself, knowing the girl couldn't see her face. She lifted her elbow and slid the envelope between the secretary's wavering hands.

"Make sure Nicole gets this," she said, then turned and walked away.

"Nice to meet you too," Rebecca yelled after her.

Jade didn't reply. She'd made her delivery, setting the

wheels in motion. The actual game would begin soon enough.

* * *

Nicole Tasoto arrived at her office in a buoyant mood. She was a little later for work than usual, mainly because of a few errands she needed to run beforehand. With those taken care of, she could focus on play testing her newest game. Watching her completed endeavor in motion would be more entertaining than the tedious development phase.

The eighteen-year-old couldn't be further from the programmer stereotype. Not only was Nicole female, but six feet tall, athletic and stunningly beautiful. The brown skinned Oriental wore her hair long, split across the shoulders of her official looking, azure business suit.

Like all women Dragonsoft employees, Nicole was discouraged from working in trousers. Her ankle-length skirt kept her thighs covered, but with her good looks and soft blue eyes, she was still a temptation for many of her male colleagues. If she wasn't the company president's daughter, she'd be the most popular date in the building.

Nicole greeted her receptionist with a cheerful smile.

"Morning, Rebecca."

"Hey, Nicole. Some crazy biker chick left this for you." She indicated an envelope on her desk. "Actually, we're inundated with psycho ladies this morning. See this weird e-mail I just got?"

Nicole stepped behind the reception, collecting the letter en route. She followed the secretary's gaze to a pop-up window on her computer screen. The typeface was small, and she had to squint to read it.

"Better brush up on your hacking skills, Silica."

The sender called herself Jade, and the domain was obviously bogus.

"Enlightening, huh?"

Rebecca clicked the e-mail delete icon and bellowed at her monitor.

"Doh! Stupid bitch. You can't even get my name right. It's Rebecca, dumbass."

"We're in the geek business," Nicole said. "Weirdos come with the territory. Are you sure that's a girl you're shouting at?"

"Who the hell knows? Or cares. So, what's your secret admirer got to say?"

Nicole tore open the envelope and inspected its contents. Photographs showed her father on stage at the convention center. She flicked through the extensive album, keeping the pictures close to her chest to prevent Rebecca from seeing.

The later images were of Toshigi chained up in a warehouse. A typed note stapled to the last photo stated the kidnapper's terms: *200,000 Dollars. 3526 Bayside. One hour from now. Come alone. Or he dies.*

Nicole's hands trembled.

"When did you get this?" she asked.

"About ten minutes ago. Why? Everything all right? What does it say?"

"I have to make a delivery." Nicole deliberately evaded her secretary's question. "If anyone asks, I haven't come in yet. Got it?"

"You're the boss."

* * *

Ten minutes later, Nicole was navigating grid locked city streets. Morning commute was in full swing, and other drivers showed no mercy. Nicole's flashy silver corvette could easily exceed a hundred miles per hour, but she was lucky to top twenty.

She chose the shortest, most direct route she could think of: east along Market Street towards the Financial District. Somewhere ahead, the Sun rose over the horizon, still low in the sky. Thankfully, tall skyscrapers blotted out the blinding light. It was already difficult enough to make progress without additional hazards to contend with.

Nicole checked her clock radio. Less than three quarters of an hour remained before the deadline. Taking no chances, she veered into the opposite lane, jumped the queue, and cut across a car waiting at an intersection ahead. Fellow motorists sounded their horns and yelled profanities, but she hadn't finished with her crazy maneuvers. She took advantage of a break in traffic, accelerated through a red light, and made a hard left turn. Her bank was two blocks to the north, in the shadow of the Transamerica Pyramid.

Nicole parked in a restricted zone and glanced in her rear-view mirror. She'd broken many laws on the way from the office, but somehow avoided attracting police attention.

She breathed a sigh of relief. Dealing with the cops would have been tricky. The toughest leg of her journey was over, but she couldn't rest easy. There was a strong chance a traffic camera had photographed her license plate, or some frustrated motorist had made a report. If so, a squad car wouldn't be far away.

Nicole calmed her nerves, got out of her corvette, and walked into the bank. While Nagoya Savings didn't have a client list to rival mainstream American institutions, over ten thousand people held accounts there. Those included her father and a high percentage of his associates. Many had valuables stashed in safety deposit boxes on the vault floor below.

Even in the lobby, security was airtight. Closed circuit cameras monitored every cubic inch of the room, and a uniformed guard stood by the entrance, automatic pistol holstered by his hip. Like most of the staff, the man was of Japanese descent. He was young, hawk-eyed and in excellent shape, a potent deterrent to criminals.

Nicole nodded an unspoken greeting to the guard and approached the teller counters. The bank had only been open a few minutes, so she had her pick of assistants. She chose the odd one out: a pale-faced American in her late twenties. An infrared motion sensor detected Nicole as she stepped up to the armored glass window, and a camera swiveled to point at her face. She smiled at the lens, trying to appear relaxed.

"Can I help you?" the woman asked.

Nicole took a deep breath, then replied.

"Yes. I'd like to make a withdrawal."

"Name and account number, please."

The teller held her fingers over a computer keyboard in readiness, but Nicole focused on an electronic ticker board above the window. Time was running out.

"Miss?"

The employee waited until she got Nicole's attention.

"Your name and account number?" she repeated.

"Nicole Tasoto. Four seven nine, three six two."

As the bank clerk entered the details, Nicole looked around. Besides her, there were five other customers. One caught her eye: an old woman dressed in a tracksuit and dark glasses. The hunchbacked crone smiled and shuffled on her Zimmer frame to a leaflet stand.

"Everything okay, Miss Tasoto? You seem kinda nervous. Is there something I should know about?"

Nicole whispered a hoarse reply over her shoulder.

"I'm fine. Could you hurry, please?"

She was more concerned with tracking the old woman's movements.

"Certainly. How much would you like to withdraw?"

She faced the window, pressed her face close to the glass, and was about to speak. Then she stopped. The woman was already suspicious. How would she react to such an unorthodox request?

Nicole had stalled long enough. "Two hundred thousand dollars," she said. "In twenty-dollar bills. Will that be a problem?"

The teller hesitated, appearing to sense the anxiety in Nicole's voice.

"I don't know. This isn't exactly normal."

"The account's in my name, right? It's my money. Just get it ready."

"Since you're asking to withdraw such a large amount in cash, I'll have to clear it with the manager first."

The woman reached for a phone receiver.

"No! Wait!" blurted Nicole.

Her loud outburst got the teller's attention, and several other peoples' too. Almost everyone turned to stare in her direction, including the old woman with the Zimmer frame.

Suspecting something was amiss, the security guard instinctively went for his gun. To Nicole's relief, the teller raised her hand to let him know everything was okay, and he stood down. Now the excitement had passed, the other customers continued with their normal business.

"Mind telling me what's going on?"

The cashier spoke in the same polite voice as before, acting like nothing had happened.

"I can't," Nicole said. "Don't you understand? It might put you in danger, too. She could be in the bank, watching us right now."

The girl shook her head, confused. "She?"

"The crazy woman who sent me the note."

Nicole kneeled down and pretended to tie her shoelace while seeking the old woman. Once again, the hunchback responded with a grin. Nicole broke eye contact with her, stood up, and pressed her palms against the teller's window. She was perspiring so heavily that her fingers steamed up the glass.

"Just help me," Nicole pleaded. "Talk to your manager if you have to, but hurry. It's my father. The woman who sent the message threatened she'd kill him if I didn't do as she instructed."

"Kidnapping. Shouldn't we call the police?"

"No! The note said to bring the money alone."

The teller nodded and grabbed her phone receiver. Though the slanted buttons made it hard to see, Nicole was reasonably certain the woman dialed an internal extension.

"Put me through to Mister Miyahara," the teller said. "Well, interrupt his meeting. This is urgent."

The cashier turned away and lowered her voice. Only snippets of the subsequent conversation were audible.

"...customer out here. She needs two hundred... don't have time... I realize what I'm asking... Yes, I think this might be..."

After yapping for an entire minute, the teller replaced the receiver and faced Nicole.

"The manager's getting your money ready now."

She saw an old Asian man through a partially open door behind the teller's window. He worked quickly to stock a leather satchel with banded wads of cash. It seemed the bank staff were responding to her request, but progress was painfully slow. She tapped her fingers impatiently on the counter.

"We're being as quick as possible," the teller reassured her.

"I don't have all day, damn it. The note specifically stated—"

"Stated what? Miss Tasoto?"

Nicole wasn't listening. A handsome, clean-shaven man who'd just walked into the bank had caught her eye.

The new arrival looked to be in his late twenties. Given he wore a trendy suit, pressed trousers and black polished shoes, Nicole suspected he was a ladies' man. He talked briefly with the security guard and flashed his wallet. There was no subtlety whatsoever in the man's approach. His shiny detective's badge was clear for all to see.

The policeman headed straight towards her. She could smell his aftershave from twelve feet away, and his wavy, light brown hair glistened with traces of gel.

Nicole shot the bank employee a hateful glance.

"I told you not to call the police."

The teller backed off, shocked at the sudden display of anger. She looked at the new arrival for help.

"Calm down, Miss Tasoto," the policeman said. "She wasn't the one who called us. That was dispatch. Your father's missing, but it seems you already knew that."

The man opened his wallet and presented his police badge. She glared at him, not at all impressed.

"Nicole, I'm Detective Kyle Travis."

# CHAPTER THREE

## *Time to Die*

When the call from dispatch came in, Detective Kyle Travis was supping his morning cappuccino at Le Cafe Tolnier. The croissants, pastries and baguettes on sale were pricier than fast food, but he preferred French cuisine to the unhealthy breakfasts served in diners and burger bars. While takeaway joints were popular among other homicide cops, they were a little low market for Kyle's tastes, and he found the bakery's customers to be more refined and sociable.

Kyle was getting to know a young blonde waitress when his partner showed up. Detective Lakeysia Symons was a veteran police officer in her late thirties. As her forename suggested, she was African American. Despite two years working together, Kyle's fashion sense hadn't rubbed off. The slightly obese, round-faced woman wore a creased, long-sleeved shirt, a cheap jacket, jeans and tattered boots. Her charcoal black hair was a mess, with an old elastic band securing her ponytail.

"See you're making fine use of taxpayers' money," Lakeysia said. "He proposed to you yet, darlin'?"

Kyle had worked with her long enough to know not to respond to the cynical jibes. The waitress wasn't so used to her confrontational style. She watched, flabbergasted, as the scruffy woman slurped her soda, a can she'd purchased elsewhere.

"Loitering isn't permitted," the server told her bluntly. "And neither is bringing in beverages from outside. I'm sorry, miss, but you'll have to order something from the menu or leave."

Lakeysia shrugged and dumped her empty drink on the table.

"No time for that. Detective Travis and I are on duty."

"Detective?"

Apparently, the girl wasn't thrilled to learn Kyle was a police officer. He cursed inwardly. Why did his partner have to open her mouth? He'd hoped to keep his profession a secret.

As usual, Lakeysia couldn't resist poking fun at Kyle's expense.

"Yeah," she said, flashing her badge and handcuffs. "Take it you didn't see the car parked out front? Don't sweat it. Travis prefers beauty over brains. I'm sure he'll make room for you on his calendar. He tell you about that? Most have just one busty girl a month, but his is special. He's got a lady for every day of the year."

"Suppose you think that's funny. And that being a cop gives you the right to boss me around."

The girl was certainly putting up a brave fight, but Lakeysia came straight back at her.

"You're welcome to stand in. Can't say I'm looking forward to studying a blood-spattered corpse or chasing the wacko who sliced him in two. Since you're so tough and smart, I can give you all the gory details and let you figure out who did it. I'll stay here, wait tables all day. Fine by me."

The waitress realized she was out of her depth and left the detectives alone. Kyle finished his coffee and watched her serve another man across the room. Accepting their brief relationship was over, he gave the girl a generous tip.

"Who's the victim?" he asked, getting to his feet.

Lakeysia filled him in on the way out.

"Asian, mid fifties. Far as forensics can tell, he was a limousine driver or valet. Matthews is waiting for us at Fifth Street garage."

"No positive ID?"

"Not yet. They're still looking for the guy's head."

* * *

Kyle rode alongside his partner in silence. It wasn't the cafeteria incident that bothered him. Lakeysia's rude interruptions in his social life were a frequent occurrence, and for girls, there were plenty more out there. No, it was the job that was wearing him down.

He'd spent five years patrolling the streets before finally making detective in September. Kyle was no stranger to the darker side of human nature. But he was homicide now, and another fresh corpse would stare vacantly back at him every other day. And more often than not, those eyes belonged to a pretty young female.

Whenever Kyle got called to a crime scene, he dreaded recognizing the victim's face. Thankfully, he didn't know too many Asian men, so the chances of that happening this time were remote. Still, Kyle regretted having a full stomach after what Lakeysia told him. Even she was more subdued than usual. Neither of them relished searching a decapitated torso for clues.

The flashing light on Kyle's unmarked car forced most drivers to give way, but Lakeysia struggled to find any maneuvering space on the congested city streets. Shortly after they passed the halfway point, the police radio crackled into life.

"Fourteen eleven, please respond."

The female dispatcher's voice was interlaced with static. Kyle snatched the communicator before Lakeysia could. If nothing else, it helped break up the tedium.

"This is fourteen eleven," he acknowledged. "Over."

"Report to a potential ransom situation at Nagoya Savings Bank, at the corner of Montgomery and Sacramento."

"Can you believe this shit? We're homicide, not kidnap specialists."

Kyle was tired, frustrated, and not in the mood for some fool's errand.

"Lieutenant's orders. We've identified the Fifth Street garage victim as Kenji Fajitsu."

"Big deal. What's that got to do with anything?"

"His employer is Toshigi Tasoto, the president of Dragonsoft. That's the video game company. According to the family maid, Tasoto never returned home last night. All indications are he was abducted."

Lakeysia covered the radio.

"And they figured that out all by themselves. Don't you just love the lady's brevity?"

"His bank manager reported a suspicious transaction," the dispatcher went on. "By Tasoto's daughter Nicole."

Kyle sat up straight, taking a sudden interest. Lakeysia leaned closer.

"Try to say no now," she whispered.

"Tell the manager to stall for time," he said. "We're en route to the location."

They were in luck. Nagoya Savings was less than three blocks away, sparing them the nightmare of traversing half the city. His partner made good progress, thanks to a lull in traffic along the last stretch.

Kyle studied the building while she parked across the street. "You stay out front," he said, unbuckling his seat belt. "It's probably best if I talked to the girl."

Lakeysia grabbed Kyle's shoulder.

"Watch your back. If this is a kidnapping, who's to say the daughter's not involved somehow?"

"And who's saying she is?"

"She might be pretty, but that doesn't make her an angel. Until we know for sure, treat her as a suspect."

For once, Lakeysia was being serious, but Kyle quickly forgot her words of wisdom when he entered the bank and saw Nicole.

The president's daughter needed no introduction. She was by a cashier's window, literally shaking with fear. The manager had followed police instructions and was in no hurry to count her money. Kyle showed his badge to the security guard.

"Detective Travis, Homicide. Don't let anyone else in. Got that?"

The Japanese doorman stood to attention. "Yes, sir. Anything you need. What's the problem?"

"Just do your job."

An old lady with a Zimmer frame brushed past Kyle and exited the bank. He gave her a brief once over, but nothing more. His eyes were glued to Nicole.

She was looking straight at him. Even with sweat

running down her face, the teenage girl was a beauty. No amount of cosmetic surgery could improve the complexion of her soft, oriental skin. Nicole's formal business suit provided a hint of social status, yet concealed none of her athleticism. The blue-eyed lady was Kyle's ideal woman: young, sexy and, above all, classy.

As he approached the counter, he realized Nicole was upset with the employee behind the window. After some words of reassurance, he introduced himself to Tasoto's daughter.

"Are you some hotshot fresh out of the academy?" she said. "Coming in like the Lone Ranger, waving your badge around for all to see."

Kyle took a step back, surprised by Nicole's unfriendly response. She was right, of course, but he wasn't used to going on the defensive with women.

"I'm being as discrete as possible."

"Are you?"

Nicole didn't appear satisfied at all.

"Well, since somebody couldn't keep her mouth shut..." She glared at the teller. "I guess you're on the case, then."

"Actually, it was the bank manager who contacted us. Like I told you before..." Kyle checked the employee's name badge. "Joanna had nothing to do with it."

"Oh."

That piece of information soothed Nicole's temper. She seemed embarrassed as she apologized to the cashier.

"Sorry if I snapped at you before. I'm a little on edge."

"I'll take things from here. Nicole?"

The detective escorted the frightened girl to a seating area. Her palm was moist and warm. Though she pretended to be relaxed, Kyle suspected she was a wreck inside. He directed her to a coffee table and sat down opposite.

"Has the kidnapper contacted you?"

"I never mentioned my father had been kidnapped."

Nicole pushed back her hair. Her response was a classic case of blunt denial, an outright refusal to cooperate. For obvious reasons, she was reluctant to share information with the police. Kyle kept up the pressure.

"Then why mention your father? Or empty your savings account? Do you normally carry that much in cash? Nicole, I can understand you wanting to keep this private. But I promise—"

She slammed some photographs and a typed note on the table. "You want to help? Okay. I'll tell you what I know, Detective. Someone has my father, and he'll die unless you give me my money. She delivered those to my office this morning."

"She?" Kyle couldn't conceal his surprise. "What did this female look like? I assume she was a stranger."

"I never saw her myself. My receptionist, Rebecca, was the one who received the package. The courier wore biker's gear, but she seemed pretty sure it was a woman."

"One hour from now," Kyle read aloud. "When did you get this?"

"About thirty minutes ago. She's going to kill him, isn't she? And since you've gotten involved, she'll..."

Nicole trailed off, whimpering as she wiped tears from her eyes. Kyle rested a comforting hand on her wrist.

"Everything will be fine. I promise. We'll be with you every step of the way."

"We? Who's—"

Right on cue, Lakeysia walked into the bank. Now the other customers had left, she spotted them almost immediately.

"Nicole, this is my partner, Detective Lakeysia Symons."

"Soon to be ex-detective." Lakeysia glanced at the note. "Short, sweet, and to the point. Gotta love that. Should I call the cavalry, Travis?"

"We could use a S.W.A.T. team. And a hostage negotiator to be on the safe side. But no choppers. I don't want to freak this wacko out."

Nicole shook her head disapprovingly. "The kidnapper said to come alone. The wording's very specific."

"Got it," Lakeysia said, ignoring the girl's concerns. "I'll go inform the lieutenant."

Shortly after she left the premises, the bank manager brought a satchel over and presented it to Nicole. Cash filled the interior of the open case.

"Two hundred thousand dollars," the manager said. "In twenties, as you requested, Miss Tasoto. I'm a good friend of your father. He and I meet often to discuss his company's finances. I hope this works out."

Nicole verified the contents and closed the satchel.

"Thank you. And I appreciate you calling the police. It was the right move, despite my reservations."

She placed her hand on Kyle's. For a moment, they looked into each other's eyes. Then the manager handed over a radio.

"Detective Travis, I took the precaution you suggested. The transmitter's concealed within the case lining. It's impossible to detect without a comprehensive scan. The receiver has a five-mile range. That should allow you to stay in contact and track the money remotely."

Nicole retracted her hand and gave the two men alternate glances.

"Transmitter? Receiver? What's going on?"

"You'll go through with the delivery as scheduled," Kyle explained. "Since we can't escort you for fear of being spotted, we'll monitor your progress and listen in by radio, just in case this mystery woman tries anything fancy. We'll surround the building, but stay out of sight. That way, once you've made the drop and your father's safe, we can grab the kidnapper."

Nicole stared at Kyle, open-mouthed.

"No! Whose crazy idea was this? What if she finds out? What then? My father…"

"Don't worry. She won't find out."

"What if she's been listening in? If she saw you arrive?"

The girl scanned the lobby. She and Kyle were the only people there, but that didn't appear to ease the girl's mind.

"It's all right," he said. "If you play this smart. And we won't move until you're both out of harm's way. Trust me." He checked his watch. "Thirty minutes. Try to remain calm, Nicole."

Nicole exhaled, then wiped her forehead.

"Easier said than done. Okay. I'm ready."

* * *

Lakeysia kept her distance, tailing Nicole's silver corvette along the back streets. Kyle urged her to drive closer, but she insisted on having two cars in between. He could understand his partner's caution, but they'd nearly lost Nicole three times already, and he didn't want to let her out of his sight.

He checked the clock radio. "Ten minutes. We're nowhere near the drop point. Damn it. Why's she driving so slow?"

"Don't ask me. Maybe she's not happy with two hundred grand and wants to collect her pop's inheritance."

Their worries regarding Nicole's hastiness proved unfounded. Once they entered the industrial sector, the daughter put her foot down, made several forays into opposite lanes, jumped three red lights in succession, and narrowly avoided a head on collision with a garbage truck.

"Think she's trying to shake us, by any chance?"

Lakeysia had trouble keeping up with Nicole's speedy, dangerous maneuvers. Pedestrians stopped to watch the sexy Asian girl tempt fate in her flashy sports car, but not everybody appreciated her driving antics.

A motorcycle officer approached from behind, siren blaring out loud. As the cop overtook the unmarked vehicle, Kyle realized the rider was a butch, unattractive female with a wart on her chin. He waved his arms frantically, trying to get her attention. When that failed, he pressed his shield against the window. Eventually, the motorcyclist noticed him, raised a hand in apology, and gave up the chase.

"Thought you liked fast women," Lakeysia said.

Kyle stared through the rear windscreen. "Did you see that stupid bitch?"

"You mean the lady doing her job?"

Lakeysia made it perfectly clear whose side she'd taken. Trust her to back the woman up. But he was determined to deny his partner an easy victory.

"Couldn't she see our dash light, for Christ's sake?"

"That's sorta difficult when it's not switched on. We're trying to avoid being seen, in case you forgot."

Kyle ignored her and grabbed the radio.

"This is fourteen eleven. In pursuit of a silver corvette. License plate ID..." He glanced through the front windscreen.

"Try looking at the car's behind instead of Miss Tasoto's," Lakeysia said.

"Tango Alpha Sierra Zero Tango Zero. We're responding to a ransom situation. There is to be no interference. You got that?"

"Nice job, Travis. Bit late in the day, though."

Kyle's partner pointed to a warehouse halfway down the street. Nicole had parked her corvette outside the front gate. She sat still, with her engine running.

Kyle scanned the surrounding rooftops. "Where the hell's our backup?"

"Out of sight, like us."

Lakeysia reversed into a parking lot, backing up from the main road. A rusted corrugated iron fence obscured Nicole's car from view.

"You left her all on her own!"

"Relax. We're keeping a close eye on your girl."

A flock of birds took flight from an advertising board opposite the warehouse, disturbed by a police squad in full body armor. Officers stood on a maintenance platform, sniper rifles at the ready. A flash of reflected sunlight alerted Kyle to S.W.A.T. team members holed up in a neighboring building, strategically positioned near upper floor windows. Some stared through binoculars, while others were busy checking their weapons.

Nicole and her police escort were the only people about. Most San Franciscans avoided this part of town, and the lowlifes who lived here were probably recovering from cocktails of alcohol and drugs served the previous night.

"Everything quiet out front," a policeman reported over the radio. "No hostiles sighted."

"You think she's feelin' up to it?" Lakeysia asked Kyle. "Point of no return. If you're worried about her, we should raid the place now, take our chances."

"No. Any sudden moves, and Nicole's father dies for

sure."

"Nicole? Seems to have stuck. Care for a word or two of advice? Don't get on first-name terms just yet. These things have a funny way of not working out."

Kyle looked at the clock. He heard his heart beat faster as the seconds ticked by.

"It's time. You expecting trouble?"

Lakeysia was busy reloading her firearm. She flipped off the safety catch, then holstered the weapon under her jacket.

"The last person who didn't got abducted, and the one before that turned up with his head missing. So yeah. I'm expectin' trouble."

Kyle was so freaked out by her comments that he jumped with fright when Nicole reported in.

"Exiting the car."

The radio transmitter the bank manager had planted in the satchel was innovative technology, and there was no loss of clarity in her voice.

"Entering the warehouse n—"

The creak of rusty hinges drowned the rest of her message out. Footsteps followed, then a loud metallic clang.

"I'm inside. Oh God. I see my father. He's tied up. I'm walking over to him."

Kyle opened the passenger door and drew his gun. Lakeysia remained behind the wheel. If she was nervous, she didn't look like it. Listening intently, he detected ambient noises over Nicole's footsteps: squealing rats, clinking chains, muffled screams and, most worrying of all, a ticking clock.

"Detective! There's some sort of—"

A ringing alarm bell interrupted her. There was a loud whoosh, and everything intensified. Rodents screeched louder, chain links clanked faster, and the agonized moans became constant.

"Father! No!" screamed Nicole.

Lakeysia grabbed the radio. "This is Symons! Move in!"

Kyle was already sprinting towards the warehouse. His partner gave instructions over the police frequency, but he wasn't listening. He reached the building a few seconds ahead of the response team.

A human fireball was chained to the floor. The Asian man writhed in agony, shaking his restraints to escape the inferno. Flames spread far, high and wide. Kyle froze on the spot. Half a dozen officers followed him in, but there was nothing they could do either. A lake of burning oil ten feet in diameter surrounded the victim, and it was impossible to reach him.

Despite the odds stacked against her, Nicole seemed determined to pull her father to safety. She raced towards the flames and raised her hands to shield her face. Kyle tackled the girl and dragged her away. She kicked and screamed, thumping his chest. Nicole was a strong woman, and he struggled to hold on to her. She elbowed him in the stomach, wrestled free, and shoved him aside.

Thick, black smoke rose from the burning petrol, so dense that Kyle choked on the fumes.

"Nicole," he coughed. "Get back!"

Lakeysia led a backup squad into the warehouse. She came to Kyle's aid while the other officers concentrated on pulling Nicole away from the fire. It took three men to pin her to the ground. After a fierce scrap, she gave up her fight and lay still, panting for breath. Her face and clothes were black from heat exposure.

"Father!"

Tears streamed down her cheeks. The police lowered

their guns and watched the flames burn, powerless to act as Toshigi's struggles became noticeably weaker. A badly roasted face was visible through the smoke. Fire ate through the handkerchief in the man's mouth. Free to speak, he called out to his daughter.

"Nicole. It was her."

Toshigi croaked, struggling with every word. He rolled his eyes and tried to face her, but some unseen contraption held his head in place.

"She wanted... you... to watch me die. She set... this whole thing... up."

"Who!?" she demanded to know. "Who did this to you?"

Her question went unanswered. Toshigi had uttered his last breath. His body grew limp, and fire soon engulfed it.

"Set what up? Father? Father!"

Nicole stared ahead, her expression a mixture of anguish and disbelief. Kyle placed a consoling arm around the girl's shoulder, but his efforts to calm her invoked only hatred.

"You killed him. My father's dead because of you. Because you interfered. Why didn't you leave me alone?"

"Nicole, I'm sorry."

"Yeah," she said, turning her back. "So you should be."

She marched past Kyle and out of the warehouse. Lakeysia watched a uniformed policewoman escort the girl to a black and white, then joined Kyle by the flames.

"Bet you twenty bucks she's faking it. Acting that good, they should give her an Oscar. I see Miss Tasoto's got you fooled. You know something. If you studied her eyes instead of her —"

"Will you leave it alone?"

Kyle stooped down to collect a charred banknote, one of hundreds that littered the warehouse floor. The flames receded, and he saw the satchel Nicole had discarded.

Lakeysia removed a notebook and a cheap Biro pen from her inside pocket. "The girl's got money to burn. Wish I had the luxury," she said, writing tidbits of information. "So, we on?"

Before Kyle could reply, firefighters rushed into the warehouse. The detectives stepped back while they sprayed dry ice over the flames.

"This isn't about money," Kyle said. "The ransom was a ploy. This psycho wanted Nicole to watch her father die. Just like he promised."

"Or find his charred remains. I'm surprised the guy lasted as long as he did."

Now the fire no longer posed a threat, Lakeysia moved closer to Toshigi's body. She slipped on surgical gloves and brushed white ashes off the dead man's hand. A glint of light caught her eye.

"Your standard, everyday thief's lock pick."

She lifted the object by its long handle.

"A chance to escape," Kyle said.

"While blindfolded and without the use of his arms or legs. I doubt even the Great Houdini would have escaped this one."

"A game he couldn't win. Wait just a minute. This guy was a big games designer, right?"

"Something like that, I guess. Not into this new age console stuff. Suppose I'm too busy solving crimes. Why don't you ask your latest girlfriend? See what she has to say."

Lakeysia nodded towards the entrance door. Outside, Nicole sat in the rear of the squad car, drinking from a polystyrene cup.

"Think she'll be alright?" asked Kyle.

"Depends if she likes coffee. Hopefully she doesn't, then she won't have an allergic reaction. She's still better off than her dad."

Lakeysia separated a dark gray shaving from the ash under Toshigi's head. She brushed sticky residue aside to expose markings scraped into a concrete brick. The killer had left a cryptic message.

"Twelve E," Kyle said. "I don't get it."

"You ever known a psycho to talk sense?"

Kyle placed the charred twenty in his partner's pocket.

"My stake. No need to waste real money. You're wrong about Nicole. Good cops don't allow previous cases to bias them. You know, not every girl is a Triad hitwoman."

Lakeysia stood up to confront him head on.

"You're the one who's biased. You think you're an expert judge of the fair sex, don't you, Travis? Let me tell you something from my personal experience. A woman's most dangerous weapon isn't a gun, a sword or a firebomb."

"Care to enlighten me? What a girl's most dangerous weapon is?"

"I'll give you a clue. They begin with the letter T. Guys like you are so busy watching the front, they don't see the knife she's sharpening behind her back."

Kyle laughed at his partner's argument. "Are you ever optimistic?"

"No. I always expect the worst. That way, I'm prepared when it happens."

# CHAPTER FOUR

## *An Uninvited Guest*

The rookie policewoman looked up at the American flag flying over the downtown precinct, face beaming with pride. Even though they'd never met, Lakeysia knew it was the girl's first day on the job. The slim redhead's uniform was neat, her handcuffs unscratched, and the truncheon on her belt polished to a shine. The veteran watched with vague interest as the young recruit removed her cap and placed it over her chest.

Lakeysia sighed. Should the new girl survive her shift, she wouldn't feel nearly as patriotic tomorrow. In a few hours' time, the rookie would be patrolling the streets. Once exposed to the city's criminal underworld, the gritty reality of tackling muggers and sex offenders would hit hard. And she'd soon realize her academy training had been inadequate preparation for the challenges ahead.

While simulated exercises captured some essence of

crime fighting, there was no margin for error—or second chances—in the real world. There was ample space for more names on the department's memorial plaque. Like many before her, the rookie was a young, spirited idealist who'd pledged her allegiance to protect and serve. She was prepared to give her life in the line of duty. But nobody had tested her ability to cope with the death of another officer, especially someone she'd grown close to.

Lakeysia considered sharing the shattering experience of losing her former partner to an assassin's bullet, in the hope the young girl would opt for a safer career path. Then she realized it was too late for that. Helpful words of encouragement would do far more good than an honest, realistic assessment. She hid her doubts behind a smile and shook the woman's hand.

"Welcome to the precinct. Symons, Homicide. So, who've I got the honor of speaking to?"

The rookie snapped to attention. "Officer Meagan Wilson, ma'am."

"No need to be formal. Loosen up a little. I ain't your commander. Just stopped to offer some guidance. If you ever make detective, apply to Vice. Less dead people to deal with. Besides, we have a real asshole for a lieutenant."

"If you don't mind me saying, shouldn't you..."

"Show respect to my superiors? I should. Page three, paragraph twenty, bullet point seven, or whatever. Let me give you some practical advice, Wilson. Criminals don't follow the police rulebook. Forget that shit and use your common sense. Otherwise, they'll be calling me down to the morgue to look at your naked, skinny body. And that's something I'd rather not do. Understand?"

"Yes. I understand."

The rookie's knees were trembling. She was probably

imagining herself on a cold, metal slab for the first time in her life. Lakeysia rested a comforting hand on Wilson's shoulder.

"Hey, you take care. Your badge doesn't mean nothing to the lowlifes littering the streets. Point your gun in their face, and it's a different story. Self preservation by crapping on the rest of civilization. That's their motto. You don't gotta live by it, but it has its merits."

Her grim observations had left Wilson downbeat and depressed. Lakeysia lifted the rookie's chin, smiled, and added a humorous coup de grâce.

"You watch your ass out there, whether or not your partner decides to."

"Thank you for being so honest with me. It's a pleasant change from..."

The girl glanced over her shoulder. Two policewomen were alone on the front steps, but she spoke quieter. "From the bullshit PC rhetoric they feed us on criminal's rights."

"Careful, Wilson. Keep thinking that, and you might end up like me. See you around."

She patted the rookie on the back and entered the precinct. They had converted the downtown offices from a hotel in the early 1950s. While most interior walls had been demolished during the renovation, the elevators were a throwback to the past. Cage doors, grinding pulley wheels and floor indicator dials had been modern equipment in their day, but replacements were long overdue.

Lakeysia suspected they'd kept the antiquated system to force the foot soldiers to exercise their legs on the stairs. Naturally, the higher ups who made policy had cozy offices at City Hall, with private 'executive' elevators included in the package.

The lift cage stopped four stories up. Homicide Division

occupied two complete floors, to the annoyance of detectives in Robbery and Vice. Their officers often complained about sharing a single office, albeit an eighty-foot square one. They'd have more to grumble about if their workload was half that of a murder detective. There were far more unsolved deaths in San Francisco than investigators, and a dedicated room was necessary to store 'cold case' files. According to rumors, some documents even predated the precinct building.

The first person Lakeysia ran into was Frances Moore, the division secretary. The sweet faced, brown-haired lady preferred a traditional shirt, long dress and high heels to the more practical outfits worn by plainclothes officers. She spent her typical day behind a desk, accessing computer records, photocopying files, and running background checks for senior personnel.

"Detective Symons."

Frances referred to colleagues by their formal titles. That led to many stiff conversations, but Lakeysia was used to it now.

"Glad I found you. Lieutenant Thorne asked me to send you his way when you got here."

Lakeysia looked at her boss' office, a partitioned area in the back corner. Venetian blinds were closed behind soundproofed windows. The big man was no doubt holding a private meeting in there.

"See the watchdog's as patient as ever. He been in there long?"

Lakeysia answered Frances' inquisitive look with a nod towards her partner's desk. Nicole Tasoto sat in Kyle's chair, answering questions from two female detectives. She paused occasionally to wipe away tears. If her despair was all an act, she was doing a convincing job.

"Twenty minutes or so," Frances said. "That's not like Detective Travis, being early for an appointment with the Lieutenant."

"I'm sure he's got his reasons. The grieving daughter, for one."

The assistant shook her head in dismay. "Does that guy date every girl he sees?"

"Just those he finds attractive. Aren't we the lucky ones? Catch you later, Frances. Got an interrogation of my own to look forward to."

Lakeysia took a deep breath and stepped into her master's domain. Christopher Thorne was the ideal poster child for the zero tolerance policy. Anyone unfamiliar with the dome-headed Texan could easily be intimidated by his broad chest, bushy black mustache and pale reddish skin tone. In another life, he would have been an actor typecast as an army drill instructor.

Photos hung behind the desk detailed his long, illustrious history with the police department: early days as a patrolman, his promotion to detective, a multitude of awards and commendations, and an unbroken seven-year stint in charge of Downtown Homicide Division. The old warhorse's poker face was wrinkly, a sign of a man past his prime, but Thorne hadn't grown soft with age.

The lieutenant brushed a fly off his suit, then got down to business. "Travis already gave me the long version. Now you've joined us, care to give your take on things?"

Thorne pushed a case file across his desk. Lakeysia took a seat beside Kyle, crossed her legs, and leaned back against the chair rest.

"Probably just a serial killer. Nothing out of the ordinary."

"Serial killer? Tasoto must have trodden on a few toes

over the years. What makes you think this isn't a one off?"

Lakeysia was about to defend her position when Travis butted in. "Could be a former employee on bad terms," he suggested. "Someone he fired, perhaps. An old colleague with an axe to grind."

The case file contained crime scene photographs that showed the remains of Toshigi's chauffeur. As usual, the forensics man had covered every angle, including the trashcan where the killer had disposed of the driver's severed head.

"Or a sword to swing. Cause of death seems clear cut. Pun intended."

Travis was determined to voice his opinion again.

"I say it's a video game freak, someone who didn't like the latest Dragonsoft offering and made her point at the annual meeting. There's nothing here to indicate a serial killer."

"Not yet," Lakeysia said bleakly.

Inwardly, she hoped Travis was right, but anybody brutal enough to chop off a man's head as part of an elaborate kidnap scheme wasn't about to stop there. Thorne closed the file, doing his best to remain hopeful.

"For now, let's go with the revenge theory. The gaming culture, eh? That's a long line of suspects. You said you thought the perp may have been a woman?"

He looked at Kyle for an answer.

"The picture of events we have is pretty vague. We're still trying to piece together the facts."

"Has the girl said anything?"

"Not yet. Jennings and Lowes are talking to her now."

Lakeysia glanced sideways at her partner. "Perhaps you could employ some of your legendary charm, get her to open up over sushi, teriyaki and sake."

"Nicole's pretty shaken up."

Of course, Travis had to defend the woman.

"I suggest you have someone escort Miss Tasoto home," Thorne said to him. "Give her time to rest, pay a visit, calm her down. Maybe then she'll be more willing to talk."

"Shouldn't be too hard," Lakeysia muttered under her breath.

Her partner reacted to her sarcasm with the usual ignorance. Once the boss had decided on a course of action, they both knew it was a waste of effort to debate his decision.

Thorne opened the blinds. Through the window, Lakeysia watched Kyle return to his desk and converse with Nicole. The two of them hugged each other tight, a further sign of a blossoming relationship. She cried into his shoulder, a trick commonly used by scheming women to lower a man's guard. Guilty or not, Travis was getting too close to her.

"What do you make of the daughter?"

Thorne was clearly thinking along similar lines.

"You want my two cents? Miss Tasoto did her old man in and there's more on the way. Either that, or she knows who did. She's definitely hiding something. Call it female insight."

"Let Travis handle her. You do a background check on Tasoto senior. Talk to his attorney. Goes by the name of Randall Forbes. He's a real slippery character."

"A sleazy lawyer. Ain't that a refreshing change?"

* * *

A record search by the ever-reliable Frances turned up some interesting facts about the deceased's attorney. Randall

Forbes had been a close acquaintance of Toshigi Tasoto since the Japanese entrepreneur moved to San Francisco twelve years earlier. He was co-founder of Dragonsoft, and a senior member of the executive board. After the president, Randall held the largest financial stake in the company.

The high-priced lawyer had no reservations about flashing his earnings in public. He owned various properties throughout the state of California and spent much of his spare time throwing exclusive parties on his luxury yacht. Every other weekend, he invited wealthy socialites, corporate bigwigs and their ilk to Fisherman's Wharf for a private get together.

It was the type of meeting where shady business deals were conducted in broad daylight. Randall's clients weren't afraid of the authorities. They possessed more than enough wealth and clout to derail any unwanted investigations into their activities.

Randall had christened his boat *Apollo*, after the god from Greek mythology. The lawyer obviously saw himself as a key figure in Toshigi's Mount Olympus. With the king dead, perhaps it was time to rename his yacht to *Zeus*.

It didn't take Lakeysia long to locate the ship. Most vessels moored at the wharf's forty plus piers were floating museums or tourist attractions. The midday tours of San Francisco Bay and Alcatraz Island had already started, leaving only historic wrecks and private launches as potential candidates. *Apollo* was the cream of the fleet: a sleek, yellow sailed vessel built for speed and privacy.

Lakeysia spotted two people on deck, but she doubted the woman massaging Randall's back was a sailor. The Asian girl's hands were soft and manicured, and her slim, artificially busty body and pink bikini suggested she had more experience navigating the male population than the Pacific.

A half naked Randall lay flat on a sun bench, sipping martini from a cocktail glass. Cool air blew in from the bay, carrying a rich, sickly aroma of wax and lotions.

Lakeysia walked up the boat's gangplank and flashed her badge in Randall's face.

"Detective Symons, Homicide. I can see you're a busy man, Mister Forbes. I promise I won't take up too much of your time."

Randall turned to his masseur. "Asuka, would you excuse us? I've got some business to deal with."

The girl smiled, rubbed his back again, and disappeared below decks.

"Sure she's old enough? You wouldn't want to screw around with a minor. The adverse publicity might not sit too well with your clientele."

Randall seemed totally relaxed as he refilled his cocktail glass.

"Asuka's my physical therapist. That's all there is to it."

"Right. And you're a strictly legitimate businessman. In case you're feeling charitable, police officers don't drink on duty."

"Good to see you know the law, detective. May I ask what this is about?"

"Toshigi Tasoto was found murdered earlier this morning."

Lakeysia broke the news as brutally as possible. Official policy was to be tactful, but she liked to catch her opponents off guard.

Randall choked on his martini. "What?" he coughed. "When did—"

"What was your relationship with him?"

"Toshigi and I were business partners." He stood up and stared incredulously. "Surely you're not suggesting that I had something to do with this?"

"I don't know. Did you?"

An outraged protest was a common response by guilty suspects, and she wanted to keep Randall under pressure as long as possible. As expected, he had an alibi ready.

"I've been here all night. Asuka can vouch for me."

"I'm sure she will."

Lakeysia stepped over a pile of revealing feminine clothes, folded her arms, and confronted the slimy lawyer head on.

"Course, she'd back you up anyway, wouldn't she?"

"What exactly are you implying?"

"Want me to spell it out for you?"

Lakeysia paced slowly around the ship's deck, stared out at the ocean, then spun sharply.

"You into mixed race relationships? Got a taste for Asian girls?"

"My personal life is not your concern, Miss Symons."

"Detective Symons," Lakeysia corrected him. "Ever had the boss' daughter aboard?"

Anger flashed in the attorney's eyes. He downed his martini and sucked his lips dry.

"I think you've outstayed your welcome, *Detective*."

Randall's cocky swagger was notably absent from the response. For whatever reason, Lakeysia's invasive line of questioning had struck a chord. She followed through, hoping to capitalize on his vulnerability.

"What? You won't answer questions without a lawyer present? You stand to inherit a fair chunk of your late partner's wealth. Am I right?"

"Since you seem so interested in Miss Tasoto, perhaps you should question her. She inherits her father's estate, not me. Now, if you're finished."

"And you, as co-founder, gain sole ownership of his company. Annual profits of forty million. Not bad for a runner-up prize."

Randall clenched his glass tight. "Detective Symons, I'm just about through listening to your unfounded accusations which, if I may say so, I find quite insulting."

"If I think of any more, I'll be sure to let you know. Don't sail too far. Wouldn't want us to get the wrong impression, would you?"

Lakeysia started to leave, but stopped at the top of the yacht's gangplank.

"One more thing, Mister Forbes. Witness reports suggest the killer may be a woman. If I were you, I'd be wary of who you invite below decks. Be a shame if something bad happened to such an upstanding citizen. Enjoy your rubdown. I would stay longer, but I really need some fresh air."

* * *

Randall only allowed his temper to flare once Lakeysia had driven away. In a fit of rage, he hurled his cocktail glass into the ocean. Intentionally or not, Detective Symons had been accurate with her assumptions. It was as if she possessed an uncanny trait for ferreting out the truth.

He was so distracted by her unannounced visit he didn't see Asuka emerge from his private cabin. It was only when she wrapped her arms around his waist he became aware of her presence.

Normally Randall would choose an attractive girl's company over business dealings, but this matter was too important to be deferred until later. He kissed the girl on the cheek and impatiently waved her below decks.

After making certain she was out of earshot, Randall collected his cellphone from its holder, composed himself, and made the call.

* * *

Shaded oriental lanterns cast a faint glow across Jade's private bedroom. Even in the dim green light, the polished blade of her katana gleamed in its support stand. The centerpiece of the inner sanctum was a king sized bed furnished with sheets to match her favorite color scheme. Its wooden corner posts were carved to resemble dragon scales, similar in design to those on the hilt of her sword. Other than that, the only furnishings were a computer desk, wardrobe, and vanity table. Bar bells and exercise machines occupied the remaining space.

When her telephone rang, Jade was practicing punches on a dummy strung from the ceiling. Torn newspaper clippings plastered the battered mannequin's body, with parts of Toshigi's face visible on the damaged scraps. The shredded article was a review of one of Jade's first games. Naturally, there had been no mention of her.

A quick glance at the answering machine revealed the caller's identity. Jade could have taken the call there and then, but Randall would have to wait until she'd finished. She focused on her target, leaped in the air, and knocked the final news clipping away with a spinning kick. Satisfied with her morning workout, Jade sat at her vanity table and activated the speakerphone.

"Suzanne." Randall referred to her by the alias she'd given him. "I wanted to offer you my congratulations on a job well done."

He masked his anxiety, but she wasn't so easily fooled. Her co-conspirator's voice was calm and composed, but nervous, pacing footsteps could be heard in the background. Something was on Randall's mind.

"I'd prefer it if you called me Jade from now on."

The killer smiled at herself in the mirror, then followed up on a hunch.

"Don't let the police concern you."

"Police?"

Randall's shaky response verified her suspicions. She brushed her hair, picturing her pawn sweating on the other end of the line.

"Don't play dumb. I know everything. With all you stand to gain from Toshigi's death, you're the obvious prime suspect. But that's why you accepted my offer. I do the dirty work while you have breakfast in bed with Asuka."

She allowed him a moment to contemplate, then continued.

"Like I said, I know everything."

"You got your revenge, didn't you?"

"And you got your money," Jade reminded him. "A satisfactory mutual arrangement. I hope I've not underestimated you, Randall. You've spent your whole life telling lies and getting cold-blooded murderers off the hook. Is it so difficult to give yourself a watertight alibi?"

"The detective who came to see me. She's smart. Be careful with her."

"A woman? That should make things interesting. Every good game needs a worthy opponent, and men are so easy to manipulate."

"Are you manipulating me?"

Randall phrased the question as bluntly as possible. Jade, not bothered in the slightest, lifted her katana from its stand and filed her fingers on the blade.

"Decapitation is a quick and painless way to die," she said. "Far preferable to being roasted alive. The chauffeur was nothing more than an inconvenience, a minor obstacle. I had no great desire to see him suffer. But Toshigi... He screwed me over. Can you imagine how it must feel to suffocate from the stench of your own burning skin? Think about that before you show the recording to the police."

"Recording? What recording?"

Randall stuttered, so it was obvious he knew exactly what Jade was referring to.

"The one you're making right now. Don't contact me again. Unless you have more dirty laundry, in which case I'd be happy to help you with the cleanup. It's one thing I'm very good at."

Jade ended the call and checked her own digital record of their conversation. Like her, Randall had taken out an insurance policy, a bargaining chip to use in the event of capture or betrayal. But that was to be expected.

She'd studied the attorney well enough to predict his every move. He would remain silent, in the hope he could somehow blackmail her later. And if Randall went to the police, he wouldn't be able to tell them anything about his partner in crime. Not even her real name.

# CHAPTER FIVE

## *Safely Back Home*

Pacific Heights could be described as a private country club for San Francisco's wealthy elite. Sprawling mansion estates dominated the hilly landscape, segregated from the outside world by wrought iron fences. Backyard swimming pools were the rule rather than the exception, while conservatories, mosaic patios and hedge mazes were not uncommon. These luxury homes were the ultimate status symbol. Prices invariably ran into seven figures, and nothing but a jackpot lottery win, powerful family connections, or significant financial success would grant a person entry into this exclusive arena.

What most impressed Kyle was how Toshigi had done it the hard way. The video game legend had amassed the funds to purchase such a beautiful residence through sheer work and dedication, building his empire from scratch. He'd named his daughter the primary beneficiary, and while Nicole could never consider the estate compensation for her loss, it was certainly an impressive legacy.

The buildings were an eye-pleasing blend of eastern and western cultures. In front of the Victorian style mansion was a modern garage with space for four cars, while the rear garden's key feature was a Japanese dojo on wooden stilts.

Kyle felt uneasy parking next to Nicole's silver corvette. Police vehicles—even unmarked ones—were chosen for their speed, handling and endurance, but his ride looked hopelessly shabby by comparison. He straightened his shirt collar and stepped onto the gravel driveway.

Topiary hedges bordered the front porch, but instead of animal figures, the leaves were shaped into Japanese alphabet characters. Kyle did not know what the message said, but he assumed it was a welcome greeting. He only hoped Nicole would show him the same hospitality.

At the crime scene, the girl made it perfectly clear she blamed the police for what happened. It was a natural reaction to hold them responsible, and her psychological wounds would probably heal. Still, Kyle wasn't happy about questioning the distraught young lady so soon after her father's death.

The detective swallowed deep, quelled his apprehensions, and rang the doorbell. A series of high-pitched notes sounded beyond the oak paneled threshold. The bell's button doubled as the nose of a blackened steel figurehead, a fancy ornament modeled after Dragonsoft's company logo. Its teeth supported a brass knocker ring, and the right eye was a peephole lens.

Kyle saw blurred flashes of pink and white through the murky glass. Somebody was weighing him up. Whoever the mystery person behind the door was, they seemed reluctant to let him inside.

"Yes?"

A woman's voice, but she didn't sound like Nicole. Kyle held his police shield up and gave the standard introduction.

"Detective Travis. Homicide."

That appeared to satisfy her. Tumblers turned, a chain slid off its hook, and bolts cranked back. Kyle counted seven locking mechanisms in total before a servant finally opened the door. Security was extreme, but Nicole had every reason to be cautious.

The family maid was a plump faced, rose cheeked brunette who looked eighteen but was probably closer to twenty-five. Her dress was the standard black uniform with matching shoes and stockings. Beneath her white cap, her hair was tied in a bun, and she carried leaning utensils in the front pocket of her apron.

"I'm Sarah," she said. The maid beckoned Kyle inside and closed the door after him. "You must be the man who called earlier."

"Yes. That's right."

He had phoned ahead, concerned a surprise appearance might have offended Nicole to the point she refused to speak with him. Then he'd have no option but to drag the girl back to the precinct, which would only upset her further. Kyle would prefer to interview her in the comfort and safety of her own living room. She'd been through enough already.

"I feel so horrible for Miss Tasoto," Sarah said. "Losing her father at such a young age. Do you have any idea who could have done such a thing?"

"Forgive me, but I'm not at liberty to discuss the case. Actually, that's why I came. If she's feeling up to it, I'd like to ask Nicole a few questions."

"The mistress is resting in the library. Do come on in.

She has been expecting you. You're welcome to wear your shoes inside, but kindly wipe your feet on the mat."

Kyle obeyed Sarah's instructions and followed her through the entrance hall. It was a vast, forty-foot tall chamber decorated with marble columns, samurai statues and oriental themed portraits. In keeping with Japanese tradition, the wooden floor tiles were mostly bare. A spiral staircase wound upwards towards the upper levels, while rooms were accessible through sliding panels.

Sarah took the lead. She led Kyle to the left, slid open one of the larger doors, and accompanied him into the library.

"Miss Tasoto," she announced. "There's a gentleman to see you."

Nicole swiveled round as he entered. To his relief, she greeted him with a smile.

"Detective Travis. Thank you for coming," she said, then addressed the maid. "It's okay, Sarah. Brew us some coffee. We'll come through in a minute."

The servant left promptly, but Kyle never saw her leave the room. He had a hard time taking his eyes off Nicole.

The beautiful Asian girl had swapped her formal business suit for a loose fitting, ruby red gown tailored from fine quality silk. Her outfit complimented her good looks, a knee length robe secured at the waist with a gold-inlaid sash.

Nicole strode barefoot towards Kyle, stopped two paces ahead of him, and folded her arms. Her stance was noble and elegant, almost princess-like. He looked up into the girl's eyes. Even without shoes, she stood three inches taller.

"I owe you an apology, Detective. You did everything you could to help my father. For all you knew, that crazy woman would have killed him regardless. It's just... I..."

She trailed off, fighting back tears. Kyle swiftly changed

the subject.

"Quite an impressive collection you have here."

He was referring to the bookcases along the circular interior wall. Tomes and parchments filled the shelves. At a rough estimate, there were over ten thousand documents, enough to rival most of the city's public libraries. Enclosed booths and reading tables were positioned throughout the room. This was a study area without the distraction of rude, noisy children, a pure center of learning that put many others to shame.

"These texts belonged to my father," Nicole said. "When Toshigi first came to this country, he was determined not to abandon his Japanese heritage. As the years passed by, he became more and more immersed in American culture. He kept these books to remind himself of his humble beginnings, a history he preferred to forget. I can't remember the last time he set foot in this room. It was so long ago."

As Nicole recounted her tale, Kyle wandered to a vacuumed preservation case. According to its label plaque, the manuscript inside was hundreds of years old. Toshigi must have shelled out a handsome sum to add it to his collection.

"I suppose the work piled up," he said.

"You mean the sales agreements piled up? My father was a self centered, capitalist pig. Sorry if I sound blunt, but I assume you want the cold, hard truth, not the romanticized version."

This was a side to Nicole that Kyle hadn't seen before: a tough, independent girl beneath the pleasant exterior. He was about to comment when a serving bell rang next door.

"Should we discuss my father's failings over coffee?" she suggested. "Sarah's prepared enough for two. You're welcome to join me."

"How can I refuse the hostess?"

Kyle accompanied her to the entrance hall.

"You don't seem too sympathetic towards your father. Were you on good terms?"

"Establishing decent working relationships was not one of his fortes. With my father, business always took priority over family. Sometimes he could be a downright miserable bastard."

Nicole showed Kyle to a guest area at the rear end of the house. He presumed this was where Toshigi would have socialized with his friends after dinner. The stylish, velvet cushioned armchairs were designed with maximum comfort in mind, while chess sets and card tables ought to keep visitors entertained until the early hours of the morning. As a bonus, the view of the back garden was simply mesmerizing. In warmer or safer times, one might open the French windows to allow ventilation. For now, insulation and security took priority.

Sarah brought in a silver tray, placed it on an end table, and poured coffee into two china cups. Expensive though it was, the cutlery was overshadowed by other items on display. Portraits by world-famous artists were framed above the mantelpiece, and priceless relics from feudal Japan exhibited in glass cases. One antique collection caught Kyle's eye: a full suit of samurai armor and weaponry restored to its former glory.

"Your father left all this to you?" he asked, choosing an armchair that faced the garden windows.

Nicole passed a cup to Kyle and took the other for herself.

"Why? Do you think I killed him for the money?"

After dropping that bomb, she sat beside him, stared

directly ahead, and stirred her coffee.

"Thank you, Sarah. That will be all."

Realizing her catering services were no longer required, the maid gave her mistress a courteous bow, pulled a feather duster from her apron, and cleaned the room.

"Nobody's accusing you of anything, Nicole. This is all routine."

Kyle leaned forward to place his hand on the girl's knee, but her sharp-eyed glare made him reconsider.

"But that's what you were thinking. I'm not stupid, Detective. I design games for a living. You can consider me an expert player. In the twelve years since my father came to San Francisco, hundreds of people have worked for him. And, as I've already explained, he wasn't the most appreciative president to serve under. Why don't you take your witch hunt there?"

Nicole's arguments were solid and logical, so Kyle followed up.

"Can you think of anyone in particular? A former employee who might have wanted to hurt your father? You said the person who delivered the note was a woman. Does that narrow it down?"

"I'm only telling you what Rebecca told me. She's my secretary at Dragonsoft. You can get the details from her."

Kyle sipped his coffee, thinking back to the crime scene. "The killer left a message. Twelve E. Mean anything to you?"

Nicole shrugged her shoulders.

"You're the detective, not me."

"You say your father has lived in the US for twelve years? Probably a coincidence. So you grew up in Japan, then?"

"No. Toshigi adopted me when I was seven."

Nicole finished her coffee and wandered to a French

window. On the way, she passed Sarah. The maid had done cleaning display cases and started on the armchairs.

"He visited the orphanage in San Jose. I'd been there ever since my parents died. I was only three at the time."

She'd avoided talking about their deaths. Kyle suspected it was a painful memory, an incident she didn't want to elaborate on.

"The visit was one of my father's publicity stunts. That was back when he cared enough to donate money to charity. I showed him my work."

Nicole turned towards a pastel portrait of San Francisco, a collage of monochrome gray skyscrapers with chunky windows. A red suspension bridge crossed wavy blue lines in the background. The colorful depiction of the Golden Gate was obviously the creation of a child, but the attention to detail was impressive.

"And Toshigi saw something in me," Nicole said. "He thought I had exceptional visual flair. The rest, as they say, is history."

A French window pane behind her shattered with a muffled bang, showering her gown with glass fragments. The terrified girl dropped to the floor. She looked to Kyle for an explanation, but he had none to give.

Then he heard a loud crack. The maid collapsed like a rag doll, fresh blood dripping from a bullet wound on her temple. Her discarded feather duster rolled away from her unmoving hand.

"Sarah!" screamed Nicole.

Kyle's experience and training took over. He threw away his coffee cup, dived to the ground, and pulled his gun from its holster.

"Stay down! There's nothing you can do for her."

She lay still, whimpering. Kyle peeked over the

armchair cushion. He'd only exposed a small fraction of his head when a second windowpane imploded. Nicole cried in terror as broken glass rained between her shaking legs.

Careful to keep low, Kyle turned to inspect the damage. The unseen assassin's bullet had shattered a display case, and the antique vase inside was literally shot to pieces. He grabbed his radio.

"This is Travis," he said, scanning the far wall whilst maintaining cover. "At the Tasoto residence, three nine one Pine Avenue. I'm under fire. One confirmed shooter, maybe more. We have a civilian down. I need backup now!"

He signaled Nicole to get behind a sofa. She shook her head, too scared to even move. Kyle lay on his side and wriggled towards her, keeping his weapon aimed at the garden.

He couldn't see anyone outside, but there were plenty of potential sniping positions amongst the foliage. His view of the lawn was severely restricted, and she—if the shooter was a woman—could well be lining up a killer shot.

Kyle extended his hand. After some hesitation, Nicole reached out and grabbed it. Her gaze was fixed on Sarah's body. The girl shook with fright, and he had trouble holding her still.

"Help me," she pleaded. "I... I can't move."

"Come with me. I'll cover you."

A touch-tone telephone rang, startling Kyle into action. A less experienced officer might have shot off the receiver, but he held his fire. Thinking the phone call could be a diversion, he kept alert for trouble. After four rings, an answering machine cut in.

"You've reached Toshigi Tasoto. Unfortunately, I'm not here right now. After the tone, leave a message."

Listening to her murdered father's voice had to be

upsetting. There was a loud beep, followed by a ten-second period of cracking static.

They waited in silence as the wind whistled through the cracked windowpanes. Then the mystery caller finally spoke.

"Sorry to disturb you, Toshigi," she said, "but I thought you were dead. You remember me, don't you? I'm the girl who arranged your funeral pyre."

Nicole looked at Kyle apprehensively. "Oh my God. It's her. She's come for me."

"I wanted to speak to Nicole," the woman said in the same chilling voice. "And to the handsome policeman keeping her company. I'm watching you right now, Detective, just like I watched you two at the bank this morning. If you hadn't been so busy chatting the girl up, she might have reached her father in time. Sorry about Sarah. She had nothing to do with this, but I was afraid you wouldn't take me seriously otherwise. Think of your maid as a henchwoman, a supporting character. Nicole, you should know those people always die first."

"Screw you! You hear me? Screw you!"

Kyle crept forward, keeping his chest to the ground. He whispered to Nicole over his shoulder.

"You stay here. Don't listen to her."

"Let's play a game. Hide and seek. Come out, come out wherever you are, so I can blow your head off."

The woman followed her sick wordplay with a girlish chuckle.

"I want you to understand that I'm smarter than you, Detective. You have no idea who I am. I could be in the same room, and you wouldn't even know it. I could kill you right now, but that would be no challenge."

Kyle reached the far wall, pressed his body against the

woodwork, and gripped his pistol tight. He shifted weight onto his lower knees, preparing himself for a shootout.

"By the end of the week, I'll be famous, and do you know where you'll be, Detective? In a cemetery, sharing a grave with that miserable bastard's daughter."

That insult was too much for Nicole to bear. She leaped to her feet and marched to the broken window.

"Shut up, you crazy bitch!" she screamed through the glass.

The girl had fully exposed herself and was an easy target for the shooter. Kyle shoved her to the floor and assumed her position by the bullet holes. He peered down the barrel of his gun, waiting for the killer to show her face.

"Stay down!"

Kyle's advice did no good. The woman's psychotic chuckling was all Nicole could hear. Overcome with terror, she sprinted to the telephone, pressed the erase message button, and yanked the receiver off its hook.

"Shut up!"

The psycho caller had pushed her into panic, and it was only a matter of time before she snapped completely and did something suicidal. Kyle had to neutralize the threat while he had the chance.

He steadied his gun and hooked his shoe cap underneath the window's locking bolt, lifting it from the floor groove. He groped for the handle, twisted it full circle, and kicked open the frame.

Frosty blades of grass crunched beneath Kyle's feet as he stepped outside. He swept the garden, using trees and ornaments for cover. He frequently turned on the spot, knowing Lakeysia wasn't around to watch his back. There was nothing this psycho would like more than to sneak up and pop him at point blank range.

Kyle heard the wail of approaching police sirens in the distance. Help was coming, but right now, he was alone. He kept his concentration, listening for any small noise that might give away the killer's position. It came sooner than he expected.

At first, the sounds were barely audible. The soft rustles and muffled crunching could have been an animal trampling through the vegetation. Then the ruckus gradually grew louder, and the seven-foot hedge that enclosed the garden shook so violently half a dozen leaves snapped off their stems. It couldn't be the wind. Movement was limited to a specific narrow section, and the surrounding air was still.

Kyle took cover behind a statue: a full size, bronze likeness of Toshigi with a square fountain at its base. As he crouched down, he felt something hard and metallic dig into his trouser leg. He lifted his knee to look.

The item in question was a spent nine-millimeter bullet casing. From here, Kyle had a perfect unobstructed view of the library wall. He could see everything: broken French windows, shattered vase, the maid's body. Behind the statue, there were two deep footprints in the soil. This was the spot where the sniper had made her nest.

Someone was coming, their footsteps soft and spread apart. The killer was making a stealthy approach. If Kyle hadn't been alerted by the earlier noises, she might have surprised him, but now he had the advantage.

The low midday sun cast a human shadow across the garden. The woman was circling towards the house, probably going after Nicole. That would be her last mistake. Once Kyle had a clear shot, he broke cover.

"Freeze!"

The suspect lowered her weapon, but elation was short-lived. His target's scruffy clothes, African American skin tone and messed up hair were very familiar. She was a killer, but definitely not the woman Kyle was looking for.

"Whoops!"

Lakeysia held her gun side on and signaled for him to relax.

"You did call for help, Travis. At least try and look happy to see me. You can rest easy. I think your date stood you up."

Kyle holstered his sidearm. "She was standing right here. Watching, waiting for her opportunity. The bitch killed Nicole's maid in front of me. Not because she didn't like her. No, it was just for bragging rights. She spent five minutes gloating on the phone."

"You seem convinced the killer's a woman. Positive about that?"

"Hey! I know a girl's voice when I hear it. Okay?"

"Yeah. I'm sure you do."

Kyle turned away in disgust. He spotted Nicole outside the open French window, gown drawn tight around her body. Her teeth were chattering. If the girl stayed in the cold any longer, she'd catch pneumonia.

"Nicole, are you crazy? Get back inside," Kyle said. "Everything's fine. She's gone."

"Don't you think you're getting a little too close to this woman?" asked Lakeysia, keeping her voice down.

"Pretty good job I was, eh? Otherwise there might be two bodies at the morgue with Tasoto name tags taped around their toes."

"It bother you why she's alive and the maid's not?"

"What?" Kyle couldn't believe what she was implying. "You think Nicole's in league with the killer? Does she look like a psycho to you?"

"Suppose she could be innocent. Who knows? Maybe this girl actually likes you."

A half-hearted comment, so he knew a punch line was coming, and his partner didn't disappoint.

"By all means, go play a game with your new friend. Just make sure she's not playing you."

Lakeysia slipped on a pair of surgical gloves and combed the crime scene. Kyle reflected on her thoughts as he returned to the house. She was wrong, of course. Nicole possibly bore some grudge against Toshigi, but there was no way she was complicit in cold-blooded murder.

What bothered him was the girl's connection to all three victims. Someone was specifically targeting the daughter and those around her, which meant she probably knew the killer personally. With any luck, recent events would encourage Nicole to be more open about her past. Kyle was convinced she was the key to the mystery.

# CHAPTER SIX

## *The Victim's Role*

Lakeysia and Kyle were still at Nicole's house when forensics showed up. Doctor Edwin Matthews had seen too many corpses to be shocked by a gunshot victim, no matter how young. The white-haired investigator scratched his beard and limped about the crime scene, studying the cadaver from a variety of angles. A female Chinese American intern took photographs, labeled pieces of evidence with numbered cards, and drew the customary chalk outline around the body.

Matthews tilted the victim's head to one side. He examined the bullet wound for a few seconds before he gave his verdict.

"The shot was fired from medium range. I'd say twenty to fifty feet away. From the direction of entry, that would probably place the shooter outside the house."

"Probably?" said Nicole. "Did you notice the broken

windows?"

The young girl made a strong case, but Lakeysia remained skeptical.

"First rule of forensics, start from scratch and assume nothing. Things aren't always what they seem."

"I suppose now you'll deduce she died from a gunshot wound. Look, could you please do something about…"

Nicole gestured towards the dead maid.

"Sarah? When Matthews gets through with the body. He's gotta make sure your story checks out. We can't rely on a single witness account."

Lakeysia inspected the shattered windowpane, taking care not to step on the broken glass.

"Or even two," she said with a glance at her partner.

Once Matthews had finished his examination, he nodded to the coroner. Miss Tasoto cried as paramedics sealed the maid's corpse in a plastic body bag. Kyle pulled the girl closer so she could rest her head against his chest.

"It's all right, Nicole. No one can blame you for being upset."

Lakeysia drew the forensics man aside.

"So, what do you reckon, doc? Three victims in six hours. That has to make your top ten list."

The doctor's assistant lifted a crushed bullet from the vase fragments, deposited it in a clear evidence bag, and brought it over for her supervisor to study.

Matthews held the slug up to the light. "Nine millimeter round," he said. "Your killer's an expert marksman. It's difficult to hit a person in the head from that distance with a rifle. This guy used a handgun, most probably a silenced pistol. A one shot kill. Your partner's lucky the second bullet missed."

"It wasn't time for him to die. This psycho doesn't miss

unless on purpose. Travis wasn't the target. Neither was the girl. They're not breathing by chance."

Matthews returned the evidence bag to his assistant. "So why kill the maid?" he asked.

"Same reason as the driver. Serial killers like leaving dead bodies. Maybe it helps them sleep at night. I dunno."

"You think it's the same perpetrator?"

It was clear from the doctor's tone that he wasn't convinced.

"You don't?"

"Different murder weapon. Different M.O. No ransom note, no sophisticated setup, no coded message. No similarity at all."

"Fact is, the victims are all connected. To the same woman. First her chauffeur, then her father, and now her maid. You believe it's all just a coincidence, doc? Trust me. This was no random shooting. It was part of the plan."

Matthews was bound to ask the inevitable follow up question.

"What plan?"

"Whatever this lunatic has cooked up for us. This isn't some video game nut acting on impulse. These are well orchestrated attacks. So far, three strikes. Two of those, Travis and Miss Tasoto, watched the victims die."

"What's your point?"

Lakeysia took a deep breath, then gave her unprofessional opinion.

"We got our work cut out. The stiffs we've seen today, they were just tasters, players in some sick game show this wacko put on for us. Our killer's smart, well organized, not afraid to take risks. And from what Travis says, might be female. The young, innocent girl next door nobody would suspect."

While Lakeysia was analyzing her quarry, Kyle had called Thorne on his cellphone. Her partner was in the thick of an argument.

"Lieutenant, I don't care about resources," he said. "Miss Tasoto was just attacked in her own home. We've already seen what this girl's capable of. I want round-the-clock protection at Nicole's residence. Three teams of two working eight-hour shifts. Starting tonight."

Lakeysia couldn't hear the boss' reply, but from the way her partner shouted back, she guessed it wasn't the response he wanted.

"The girl dies, and it's on your head, not mine. Anything happens to Nicole because you refused to give her protection, and I'll see to it you shoulder the blame. Yeah, I'm aware you outrank me."

"That's love for you, Matthews," Lakeysia said. "It can drive a guy crazy."

Kyle was so infatuated with his new girlfriend that he wasn't afraid to talk down to the lieutenant. Fortunately for him, the gamble paid off.

"Thank you, sir."

Finally calming down, he terminated the call and gave a thumbs-up signal.

"Wouldn't count on you being a detective when all this is over," Lakeysia said. "Take it Thorne agreed?"

"Yeah. Not that it'll do any good."

"Do you think she'll come back?" asked Nicole. "Try again? Because if she does, that bitch better —"

"No," said Kyle, contradicting his previous arguments. "Our girl's too smart for that. But right now, you're the only lead we've got. I'm just covering the bases. That's all. I don't want anything to happen to you."

Lakeysia whispered in Nicole's ear. "Not until you

dump him, anyway."

Her private remark brought a smile to her face, though it soon disappeared.

"My father, and then Sarah. Why them and not me? What does this crazy woman want?"

"We were hoping you could give us some input on that."

Kyle handed Nicole a business card.

"Here's my number. If you remember anything that might help, or if you need someone to talk to, call me. Okay?"

"Okay."

"We'll catch her. You have my word."

Lakeysia buttoned her coat. "Perhaps you two should spend the night together. This nutter seems to enjoy performing in front of cops."

"I think Nicole needs some time to herself."

"Then we should go home, Travis. Get some rest. We'll need it."

Kyle joined her by the door.

"So, do you still reckon Nicole's guilty?"

"You bet. The question is, of what? Liking you, withholding information, or conspiracy to commit murder one?"

* * *

Charlie Horwick turned to the last page of *Jade Dragon vs. Doctor Takamura*. The aging night manager had read the comic book countless times, but this issue was his favorite, the one where the ninja heroine battled a mad scientist with a miniaturization cannon.

He ought to be watching the security monitors, but there was never anything interesting to see. After another hectic day of business, the Dragonsoft Development offices were now closed, and everyone else had left hours ago. Apart from the secretary, Rebecca Masters. A single mother, she needed the extra cash and so worked late often.

Charlie squinted, struggling to read the last speech bubble. Then he realized the page had darkened. For the second time in a week, his reading lamp required a new bulb. The watchman tossed the comic book on his desk and reached for a supply drawer. He froze, staring at the security footage of the front approach. A black motorcycle was parked on the tarmac outside.

Charlie scanned the monitor screens, but found no sign of an intruder. On another night, he may have checked it out, but the murders of Toshigi and two staff members were still fresh in his mind. Police had interviewed all Dragonsoft employees during the afternoon, and the killings were national headline news. Although the authorities had kept the exact details under wraps, the deaths must have been pretty gruesome to cause such a stir. Charlie was in his fifties and unarmed, no match for a crazed killer.

"Not very brave, are you?"

A gloved hand flipped the lamp switch. The focused beam shone directly into Charlie's eyes, leaving him dazzled.

A tall, feminine figure stood before his desk. She wore biker's gear, a black leather outfit with a crash helmet concealing her face. The woman had one arm behind her back, holding something long and metallic that glimmered between her legs. She dragged its pointed end along the floor, creating a horrid scraping noise.

Charlie wasn't taking any chances. He groped for an alarm button under his desk.

"Do I know you?" he asked, stalling for time.

"Yes, Charlie. I believe you do."

Polished steel flashed before his eyes. Before he knew it, the woman in leather had a blade against his throat.

"I wouldn't touch that button," she said, "unless you have a noble sense of duty to your dead boss."

To emphasize her seriousness, the girl twisted her weapon. The sharp edge was so close it shaved hairs from Charlie's neck. The biker held him at sword point, lifted her helmet, and threw it aside. Long, golden blonde hair draped over her shoulders.

The woman leaned forward into the light. "Recognize me now?" she asked, staring into his eyes. "I've had quite a makeover."

She spun the comic book round, closed it, and glanced casually at the title.

"Jade Dragon, my favorite game character. At least, she was before that greedy bastard Toshigi milked her for all she was worth. Of course, I never made a dime from any of the stupid spin offs. Do you think that's fair, Charlie? Well, do you?"

She pushed her sword into his throat, prompting him for a reply.

"No," he said hastily. "I don't."

"Would you have the courage to say yes if you did? Or do you consider yourself too important to die?"

Charlie's memory had grown weaker with age, but he knew the woman's voice from somewhere, and he was sure he'd seen those bright green eyes before. Could it be that game developer who used to work upstairs, the one who shared an office with Toshigi's daughter?

"Do you like girls with swords?"

The biker asked her question with a sadistic smile. She rotated her blade, peeling flakes of skin from Charlie's neck.

"No? How about martial arts? Fighting babes?"

With blurring speed, the intruder struck his nose with her palm. Before the pain could even set in, the woman dropped her sword, vaulted on the watchman's desk, and kicked him off his chair. He landed on his back, blood dripping from his nostrils. The fall knocked the wind out of him, and he barely held onto consciousness.

"Admit it, Charlie." His attacker jumped down, landing next to him. "You were envious of me. I was this big, successful games designer, and you were nothing but a lowly security guard."

It took all Charlie's strength to pull his body within range of the alarm switch. The woman chuckled, watching him exhaust himself. When the manager's fingers were an inch from the red button, she grabbed his hand, extended it, and pressed her foot against his shoulder. He heard—and felt—his bones creak with tension.

"But you see, I'm good at what I do. And you're not."

She broke Charlie's arm with a single, well-placed blow to his elbow. A quiet crunch preceded unbearable pain. Paralysis seized him, agony and fear rooting him to the spot.

"Please," he sobbed. "Please. No more."

The woman adjusted the monitor controls. One image flickered, then changed to show the president's greeting room. Rebecca typed at her workstation, unaware a psychopath was watching through the surveillance camera behind her.

The blonde girl placed something on Charlie's chest and folded his arms across the top. It looked and felt like a toy plastic sword, but the old man couldn't care less. He just wanted his suffering to end.

The woman zoomed in until the secretary's face filled the screen.

"Poor Rebecca. The pretty damsel in distress is going to die. And it's all your fault, Sir Charles. You could have sounded the alarm, but you chose to beg for your own worthless life instead. Not a chivalrous thing to do. You're a knight, a guardian. You were supposed to protect the citizens of your castle, but you failed. And that's unacceptable."

Having passed judgment, the woman kneeled down and gently lifted Charlie's head off the ground. She grabbed a tuft of his hair and snapped his neck with a single, powerful twist of her forearm. Death was mercifully swift.

* * *

Jade made a brief trip outside to collect her knapsack, then returned to the office and took the elevator to the top floor. She was careful to replace her helmet on the way up. A few years ago, Toshigi had installed surveillance cameras throughout the building. He claimed it was to protect his employees, but the real reason was to discourage slackers and corporate espionage. Sophisticated counter measures protected the network, making it impossible to disable the system without alerting the private security company.

There was only one camera in the lobby, so it was easy for Jade to keep her back to the lens. The upper levels were much more secure. Three separate devices monitored the approach to the design office, with a fourth in the reception area itself. It was crucial that she kept her face concealed. Even in her blonde wig, someone would surely recognize her from surveillance footage.

Jade drew her tranquilizer gun as she walked along the corridor. Like the night watchman, Nicole's secretary had a role to play before she died.

Rebecca looked up from her workstation, alerted by Jade's echoing footsteps. She screamed, recoiling from the woman who marched towards her.

"Who are you?" she whimpered.

Jade dropped her knapsack and raised her pistol.

"Probably the last person you'll ever see."

Quivering with panic, the timid secretary unzipped her handbag. She tossed out a pile of cosmetic items and clumsily retrieved her revolver. Jade knew her target carried a firearm. That's why she'd readied her tranquilizer in advance.

The killer fired a dart into her victim's neck. The sedative spread quickly through a person's bloodstream. Rebecca was rendered her numb and powerless within seconds. She had no chance to aim her weapon.

Jade pried the gun from the girl's fingers, released the chamber, and emptied the bullets onto the floor.

"We can't have you cheating, can we?"

Rebecca's eyelids fluttered open and closed. She attempted to speak, but could only whimper and squeal. The secretary's pupils were dilated. She was fighting a losing battle to even stay awake, let alone confront her attacker.

Jade discarded the revolver, then pulled out the dart. She dropped it in a wastebasket and dragged Rebecca into the next room.

Dragonsoft's chief developers shared the same workspace, a spacious office with a postcard view of San Francisco. Only visitors could enjoy the scenery. The company assigned all programmers places behind a long, plastic table. Chairs, computers, and keyboards were fully integrated into the structure. Employees worked with their backs to the window all day, constantly in the scope of surveillance cameras. To remind them whom they served, the president had mounted a silver framed portrait of himself on the far wall.

Jade lifted Rebecca off the floor, carried her over to the desk, and sat her down in Nicole's chair. The head designer's seat was in the center, directly opposite the painting of her father.

The assassin removed a set of chains from her knapsack and used them to bind Rebecca's ankles and chest to the backrest. She pulled the restraints tight, securing the links with combination dial padlocks. She strolled to the portrait and defaced it with a single swipe of her katana, cutting a straight horizontal line through Toshigi's neck. As the canvas flopped down, she stowed her sword away in its sheath.

Now that Jade had vented her frustration, it was time to wake her prisoner. She filled a plastic cup from a water cooler, then poured the chilled liquid over Rebecca's head.

The secretary jerked upright. She wiggled her knees, attempting to shake off her drowsiness. To speed things up, Jade rolled up Rebecca's sleeve, slammed the girl's limp forearm on the desk, and squeezed her fingers.

"You must be wondering why I've left your arms free."

She smiled as her victim winced in pain.

"Well, even the world's greatest hacker would have a difficult time if she had no hands to type with. Should we see how you manage?"

Jade slowly unsheathed her katana. The sedative was wearing off, but Rebecca was still too weak to fight back. She cried out as her attacker raised her sword high and slashed down. The blade chopped its target cleanly in two.

Sparks flew in Rebecca's face. The swing had severed an electric cord, missing the girl's hand by the width of a little finger. With no power, the desk lamp went dark, leaving

Nicole's computer terminal as the only light source.

Jade released her victim's wrist. Able to move again, the secretary nursed her arm back to good health.

"What do you want?" she asked, her voice dry and exhausted.

"I'm surprised, Silica. You have a reputation for remaining calm under pressure."

She dropped the power cable under Nicole's chair, took off the girl's shoes and socks, and then wandered off into the shadows.

"My name's Rebecca Masters, you freak!"

Yelled in defiance, but she couldn't hide her fear.

"Tonight," Jade said, returning with the cooler, "you get to play Silica. Look. You've got the best seat in the house. Should be fun. Like I told Toshigi, all good games need a time constraint. What do you think? Water clocks were popular in ancient times."

She placed the plastic container next to Nicole's computer and thrust her sword at the tank, puncturing it near the base. As liquid dripped from the skewered cylinder, the killer vaulted over the desk, sat facing her victim, and ushered the water towards her.

"You just gonna watch me die!?" Rebecca shrieked. "Is that it?"

Jade leaned back across the table and stretching her arms.

"You could always look for the combinations I buried in the text of the e-mail. Then you could free yourself before it's too late. Three sets of numbers to find. I suggest you work quickly."

"What e-mail?"

Rebecca looked at her assailant, the cooler, then the electric cable. Water spilled over the edge of the desk, and the pool beneath her chair was spreading towards the exposed wire.

"What e-mail?" the girl repeated.

"The one I sent to Nicole's computer ten minutes ago."

"This your idea of a joke? I don't know her password!"

She pulled the chain around her chest, but the padlock clasped it in place. The prisoner rocked back and forward, attempting to free her legs. She toppled sideways, unbalanced by her weight.

Jade caught Rebecca with her foot and lifted her into an upright position.

"Careful, Silica. You might fall, then you won't be able to use your computer."

"Stop calling me Silica!"

"It's your name, isn't it? You're supposed to be an expert hacker. Breaking into Nicole's account should be trivial for someone as intelligent as you. You can't say I gave you no warning. I told you to brush up on your skills. Remember?"

Frustrated by her failed efforts to escape, Rebecca caved in to Jade's wishes and played along. The secretary typed on the keyboard, attempting to access Nicole's private account. She correctly deduced the username since it had the same logical structure as a company employee, but she could only guess what the password might be. She tried many possibilities: hobbies, video game titles, names of work colleagues.

Each time, the computer responded with an *Invalid Login* prompt. After twenty attempts, Rebecca gave up and buried her head amongst the keys.

"Go to hell, you weirdo bitch," she cried. "Go to hell!"

Jade sat up and stroked Rebecca's face.

"Very disappointing. I expected more from you."

The water was now within an inch of the live wire.

Rebecca had a minute left, if that. Her resistance broken, she could only beg.

"Kill me, if that's what you want. Just don't hurt my kid."

"I wouldn't harm an eight-year-old boy. What kind of woman do you think I am? He'll have to attend his mother's funeral, but then, so did Nicole. It didn't stop her from being successful. What did you accomplish with your life?"

"Why are you doing this? Why? Who the hell are you?"

"We were good friends once. Don't you remember me?"

Jade threw back the secretary's head, leaned in close, and raised her helmet visor.

"How about now? Do you like my new hairstyle?"

Shadow masked jade's face. The only clearly visible features were her long, blonde hair and bright green eyes.

"Len—", Rebecca began.

Before she finished saying the name, a loud fizzling noise caught her attention. The secretary lifted her legs a fraction of a second before the water lapped over the cable.

"Sorry, Silica," Jade said, "but your time's up. And you failed. Watch your feet."

She chuckled and kicked Rebecca's kneecap with her heel. The girl's foot landed in the pool with a splash. Rebecca convulsed violently, eyes bulging as electricity coursed through her body.

The killer stamped on the secretary's toes, trapping them beneath her boot. The leather sole kept her insulated, allowing her to watch in total safety.

Steam obscured Rebecca's shaking legs, and the shock was so great her hair stood up on end. The chains clanked as her reaction became increasingly violent and erratic. Her screams turned to choking coughs. Blood sprayed from her mouth, an aftereffect of biting her tongue. After nearly ten seconds of resistance, Rebecca fell silent and collapsed lifelessly in her seat.

The killer shut off the power and climbed off the desk. She grabbed Rebecca's charred hand and slid a farewell token onto her index finger. It was a cheap plastic ring with the letters 'Si' etched into the fake gemstone.

Jade left the building, pausing by the front reception to leave yet another hint for the cops to find. She mounted her motorcycle and rode back towards San Francisco.

She was disappointed with her victims so far. Faced with adversity, Rebecca had come up hopelessly short and —just like the others—had refused to play the role assigned to her. Although Jade's game designs ensured none of her targets could win, she'd gone to great trouble to plan their deaths, and would have liked to see at least one go down fighting.

Toshigi, Kenji, and Rebecca were pathetically easy prey. Eliminating the maid while evading police detection had been a little trickier, but still much easier than Jade had expected. Perhaps it was time for a bonus kill, some victim who might offer more of a challenge.

After some consideration, she decided to raise the stakes. The assassin selected a target she thought would be a suitable test of her abilities. There was likely to be a strong police presence around the house by now, which ought to provide worthy opponents to deal with. And it would be another opportunity to play a game with the detectives.

After reaching the city limits, Jade circled the block three times. Every so often, she changed lanes without signaling. When she was certain nobody had followed her, the killer headed for her next destination. Pacific Heights.

# CHAPTER SEVEN

## *A Bonus Kill*

Officer Meagan Wilson doubted her first day could get worse. On her initiation beat so far, the rookie had broken up a catfight between two overweight women in a department store, pulled over a drunken truck driver (and remained calm during the ensuing profanity), and provided street directions to lost tourists.

The detective she'd met outside the precinct had been right about one thing. Life as a policewoman was nothing like academy training. Shooting paper targets and running the assault course may have been danger free, but those exercises had at least taxed her brain and provided some excitement.

Meagan's designated partner was Rico Asante: an obese, hairy-armed Mexican with a severe case of bad breath. His body odor was so foul that she drove with the side window lowered. The city's polluted air was almost refreshing by comparison. The Sergeant had assigned Rico to break Meagan in, but so far he'd done nothing but offer poor advice and leave all the legwork to her. Perhaps he was taking advantage of her rookie status, or maybe he was just lazy. Either way, his laid back attitude was driving her insane.

"Rico, do all cops end up so washed out? Because if they do, I'm quitting right now."

Not surprisingly, he didn't reply. It was difficult with pastry, cream, and chocolate stuffed in his mouth. The Mexican hadn't stopped eating since they'd arrived at the mansion, and he still had plenty of doughnuts left in reserve. He licked his sticky fingers, reached into a box between his legs, and selected another.

"Want one?" Rico asked, clearing his throat.

"Why? So I can take your place as the fat, lazy slob? They do come with napkins, in case you didn't know."

Meagan wasn't usually so critical, but she was appalled by his lack of manners.

The rookie peeked through her binoculars. Everything was quiet around the house. She pictured Miss Tasoto curled up on a Persian rug by her fireplace, playing video games on a giant screen while her bodyguards sat outside in the freezing cold.

Meagan supposed she shouldn't be so harsh. The girl had just lost her father and witnessed her maid's execution, and must be terrified she might be next.

That said, it wasn't as if Meagan and Rico had volunteered to be her babysitters. As a fresh recruit, she had no say in the matter, and she doubted he was well respected by his peers. Since nobody else wanted to work the graveyard shift, the sergeant had assigned the job to them.

"Should I take a look?" her partner asked, reaching for

the binoculars.

Meagan snatched her hand away. "And smear the lenses with your sticky fingers? No, thanks."

It was the first time he'd offered to assist her all night, but his generosity more likely stemmed from boredom than a sense of duty. Besides, the thought of having nothing to do except wait was enough to put Meagan off. She rubbed her eyes and glanced at her watch. It had been a long day, and there were still three hours left until shift change.

"This is a complete waste of time," she said. "If the investigating officers believed the killer would return to the crime scene…"

"They would've stayed to spring the trap. We got the shit end of the stick. Get used to it. We're only good for —"

"Ssh! Quiet!"

Meagan heard a motorcycle engine, but the noise was faint.

"It's getting louder."

Rico stopped munching his doughnut and listened. Meagan turned her binoculars from left to right, scanning the approach. She eventually settled on right, the direction the sound was coming from.

The vehicle was somewhere beyond a slope in the road. A single headlamp appeared over the crest of the hill. Meagan kept a steady watch. As the motorcycle drew close, she grabbed her pistol grip and flipped off the safety catch.

An orange bike zipped past with a loud, high-pitched whine. The riders were two joyriding teenagers, a boy and a girl. Both screamed with excitement and were either stoned or drunk.

"Stupid kids."

Meagan watched them disappear round a bend. She would have relaxed, but something about the engine sound wasn't quite right. There was a distinct echo, a dull chugging noise mixed in with the whine. Almost as if someone was using another bike to cover their own presence.

Both noises faded, but Meagan remained tense. On impulse, she grabbed her binoculars and focused on the house's exterior wall. Her search for the phantom biker proved fruitless. She was about to pass off her suspicions as paranoia when she spied someone on the side path.

Her grip tightened around the tubes as she concentrated on the shadowy figure. It was hard to tell for sure in the poor light, but Meagan could swear the intruder was six feet tall.

"Rico, we got trouble. Call it in!"

She drew her weapon and exited the car. Her partner looked dumbfounded at first, then aghast at having to do some police work.

"Meagan!"

The doughnut box fell off Rico's knees, contents scattering over the carpeted floor.

"Shit. This better not be a wild goose chase. You sure you saw something?"

"Yes! What the hell are you waiting for? Call for support."

Rico raised dispatch on the two-way radio.

"This is Asante. We have a possible intruder at the Tasoto Residence. Send backup now."

He pulled out his gun and joined Meagan on the front drive.

"We stick together," he said. "Watch each other's backs."

"I know the drill."

Meagan tried to sound confident, despite being anxious as hell on the inside.

Rico nodded and beckoned her to follow. He led the way, hugging the mansion wall. The experienced patrolman checked walls and bushes while she covered the rear.

In contrast to Rico's soft footsteps, Meagan's were loud and clumsy. She staggered backwards along the side gravel path, too afraid to look where she was going. For all she knew, a killer could be concealed in the darkness waiting to strike, and she didn't want to leave herself exposed.

It was a relief when they reached the rear garden. The soil was solid, and Meagan had an easier time maintaining her balance, though her gun still wobbled in her unsteady hand. She cursed herself for being so impatient for action. Providing directions to tourists was hardly thrilling, but far less intimidating than pursuing a murder suspect.

"Only one way in," Rico said, studying the garden's layout.

Meagan checked feasible routes into the house. All but two were sealed tight, and the planks nailed across the broken French windows were intact.

"No sign of forced entry," she noted. "The intruder's still outside."

"If there is an intruder."

Rico made no effort to hide his skepticism. The officers swept the backyard, working side by side to cover ten thousand square feet of grass, shrubbery, and garden ornaments. Shadows shifted with the tree movements, and the wind chilled Meagan to the bone.

It was like being in a horror movie, cast as the helpless victim of an unknown stalker. Meagan's stomach churned, and her pulse rate quickened. She could sense someone watching, but a thorough search of the grounds failed to reveal an intruder.

Not counting the house itself, there was only one place

left to check. Rico signaled Meagan to cover him, crawled on all fours, and peered beneath the wooden foundation of the dojo. A squirrel scurried between the support stilts, scrounging for food in the dark brown soil. But there were no other signs of life, animal or otherwise.

After declaring the coast clear, he stood up and grabbed the dojo's door handle. Meagan took position at the bottom of the steps, ready to fire if necessary.

Rico flexed his fingers and pulled back the sliding panel, to be greeted by nothing except darkness on the other side. He looked around for a light switch, but couldn't find one.

"You stay outside," he told Meagan. "Make sure nobody sneaks up from behind."

His blatant deviation from protocol troubled her.

"Rico, aren't we supposed to stick together?"

"Cover the rear, damn it. I call for you, then you come in. Else stay put. It's dark in there. Don't want you shooting at me by mistake."

Before Meagan could argue, he entered the building alone and vanished into the shadows. Reluctantly, the rookie did as asked. She stood with her back to the wall and played the lookout. Had she looked up at the dojo roof, she may have seen the attack coming.

The two-footed lunge caught her by surprise. The unseen attacker kicked Meagan between the hips, sending her flying forward. Her skull cracked against the hardened soil.

Meagan lay paralyzed, unsure whether it was the blow to the head or sheer terror that prevented her from moving a muscle. Someone dressed in a black leather jumpsuit stood on her hand and disarmed her. The weapon slid across the grass, out of reach.

"Rico!" she cried out. "Rico!"

The attacker wrapped a thin wire cord around her throat and pulled it tight, silencing her cries for help.

Meagan kicked and struggled, but it was to no avail. She was still weak from the initial blow, and the strong-armed killer had no trouble dragging her underneath the dojo. She heard thumping above, then saw Rico's feet on the front steps.

"Meagan!" he yelled. "Meagan! Where are you?"

The intruder tightened the wire garrotte around her throat. She attempted to call out to her partner, but the words choked in her mouth. Strength fading, Meagan flung her elbow at the attacker's face, knocking off the biker's helmet.

The pale-skinned blonde—was it a woman?—threw her backwards and shifted on top, effectively pinning her to the ground. Rico paused by the discarded gun.

"Meagan? Meagan!"

He shouted her name several times, running frantically back and forth.

"Your partner seems lost," the attacker said, pulling her garrotte even tighter. "If only you could call for help. Aren't bodyguards supposed to protect people? Try starting with yourself, you skinny bitch."

Meagan clawed at the wire around her neck, gasping for breath. Her vision spun, and she saw a glowing white light on the horizon. She punched and kicked, but her blows were timid and increasingly desperate. After a minute-long struggle, she relaxed and slipped into a peaceful, endless sleep.

Before she passed out, the last thing Meagan heard was a psychotic, girlish chuckle.

* * *

Jade waited thirty seconds before she loosened her garrotte. Though the redhead had stopped moving, the killer wanted to be sure she wasn't playing dead. Satisfied the cop wouldn't miraculously spring back to life once she let go, she released the girl and retrieved her helmet.

Taking on armed opponents had felt rewarding, despite her victim being physically weak and inexperienced. The excitement of strangling a policewoman to death under her partner's nose had made the trip worthwhile. Now it was time to deal with the other one.

Jade crawled to a decent vantage point, unzipped her jumpsuit, and unsheathed her katana. The Hispanic cop had stopped chasing shadows. He was standing twenty feet away, panting with exhaustion. The assassin found it ridiculously easy to sneak up behind the fat Mexican and tap him on the shoulder.

He turned around. "You almost gave me—"

Before the bumbling fool realized he wasn't talking to his partner, Jade sliced off his weapon arm.

Rico screamed in pain as blood poured from his severed elbow, turning frosty grass from white to red. The detached limb fell beside Jade's feet, fingers still clutching the pistol grip.

The murderess chuckled at the fat cop's plight, watching him limp about the garden. She knocked him onto his back with a high kick and plunged her sword down into his stomach. The blade passed all the way through into the ground below, pegging him into place.

"Meagan was looking for you earlier, Rico," Jade said. "Calling your name."

She lifted Rico's three remaining limbs off the bloodstained soil, breaking each with a powerful stamp. He screamed at the first attack, but could only groan after that.

"Too bad you couldn't hear her."

"No. Don't kill me."

His whimpers gave way to pitiful, babyish squeals. The killer dragged Meagan's corpse out from underneath the dojo and dumped it face up in the garden. She stripped the dead policewoman of her uniform, removing her shirt, trousers and shoes.

"Your partner's so beautiful," Jade said, straightening the red hair. "That's why I strangled her. I wanted to avoid tarnishing her skin. I know what it's like for a young woman to be robbed of her dignity, to suffer abuse from those in power. To be taken advantage of. I didn't want to put her through that. None of this applies to you, Rico. You're an ugly bastard."

Rico's eyes widened in horror as Jade gripped her sword hilt. She stood on his chest, using the leverage to pull her katana free. Blood covered the lower blade, a deep red sheen that glistened in the moonlight.

"Don't worry. I'm not going to kill you. Because I need you to give a message to your friends on the police force."

Jade grabbed Rico's chin, held it steady, and used her weapon to carve four alphanumeric characters across his forehead. *18-A.*

* * *

Kyle hadn't seen Candy Watson for seven months. The curvaceous, sandy-haired marketing analyst had gained a few pounds since then, but still attracted many a bachelor's eye as she walked into Luca's Bistro. The Italian restaurant was popular with dating couples, featuring live stage music and an award-winning wine list. During peak hours, it was essential to reserve a table in advance.

Kyle straightened his tie, ensuring he looked presentable. He thought it strange that Candy had gotten in touch again. She had, after all, made it quite clear their relationship was over. When he first met her, she was a rising star at one of the city's prestigious electronics firms. They became romantically involved following a chance meeting in a coffee bar.

Many of Kyle's previous girlfriends had found what he did for a job scary, but Candy was different. She took great interest in his work, and actually enjoyed the company of a man who lived dangerously. Or so he had believed.

Kyle recalled the fateful evening when he'd brought a bouquet of daffodils to Candy's apartment, only to discover her in bed with an older guy. Her secret lover turned out to be the vice president at her agency. She was having an affair with her boss to further her career, and had no scruples with dating two men at once. When Kyle confronted her the following day, she dumped him without so much as an apology. Their love had been a charade.

Now Candy had expressed a desire to see him again. On the phone, she'd said she regretted her mistake. Obviously, things hadn't worked out too well with the VP. Despite the girl's romantic flip-flopping, Kyle had accepted her invitation to buy him dinner. Though he was disappointed not to be eating with Nicole, she needed some time alone, and he had the evening free. So why not?

"Are you ready to order?" the server asked.

"Yes," Kyle said. "The lady will have the Pasta Supremo with a Caesar Salad."

The waitress jotted his choice down in shorthand.

"And you, sir?"

"He'll have the same," Candy answered for him. "And to

drink, we'll share a bottle of your Golden Creek Cabernet."

She let the staff member collect the menus, waited until they were alone, and unbuttoned her jacket.

"Pasta Supremo. That brings back fond memories."

She was recalling their previous visit to Luca's Bistro, some eight months ago.

"And a few bad ones. How's… Terence doing?"

Kyle stalled on purpose. He hadn't forgotten the name of his competition.

The waitress brought a bottle to their table, uncorked it, and poured two glasses of wine.

"Terence is doing fine," Candy said after the girl left. "Though you know these corporate types. They can be extremely dull."

"I'm sure there are exceptions. So what's the story behind our sudden reunion? What are we honoring tonight?"

Kyle raised his drink. She responded to the toast, clinking her wine glass against his.

"To adventure. That's what I miss the most. Your detective stories."

"My stories? Things aren't so glamorous in the real world. Believe me."

Candy stroked Kyle's hand. "You've taught me a trick or two about police work, like how to be observant. I don't see a ring around your finger. So, you haven't tied the knot yet? I'm surprised some lady hasn't snagged you by now."

"That's because I'm still looking for the right girl."

In his mind, Kyle weighed the woman seated across from him against Nicole.

"Someone beautiful," he said. "Exciting, mysterious."

"And do I fit that description, Detective Travis?"

Kyle's cellphone rang before he could answer.

"Pardon me." He reached inside his jacket. "Probably my partner. She usually calls when it's inconvenient."

Candy gave him an inquisitive glance. "She?"

"I never mentioned Lakeysia? Don't worry. She doesn't even qualify for your league, and she'd never mix business with pleasure."

"I bet you would."

Candy's seductive smile eased the tension, but Kyle frowned when he saw the caller ID. Curiosity got the better of his date, and she leaned across the table. He tried to conceal the information on his phone's LCD screen from her, but wasn't fast enough.

"Who's Nicole? Do you mix business and pleasure with her?"

For a second, Kyle considered telling a little lie, then he realized Miss Tasoto could be in danger. In two minds, he answered the call.

"Everything okay?"

"Detective Kyle Travis, Homicide."

The woman's icy introduction turned his knuckles white. It was the killer. Her voice was unmistakable.

"I like your business card. It's nice and official. You should have chosen your bodyguards more carefully."

Candy slammed down her glass in anger.

"Hi, Nicole," she shouted into Kyle's cellphone. "I'm the girl he stood you up for."

"Shut the hell up, Candy!"

Kyle covered the phone as he yelled. His date gave him the finger, gathered her belongings, and stormed away from the table. But his thoughts were elsewhere.

"What do you mean?" he asked the psycho woman.

Kyle had already connected the dots. He waited for the killer's answer, terrified of what it might be.

"Did I catch you at a bad time? I'm so sorry. And to think Nicole trusted you. Instead of being here to protect her from me, you'd rather have supper with Candy. Is she sweet, detective? She sounds like it."

"What have you done?"

"It wasn't very good police work, placing her life in the hands of an overweight Mexican and a silly girl who should have stayed in high school. Now it's just her and me."

"You're bluffing."

The killer chuckled. There was an agonizing wait before she spoke again.

"Come on, Detective. Surely, you know me better than that. You'll find your dead colleagues in the back garden, next to your lady friend."

"Touch her and I swear—"

A dialing tone rang in Kyle's ear. The caller had hung up on him. Either she was lying and wanted to test his nerves, or she really was planning to kill Nicole.

Kyle put neither possibility past this audacious woman. He threw payment on the table, left the restaurant, and informed dispatch of the situation. The Tasoto residence was four miles away, on the other side of town. Even if he drove at top speed, there was no chance of reaching her in time.

* * *


Jade tore Travis' business card into tiny pieces, then blew the confetti off her leather glove.

As the strips floated to the ground, she replaced the telephone receiver on its stand. It was amusing how the detective had unwittingly given his nemesis a personal number. Now she could reach him whenever she wanted. Threats against Nicole's life were his weakness, one the killer intended to exploit as the game progressed.

She trode carefully past the broken wood and glass, the wreckage from the shattered French windowpane. The barricade had yielded to Jade's sword, but her presence in the house had triggered a motion sensor alarm. Loud shrieking reverberated through the mansion halls, but she knew the police wouldn't arrive for a few more minutes. Even though Detective Travis would have radioed for reinforcements, there was plenty of time to do what she needed to.

Jade exited to the entrance hall, drew her katana, and climbed the staircase to the upper floor. She had spent four months in training to prepare, so moving silently had become second nature. A small child would have made more noise.

From outside the house, the assassin heard screeching tires and wailing sirens. The front downstairs windows flashed blue. As expected, the dead girl's colleagues had arrived to save her.

Uniformed grunts were too predictable to be anything more than a slight nuisance. They would search the garden, the lower floor rooms, and finally upstairs. Jade could easily perform her last act and disappear long before anybody found Nicole.

The killer smiled in triumph. Her detour had been a resounding success. The cops had tried to stop her and failed. Despite all the hints they'd been given, they still didn't have a clue who she was.

# CHAPTER EIGHT

*Mourning the Dead*

Outsiders categorized Americans as either rich or poor, but those who rented places on Telegraph Hill were somewhere in between, wealthy enough to live downtown but unable to afford anywhere nice. The view from Lakeysia's third-floor apartment was better than those from ground level, but not by much. While some residents could see Coit Tower and Bay Bridge, her window looked upon a derelict hotel building across the street. Lakeysia hadn't dusted or vacuumed in a month. Regardless of how often she cleaned her place, new dirt always replaced the old.

The evening news broadcast featured a special report on the growing number of girl gangs in inner city Los Angeles, a statistic the presenter referred to as "a disturbing trend". Lakeysia switched the television off and took a break from her homework. She had no wish to listen to an inaccurate, sensationalized account of crime in Southern California. Female gangsters were hardly a recent phenomenon, and certainly not worthy of discussion. Especially after what happened three summers ago.

Lakeysia still vividly remembered Carl Brewster. The two detectives had been engaged for five months, and were about to become partners in both marriage and Homicide Division. They'd talked about quitting the force to start a new life in the country and escaping from the nightmare of South Central.

Then Carl was killed, a week before the wedding. The shooter was Mei Tan, a name that Lakeysia would never forget. When someone takes away a loved one, it leaves a scar that never heals.

The incident occurred during a dawn raid on a suspect's residence. The two partners and four other cops were after Lao Ching, a Chinese Triad boss wanted for the murder of a nightclub owner. After a bloody shootout with his bodyguards, the assault team cornered the crime lord in his bedroom.

A naked, Oriental girl cowered behind the bed sheets, screaming as police stormed in. Mei Tan played the part of the innocent hooker to perfection. While the detectives concentrated on disarming Ching, the female assassin pulled a laser-sighted handgun from under her pillow. In one fluid move, she rolled on her back and shot Carl between the eyes.

Lakeysia returned fire. She put three bullets through Mei's heart and two in the girl's brain. A single, well-aimed round was normally enough to kill a person, but she wanted to make sure. The desire for vengeance clouded her thoughts, and there would be no opportunity to claim self defense later.

She knew Carl was dead before she ran to his side. Her partner was wearing a bulletproof vest, but it only protected his body, and the hitwoman had shot to kill.

Everyone on the team, including Lakeysia, had assumed the girl was no threat. Their poor judgment had cost her fiancée his life.

After the funeral, Lakeysia's outlook became increasingly cynical, and she never entered a relationship again. She later learned Mei was Ching's top assassin, his 'go to' enforcer for contract hits. It was she who'd murdered the club owner, posing as an escort girl to get him alone in his office. Perhaps that's why Lakeysia didn't trust Nicole. She viewed every woman she met as a potential killer.

She ate her last slice of Hawaiian pizza and studied the photos one more time. Matthews had documented the warehouse crime scene thoroughly: the '12-E' message, the thief tools on Tasoto's chest, the ransom note.

Lakeysia scanned the prints for clues the murderer hadn't intended to leave behind, evidence that they had overlooked. Despite spending two hours with a magnifying glass, she still couldn't find a thing. She had learned the perpetrator was careful, intelligent, and manipulative, just like Mei Tan.

Kyle hadn't jumped to the wrong conclusion at the estate. The killer was a woman, and maybe the one he was getting too close to.

The telephone rang, but Lakeysia decided not to answer. It was probably a telemarketer selling cable TV packages or offering to reduce nonexistent mortgage payments. Her assumption proved incorrect when Thorne left a message on the answering machine.

"Symons. Just thought you should know. The stakeout team at Miss Tasoto's home called in. Something about an intruder."

Lakeysia grabbed her phone. "I'm on it, lieutenant."

"Could be a false alarm. Wilson's new, and a bit

jumpy."

"Wilson? Meagan Wilson?" She raised her voice in disbelief. "It's her first beat. Who the hell put a newbie on duty? The grim reaper?"

Lakeysia slammed down the receiver, retrieved her car keys from under the pizza box, and left her apartment. She was genuinely afraid for the young girl. Dealing with this psychopath was dangerous for anyone, but a rookie like Wilson was way out of her depth. As Thorne said, it could just be a false alarm, but deep down, Lakeysia knew the threat was for real.

* * *

Lakeysia's concern grew when Thorne informed her Travis was also on his way to the mansion. Apparently, the killer had called to threaten Miss Tasoto's life.

Soon after she crossed the district boundary into Pacific Heights, three squad cars converged to form a convoy behind her station wagon. She sped up, turned through the estate's gate, and swerved to a halt in the driveway. Uniformed officers joined her by the front steps, armed and ready.

"You four! Go round the rear!" she said, directing them with her pistol. The wailing burglar alarm made it difficult to issue verbal instructions.

That left two men for backup. She signaled them to cover her as she approached the entrance, took a pace back, and kicked a spot just below the handle. The door swung into the neighboring wall with a loud crack, chipping the stonework. But she needn't have exerted herself. All the locks had been disengaged. Someone was expecting them.

Lakeysia spearheaded the assault. She advanced into

the hall, anticipating trouble at any moment. The lights were on, and a sliding door was open at the far end.

"Check downstairs!"

While the other cops searched rooms on the ground floor, she ascended the spiral steps. Dirty boot marks marred the wooden tiles. The footprints formed a trail that led upstairs and across the landing to the master bedroom.

Well aware of the killer's passion for playing games, Lakeysia ignored the tracks and checked other areas first. Unlike her relatively tiny apartment, there were several sleeping chambers, connecting bathrooms, servants' quarters and even an observatory.

"Detective Symons! Out here!"

The shouts originated from the back garden. Through a landing window, she saw four officers standing around a half naked, red-haired female.

It was Officer Wilson. A Hispanic man lay on the grass beside her, face covered in blood. From the way the other cops tended to his wounds, it appeared he was still alive. Meagan—left alone—hadn't been so lucky. Lakeysia's worst fears had come true. On her very first day of real action, the rookie had fallen victim to a serial killer.

It required all her professionalism to contain her anger and keep a cool head. She saved her mourning for later and retraced the footsteps back to the master bedroom. Lakeysia took cover behind the wall and slid the panel open with her foot, keeping both hands on her weapon. She pivoted round, checked the ceiling beyond the doorway, and stepped into Miss Tasoto's fantasy world.

Lakeysia had seen hundreds of bedrooms in her career. Most of them belonged to drug addicts and other lowlife scum, but this one was marketable as a Japanese emperor's palace. Furnishings included a velvet shrouded, four-poster bed, an outside balcony, and a closet the size of a typical hotel room. Nicole's play zone was every teenage boy's dream. Besides the latest console systems, it had everything the avid gamer could want: a cinematic TV screen, light guns, network linkups, and a library of software from the entire Dragonsoft collection.

Lakeysia had no interest in any of this. She stayed by the entrance, ignoring the obvious footprint trail that led to the en suite bathroom on the right. The connecting door was partially open, but she suspected the killer had set a trap.

She proceeded with caution. Her first port of call was the bed. She slowly approached the velvet drapes, pulled them aside, and thrust her gun forward. The freshly made linen sheets were undisturbed. If the murderess was still around, she lay in wait elsewhere.

Squelchy feet alerted her to the woman's presence. The second clue was the sound of a wardrobe door clicking shut, and the third was a faint, feminine shadow on the bedsheets. The killer was standing right behind her, wielding a long and thin object two handed.

Lakeysia kneeled down, as if to look under the bed. Then she quickly dropped to the floor, rolled over, and took aim at the woman by the wardrobe.

It was Miss Tasoto. She wore a peach bathrobe, and her face and hair were soaking wet. The weapon she carried wasn't a sword, but a twin-barreled shotgun.

"Nicole! It's me."

Lakeysia kept her pistol aimed at her, just in case. Then the girl relaxed and lowered her arms.

"Detective Symons. Thank God. She was right here, in this room. I was taking a bath when the alarm went off."

Lakeysia placed a finger to her lips, motioned Nicole to remain still, and ·opened the bathroom door. She concentrated on the potential threats ahead, theorizing that if Miss Tasoto wanted to kill her, she would have pulled the trigger already.

Thick steam filled the air, making it hard to see. But this was evidently a wealthy person's home. Silver-plated shower fittings were a few cuts above the norm, and the tiles were ceramic instead of plastic. The mist got progressively thicker towards the tub: a ten-foot wide, circular pool with glowing, crystal lights embedded in its decorative rim. The surrounding floor was damp from condensation, and the muddy footsteps ended near the edge.

Once again, Lakeysia searched the least obvious hiding places first. She drew back the shower curtain to check for concealed intruders. Discovering no surprises, she grabbed a bottle of designer shampoo and lobbed it into the tub.

She heard the glass container roll about the tub's interior before coming to rest. Either nobody was inside, or the killer was an expert at dodging projectiles. Lakeysia assumed the worst scenario and sprinted across the wet floor. She slid next to the bathtub and aimed her pistol over the side.

The hot water valve was open. Steam evaporated from an ankle deep pool, clouding her vision. The level remained more or less constant, with liquid draining out through the plughole at roughly the same rate it poured in.

Lakeysia shut off the faucet and wiped condensed vapor from her eyes. As the humid fog cleared, she noticed something written in the tub's bowl. It was a message in blood, still wet and fresh. *Alas, Poor Rebecca.*

Lakeysia holstered her gun and switched on her radio.

"This is Symons. Get somebody over to the Dragonsoft office tower in Twin Peaks. Right away."

"Detective?" Nicole called out as she entered the

bathroom. "What's wrong?"

Lakeysia barred her path, but she had already seen the message.

"Oh, God! Rebecca. No! Please. Not her. Please God, no."

Nicole stumbled forward and collapsed in Lakeysia's arms, eyes flooding with tears. The detective embraced her, giving the girl a firm shoulder to cry on. Miss Tasoto buried her face in Lakeysia's suit, making it awkward to tell if her mourning was real or merely staged.

Lakeysia was having second thoughts about Nicole's guilt. If this was a performance to gain her trust, then it was flawless. It was possible her opinion of Miss Tasoto had been colored by the events that led to Carl's death. Or perhaps she really was a brilliant actress, an assassin even deadlier than Mei Tan.

* * *

Paramedics lifted Rico Asante onto a stretcher and wheeled him towards a waiting ambulance. He was barely conscious, having received emergency on-location surgery. In truth, he probably wished the psycho had strangled him instead of his partner. The medics had disinfected and bandaged Rico's severed arm and stomach wound, and encased his other limbs in plaster. Should the physical wounds heal, memories and nightmares would likely haunt him forever.

An extra cloth was wrapped around his forehead, but that didn't hide the killer's message. The bloody red lettering had diffused through the white material. Lakeysia jotted the '18-A' clue down in her notebook.

She stood outside the ambulance's rear doors, with a female Hispanic officer by her side. The cop waited with her cap off and her head lowered, a mark of respect for her fallen comrade. As the paramedics pushed Rico into the ambulance, the policewoman asked him a question in Spanish. Lakeysia had a basic knowledge of the language, enough to understand her simple query.

"Who did this?"

"Un demonio hermoso con los ojos verdes," Rico coughed.

His response was beyond Lakeysia's translation skills. She turned to the Hispanic woman.

"What did he say?"

"That the killer was a beautiful demon with green eyes."

"Appreciate the tip."

Lakeysia gripped Rico's hand as the ambulance crew connected him to a blood drip. Then they closed the doors. She watched the vehicle drive away, wheels tearing up the garden.

"He's my best friend on the force," the officer said. "You nail the bitch responsible, you let me know."

Lakeysia glanced up at the master bedroom window. Two images were silhouetted on the curtain: a man and a woman. The figures embraced and became one.

"Oh, we'll catch her. Rest assured, my partner and I are working on it day and night. You say you're the guy's friend?"

"His only real one. Nobody's got much time for Rico."

"Have some pity for the new girl. Think you could make friends in a day?"

Lakeysia looked across the garden, to the spot where the paramedics sealed Meagan inside a black body bag. Her mobile telephone beeped. She checked the digital screen. The caller was Lieutenant Thorne, the perennial bearer of bad news.

* * *

Kyle wiped Nicole's face and wrapped a towel around her hair. She sat on her bed, facing away from the bathroom. The girl was in complete shock. She couldn't keep still, and the mattress springs creaked whenever she shifted her legs.

"Everything's fine."

Kyle brushed a spot of water from her cheek.

"You're safe now," he said.

"No. I'm not. That's what you said this morning. You told me she wouldn't come back."

He sat beside her so she could rest across his lap.

"I want you to think carefully. Do you have any idea who this woman might be? What her agenda is?"

"Who cares what her crazy agenda is?" Nicole screamed, sitting up. "I don't even know who she is. You're the detective, aren't you? You find out!"

Heavy footsteps came from outside the bedroom. Lakeysia marched through the door and straight up to them.

"They just found Rebecca. She's dead, electrocuted in her office."

"Oh God," Nicole said.

If Lakeysia was sympathetic, it didn't show one bit.

"Or should I say your office? Seems our mutual friend made a stop in Twin Peaks tonight, bumped off your secretary and the night watchman. Funny, isn't it? How all these deaths seem to revolve around you. I wonder why."

"How the heck should I know?" Nicole asked, turning to Kyle. "First you accuse me, and now your stupid partner. I'm not the one who killed them."

"Hey!" he said, shifting the blame. "This young girl has

been through hell tonight. Knock it off."

Lakeysia ignored him. She grabbed Nicole's bathrobe and yanked her forward.

"Why are you protecting this woman, Miss Tasoto? You know who she is? Eh? She a friend of yours? Or are you holding out because you haven't found a scapegoat yet?"

Kyle chopped away his partner's hands, stood up, and locked eyes with her.

"Lakeysia, we need to talk. Now."

"All right. Let's talk. Me and Travis are going to step outside. Leave you to mourn the dead. This woman's one smart bitch. Must think she's real brave killing a rookie, an old man, a secretary. But I'll get her. Want to know why? Because I'm smarter than your lover boy. Don't play innocent with me."

Kyle followed Lakeysia into the corridor and gently closed the door behind her.

"I don't appreciate the way you assaulted Nicole back there. I realize the girl might seem like a reincarnation of Mei Tan to you, but that doesn't make her a killer."

"What? You're upset because I touched up your girlfriend? She may not be guilty, but that woman's hiding something. And I want to find out what that is before more people turn up with body parts missing. Part of my job description. Yours too, in case you forgot."

Her arguments didn't sway him. She was clearly biased by previous events.

"That doesn't justify what you did."

"Someone's gotta be the bad cop. Eighteen. That's how old Meagan Wilson was. Same age as your girl. Want Miss Tasoto to get choked to death? No? Then you find out what she's not telling us. Use a more delicate hands-on approach if you like. Whatever it takes to convince her to talk. See you later, Travis. I'm gonna comb the crime scene for clues."

"Yeah. Why don't you do that?"

Kyle stepped back into the bedroom and slammed the door closed.

* * *

Police had established a perimeter around the Dragonsoft office tower. Three burly officers checked the ID of everyone who wished to enter, and nobody was allowed through the cordon without authorization. A couple of news vans were parked next to the patrol cars, and Lakeysia spotted one prominent TV anchor making a live report. Word of the killings was spreading, but the press vultures hadn't yet shown up in full force.

Lakeysia drove as close to the building as possible. She had no wish to discuss the lack of progress with television reporters. The detective presented her shield to the officer on duty, ducked under a web of crime scene tape, and entered the lobby.

Matthews and his female assistant had already arrived, and were dusting the night watchman's body and desk for fingerprints. It was a tedious but necessary task nobody expected to bear fruit.

"His arm's broken," the doctor said, examining the corpse. "So is his neck. Guy didn't stand a chance."

Lakeysia slipped on her surgical gloves.

"Fairness isn't a word in this nut job's dictionary. You should see her latest escapade. She strangled a rookie cop to death, then sliced his partner up for good measure. Broke a few bones first. Apparently, it's not enough to kill her victims. She has to make them suffer, get up close and personal."

"Seems you were right about the killer being a girl."

The way Matthews said it betrayed an old-fashioned view of the fair sex. The naïve doctor had trouble believing a woman could be capable of such violence. Murder maybe, but not brutal torture. Lakeysia knew that was a fallacy.

"Or possibly an Amazon. You tell me, doc. How strong would a pretty little thing have to be to pull this off?"

"Hard to say. Any powerful adult, male or female, could have easily beaten up this man."

Matthews' opposition was slowly waning.

"This was an act of precision rather than brute force. I'd be fairly confident the killer's an expert in some martial arts discipline, but don't ask me which."

"A kung fu addict, eh? Perhaps she learned the moves from one of those fighting games."

Lakeysia watched herself on the security monitor. A camera was on the ceiling opposite, pointed straight at her. Matthews read her thoughts.

"We already checked the footage."

The doctor's assistant pressed some buttons. An image showed a recording of the murder. The killer was a tall woman dressed in black motorcyclist's leathers. Long, blonde hair masked her identity, and she was careful to avoid looking at the camera.

"Kari watched the whole thing," Matthews said. "A genuine snuff movie. Not one clear picture of the girl's face. She's a lucky bitch, I can tell you."

"That's not luck. It's premeditation. What's that on the dead guy's chest?"

Lakeysia pointed at the sword under the night manager's hands.

"A child's toy from the look of things. There's a pattern scratched on the hilt."

She kneeled down to inspect it. The markings Matthews referred to weren't part of the toy's design. The killer had supplied her own artistic touch, carving a medieval style coat of arms into the plastic.

"She likes her games," Lakeysia said, sketching the figure in her notebook. "Can't wait to see the deep fried secretary."

Two minutes later—when she arrived upstairs—she cursed her wicked tongue. She was known for her quips, which often lightened the mood at murder scenes, but her comment about Rebecca was too accurate to be humorous. Thorne had told her the M.O. was electrocution, but knowing the cause of death in advance didn't prepare Lakeysia for the horrific sight that awaited her in Nicole's office.

Rebecca's face was black, barely recognizable beneath a mass of twisted hair. Solidified blood surrounded her bare feet. In her desperation to escape the electric chair, the secretary had cut her ankles on the restraints. With hindsight, the maid and chauffeur were fortunate to die quickly. The other victims had all suffered.

Matthews joined Lakeysia by the body.

"The chains and padlocks are the same as those on the first victim. Fairly easy to come by, nothing that would help your investigation. However, we found this in the trashcan."

The doctor showed her an evidence bag. It contained an anesthetic dart, ammunition used in a tranquilizer pistol.

"The killer puts her victims to sleep," she said. "Then they wake up to a living nightmare. Seems Rebecca was trying to access Nicole's e-mail account."

Lakeysia nodded at the computer screen. Someone had typed the user name *NTasoto*, but the password field was blank.

"We'll need to ask Miss Tasoto for the login details. I know a man close to her."

She dialed a number on her mobile phone. Her partner took a few seconds to take the call. Apparently, he was still upset with what had happened earlier.

"Travis," she said when he finally answered, "see if you can find out the password for Miss Tasoto's office computer."

Rather predictably, he stonewalled her.

"May I ask what for?"

"Cause it might help us nail a psychotic killer. That a good enough reason for you?"

Her irritated response produced the desired effect. She heard Kyle talk to Nicole in the background, though their voices were too quiet to discern what was said.

"Cyber maiden. All one word," Kyle relayed after some discussion. "Then a hyphen followed by the digit four."

"Cyber maiden dash four. Got it."

Lakeysia closed her cellphone and entered the password. Nicole's online mailbox contained three unread messages. The newest, sent by a user named Jade, had an obviously bogus domain address and the subject *Attention: Stupid Cops*.

"Think this was meant for us?"

Lakeysia opened the message. It was a single line of text. *The combination is 14O. Jade Dragon.*

Matthews tried setting the padlock dials based on the cryptic clue, but with no success.

"Why bother sending that e-mail if it's not the right combination?"

"Nicole's password was alphanumeric, doc. No chance of Rebecca guessing it. Another of our wacko's no-win situations. That's not a zero. It's the letter O. Fourteen-O. Fits with twelve-E and eighteen-A."

Lakeysia pulled out her notebook then scribbled '12E 18A 14O'. Purely on instinct, she wrote out the English alphabet, and numbered each character one through twenty-six. She converted the numbers to the corresponding letters to get a strange word.

"Lerano," Matthews read over her shoulder. "What's that?"

She crossed out the text.

"I think you mean who. The killer came here before the house. The right order's Tasoto, Rebecca, then Rico Asante. Fourteen-O goes in the middle."

Seeing the doctor was confused, Lakeysia wrote out the letters in the rearranged order to explain her theory.

"Lenora," he said. "That's a woman's name."

Lakeysia snapped her book closed.

"Got it in one, doc. Could be a screwed up interpretation, a false lead, or the name of our favorite psycho."

# CHAPTER NINE

## *Green Eyed with Envy*

"We found something under the front desk!"

Doctor Matthews' assistant dashed through the elevator doors and announced her discovery as if it were a world-shattering event. Lakeysia logged off from Nicole's account, not excited in the least.

"Hope it's a stash of rare coins. Then we can split if fifty-fifty."

She followed Matthews and Kari down to the lobby. It was hard to be optimistic about any physical evidence her quarry may have left behind. So far, the killer had presented them with nothing except riddles and corpses. This woman wasn't prone to making mistakes.

The finding turned out to be a single, two inch-long strand of blonde hair. Lakeysia double checked the surveillance recording of the manager's murder, and held the sample against the monitor glass to make a direct comparison. The colors were identical.

"This is where the killer was standing," Matthews said, bagging the hair with a pair of tweezers. "It's authentic, in my opinion."

"Seems that way. But suppose the guard was shagging a blonde beauty on the side? Did his stuff under the desk so they wouldn't get caught on camera?"

The doc laughed, playing down her claims.

"The night manager was fifty-three. A little old, don't you think?"

"Same applies to you. Would you say no to a sexy girl?"

Matthews hesitated to reply, and his assistant looked uneasy as well. The Chinese American intern pretended to search a desk drawer, but Lakeysia sensed she was avoiding eye contact.

"I see you've taught her how to play doctor," Lakeysia said quietly. "Another guy with the hots for an Asian beauty. That's three in two days. I'm feeling left out."

Lakeysia grinned, then let it slide. He wasn't married, and she didn't want to dwell on his personal life.

"How soon can you do an analysis?"

Matthews was eager to change the topic. "I should have the results ready by this afternoon."

"Get back to me."

Lakeysia hoped to escape before Thorne made an appearance, but she never reached the door. The lieutenant wasn't in a good mood, or even a mild one.

"Symons," he said, hands on hips. "Let me clarify the situation for you. I have the DA breathing down my neck, a media circus outside, and a rookie officer's funeral to attend. I'm supposed to give a press conference within the hour. So, what do I tell them? We've yet to come up with a single concrete lead?"

As always, arguing with Thorne was pointless, but Lakeysia tried her best.

"We found a hair sample that might belong to the killer."

"And it might actually be useful if you had a suspect to run a DNA comparison test against."

"Lieutenant, I believe Nicole Tasoto knows who's responsible for this."

"That a hunch?" he asked.

"Yeah, but a solid one, all things considered. Whoever killed the president has a score to settle with his baby girl, too."

Thorne paused to think, searching for a flaw in Lakeysia's logic. "Possibly," he said. "I want the daughter brought in for questioning."

"We already tried pressing her for information."

The lieutenant stepped closer and breathed on her face. His way of saying she wasn't doing enough.

"Then press a little harder. Some lunatic murdered three people tonight. I'd say it's time to take off the kid gloves. Wouldn't you agree?"

* * *

Lakeysia asked Frances to prepare coffee before the interview. It was lukewarm and tasted horrible, but she needed an overdose of caffeine (or whatever substitute the manufacturer used) to stay awake. She'd been on the job for thirty hours non-stop, and wanted to be fresh for the upcoming duel of words with Miss Tasoto.

The room itself was downright ugly: a cream painted, windowless box with plastic furniture. The table was basic and the hardback chairs were dangerously uncomfortable, a world away from the velvet cushions of Nicole's mansion.

Lakeysia glanced at the clock on the wall. It was a basic analogue model that somehow kept perfect time. Miss Tasoto had reported to the front desk ten minutes ago. Naturally, Kyle had insisted on being her personal escort.

When the happy couple finally showed up, they were at each other's throats. Nicole wore a designer dress and an expensive sapphire necklace. She could have passed for a fashion model, and certainly behaved like it.

"You want to explain what this is about? Am I a suspect? You must be getting pretty desperate."

"We just need to ask you a few questions," Kyle said, showing her to a seat. "That's all."

Nicole remained standing and shoved the chair aside. A defiant outburst was coming.

"Questions about what?" she asked.

Tired of their petty arguing, Lakeysia took charge. "You can start by telling us about Lenora."

It was speculative, but all she had in her armory.

"Le... Lenora?"

The girl obviously recognized the name.

"Let me guess. It's a long story. Tell you what. Travis can fetch some lunch while you fill me in. You like Japanese?"

Nicole collapsed into the chair. "Anything. I don't mind."

Lakeysia had deliberately kept Kyle out of the loop, and he had trouble following her line of questioning.

"What's this about?"

"The lady asked for something to eat," she said bluntly.

She wanted him out of the picture so she could interview the girl without his interference. He took the hint, slamming the door on his way out. Lakeysia switched on a tape recorder.

"So, who's Lenora?" she asked, tossing her notebook on the table.

Nicole glanced at a mirror on the far wall. She had probably seen enough cop shows to know it was a front for an observation room.

"Don't worry, Miss Tasoto. It's just you, me and our lieutenant. No Lenora, so go ahead. Spill the beans. Right now, you're the only other suspect I got on my list. Want it to stay that way? Fine with me. If you'd rather have your ass off the hook, start talking. Your call."

Nicole looked down at her dress and scratched her leg. Several seconds went by before she spoke.

"I assume you mean Lenora Knight."

"Is there more than one Lenora in your life?"

She shook her head.

"Well, that's the Lenora I mean." Lakeysia opened her notebook and flipped to a blank page. "Tell me about her."

Nicole took a breath. "We worked together at Dragonsoft. I was only sixteen, but my father valued my creative input, so he had me help with games development when I wasn't in school."

Lakeysia scribbled down the essentials.

"We? So it was just you and her?"

"No. There were two other girls. We received a lot of abuse from male colleagues. They weren't used to the idea of female game designers at Dragonsoft. It was pretty tough going."

"Yeah, it must have been hell." Lakeysia feigned sympathy. "Being the only daughter of a millionaire. I grew up in South Central L.A., so I kinda see where you're coming from."

"Quit treating me like some spoiled, selfish brat! My

parents died when I was three, so spare me the hard childhood story."

Lakeysia finished taking notes, careful to give no reaction to Miss Tasoto's outburst.

"Okay, then. I'll stop treating you like a brat. Let's concentrate on this all-girl band of yours."

"We formed our own programming group, the Cyber Maidens."

"And you're Cyber Maiden Four," Lakeysia said, recalling Nicole's password. "Figured you'd be number one, being the old man's daughter."

The suspect sat up, hands clenched into fists.

"We all treated each other as equals. Except for Lenora."

From Miss Tasoto's tone, it was obvious she no longer considered 'her' a friend. Lakeysia suspected she was about to get the dirt on Lenora.

"She claimed I stole her design ideas. She threatened to take my father to court over it, sue him for millions. And then he blamed me for her actions."

"So did she? Take your father to court?"

"No. The judge threw out the case because she had no proof. Want to know why she didn't? Because it never happened! She was nothing but a lying, cheating bitch who got what she deserved."

Lakeysia closed her notebook and sat with her arms folded.

"Is that your professional opinion, Miss Tasoto? I'd say she's more like your run-of-the-mill psycho."

Nicole took her time to respond, as if grappling with the notion. "Do you really think Lenora could be the killer? She'd have reason to hate me and my father, but..."

"Or it could be another member of your sisterhood. Do the other two girls hold a grudge against you?"

"Iris? Hannah?" she scoffed. "No. That's ridiculous."

Based solely on Miss Tasoto's testimony, Lakeysia couldn't discount them as suspects.

"So, where are your pals now?"

"I have no idea. I lost touch with them. The Cyber Maidens split up after my father fired Lenora. Hannah works at a dance club on Broadway, I think. I can't remember which one. Iris? I haven't heard from her in years. We were such a close-knit group. That bitch ruined everything."

"So, she's no longer employed by Dragonsoft." Lakeysia tapped her pen against her notebook, watching Nicole closely. "She could be our woman, but one thing don't fit. Two hundred grand in your account. That's a lot of money for a child, even the heiress to an empire. Very convenient, you having access."

"I'm eighteen, Detective. And my father gave me that account. I wasn't supposed to touch it. He was temporarily storing the funds under my name. He said he didn't want to keep all his company profits in one place."

"Also saved himself a bundle on income tax, but I'm sure that wasn't intentional."

"So Toshigi fiddled his taxes. He was in business to make a profit. I wouldn't put it past him. Sorry, but I still don't understand what the big deal is."

"I'd call two hundred grand a big deal, but then I'm not some selfish, spoiled brat."

Lakeysia smiled at Nicole, ignoring her unfriendly reaction.

"My question is, how did Miss Knight know you had so much in your nest egg? Was it common knowledge? I can see why you'd brag, but…"

That seemed to stump her. "Maybe Lenora has an

accomplice. Someone in my father's accounting division who leaked the information."

"You mean Mister Forbes' division? It's his company now. Makes you wonder, don't it?"

Lakeysia pulled a manila folder from her jacket, unwound the fastener, and spread the contents before Nicole. The girl looked through the crime scene photographs one by one. Each showed a clue left by the killer: the plastic sword on the night manager's chest, the ring around Rebecca's finger, the thief tools on Toshigi's charred body.

"This lady likes her calling cards," Lakeysia said. "Make any sense to you?"

"That's the crest of Sir Charles of York. He was a knight in *The Templar Legacy*, a pioneering hack and slash RPG. Or a role-playing game. The markings on the ring are the signature of Silica, the teenage computer hacker from *Ultimate Heist: Tokyo*."

Lakeysia nodded. The gamer lingo was incomprehensible, but she didn't want Miss Tasoto to stop.

"And my father was dressed as Black Ghost, the cat burglar from *Ghost in the Night*. They're all characters, Detective. And the Cyber Maidens designed the games that feature them. So it has to be Lenora."

"Ah, the plot thickens," Lakeysia said, collecting the photos. "Don't seem so surprised. You look like the kid who forgot to do her schoolwork."

"What are you saying?"

Lakeysia leaned across the table.

"I know when I'm being lied to. Level with me, Nicole. You stole Lenora's game ideas, and now she wants to get even."

The girl gritted her teeth. "Just because I used—"

"So, you're not the saint Travis seems to think you are."

Lakeysia slid the photos back into the folder. A moment later, Kyle entered the room with two takeaway bags. She switched off the tape recorder, stood up, and smiled.

"It's okay, Travis. We're done. Now you can take Miss Tasoto home. Try not to mess up her lovely four-poster bed too much."

"Lakeysia! What the hell?"

Her partner offered her a bag, but she ignored him and left the room. She'd eaten enough Japanese nuggets for today, and the daughter had thrown her a fortune cookie.

Her story about Lenora filled in all the blanks. Nicole might have stolen a few game ideas, but unless the girl was a frighteningly good liar, she was no killer. Lakeysia felt she owed her an apology, but now wasn't the time.

Kyle was right about Mei Tan biasing her, but he'd feel better about things after he won the bet. Lakeysia refused to admit she was wrong until the case was officially closed. Perhaps the daughter had designed the perfect murder spree and was playing her part to perfection.

After leaving the interview room, Lakeysia returned to Homicide and presented Frances with a summary of Nicole's statement.

"Run a search on Miss Tasoto's former group. Give me their names, last known whereabouts, the full shebang."

"Any idea where to start?"

"Try game sites," Lakeysia suggested. "Web zines, chat rooms for girl geeks. They're Cyber Maidens, so look in cyberspace. Where else would they be?"

* * *

The forensics lab was below ground, next to the precinct morgue. Coroners delivered via the old hotel service entrance, thus avoiding the need to carry body bags through the front door. The cold storage area was still in use, though the freezers no longer contained food, and it wasn't ham and beef that got sliced up on the steel tables. Water pipes rattled and squeaked behind grimy brick walls, and turquoise strip lights made it seem much colder than it actually was.

Spiritually inclined people might have thought of the morgue as a holding chamber for those awaiting the afterlife. Lakeysia considered it the police department's version of hell, a seldom-visited tomb that reeked of the dead. It was the one place on Earth nobody wanted to end up.

Lakeysia hurried through the freezer and into the laboratory. It was marginally warmer than the morgue thanks to electric heating, but still cold enough to see her breath. The doctor was with his assistant, though his eyes were on another woman's hair. With tweezers, he took the blonde strand from its evidence bag and placed it on a glass slide.

Matthews peered through his microscope, adjusting the focus knob until he was satisfied.

"The specimen's not artificial. It came from a female Caucasian. Late teens, possibly early twenties. The hair's dyed, and it was done recently. Blonde's not the natural color."

"Our girl's a redhead," Lakeysia shouted. "Ain't that right, doc?"

Matthews and Kari both jumped as she announced her presence. It was rare for an officer to visit the forensics lab without making an appointment. Nobody passed through the morgue unless it was necessary, and they wanted someone living to be waiting for them when they arrived.

That was one procedure Lakeysia usually followed, but she needed an immediate answer to her question. The doctor was quick to provide one.

"Yes. The sample's from a redhead. My first guess would have been a brunette, except you're not guessing. What's the fresh evidence you're desperate to show me?"

Matthews was referring to the photographs in Lakeysia's hand. Frances had struck gold, finding a picture of the Cyber Maidens with a single internet search. The digital photo was taken at an award ceremony two years previously, less than a month before the group's breakup.

"Mafia gangsters recruit heavies, Miss Tasoto recruits game designers," Lakeysia said.

She presented her first photograph to Matthews. It was a color printout of the image France found on the Internet.

"You might say this was her family. Meet the Cyber Maidens, doc. Sure you recognize Nicole. That's Hannah Davies, and Iris Levier."

Miss Tasoto wore yet another formal outfit. Lakeysia hadn't seen this pearly white blouse before, but the rich girl probably had a dozen fancy dresses.

She stood in front of the others, clutching a crystal award plaque engraved *Jade Dragon - Game of the Year*. Hannah and Iris were on her left side. Both had several years on their colleague, if not access to her expensive wardrobe.

Hannah was the pretender to Miss Tasoto's throne. The five foot nine, platinum blonde dressed liked a high school prom queen, right down to the fake silver circlet. Iris couldn't care less about appearances. Her spiky hair was dyed purple, and her nose and ears pierced with brass rings. Black jeans, choker and a leather jacket completed the goth look.

"Bizarre little club, ain't it? The lady over here is Lenora

Knight, the Cyber Maidens' contender for the world's strongest woman. Looks a real happy one, don't she?"

Lakeysia showed Matthews her second photograph, a blowup of Lenora's face. The prime suspect was a tall, thick-shouldered girl roughly the same age as Nicole. The blood haired teenager wore a dark green tank top that emphasized her lean, muscular build. With her powerful arms, Lenora would have no trouble besting the average male in a wrestling match. The other girls all smiled at the camera, but she stared forward with a bitter expression.

"Believe me, doc. You're better off sticking to Asians," Lakeysia said. "They say blondes have more fun. Seems Miss Knight wanted to test the theory."

The detective handed over her third and last photo: a close-up of Lenora's bright green eyes.

"That's her. She's our girl. Strong, focused, determined. And green eyed with envy."

* * *

The police assault team waited for Lieutenant Thorne to give them the green light. According to her driver's license records, Lenora's last known residence was a penthouse apartment in Outer Richmond. All Frances' research showed she lived alone, but nobody was taking anything for granted. Undercover officers had established roadblocks at both ends of the street, and warned the neighbors to remain indoors.

The cops occupied the unit one floor below. A technical specialist stood on the dining table, directing an optical fiber he'd inserted through a drilled hole in the ceiling. Richmond had its fair share of Edwardian houses, but over recent years, real estate moguls had transformed the residential landscape by building ultra-modern condos.

Lenora lived atop a brand new tower block, in a space-age apartment that came with a private gym, indoor pool and sauna. Her furniture was sci-fi junkie material: chrome futons, vibrating bed, lava lamps and automatic sliding doors.

"No trace of the suspect," said the technician. "Or any booby traps."

Lakeysia secured her bulletproof vest. "Somebody sign me up for games design at San Francisco Tech. She and Miss Tasoto got my place beat hands down."

"I don't think Knight is here, lieutenant," Travis said. "She probably knows we're on to her. Odds are she's long gone."

"We deal in facts," Thorne reminded him. "Not odds. This woman's already killed a cop and left another in bits and pieces. You don't let your guard down, not for one second. Not until I give the all clear. You got that?"

The lieutenant waited for the technician's go-ahead, then gave his starting orders.

"Okay, guys and girls. We're on."

The assault team leader led his unit into the corridor and up the stairwell. He paused outside Lenora's apartment, signaling his officers to hold their positions. One man carried a battering ram to use on the suspect's door.

Lakeysia waved him back and produced a master keycard she'd gotten from the building manager. Thorne took the card and slid it into the reader. A diode lamp changed from red to green. The unit commander counted down from three with his fingers, then turned the handle.

"Police!"

The leader went through the door, and Thorne followed. Officers stuck to the plan, splitting into pairs to secure the apartment.

Lakeysia and Kyle took the bedroom. The bosses and a female officer swept the gym, bathroom, and sauna. Meanwhile, the assault commander and the rest of his men searched the living area and kitchen.

The place had been completely cleaned out. Other than furniture and appliances, there was nothing to suggest the unit was still occupied. Refrigerators, cupboards and storage closets were all empty. The dining table was spotless, the bed sheets and pillowcases fresh, and the bathroom towels unused. All the carpets smelled of cleaning fluid, and the kitchen tiles shone like new. It was as if Lenora had never lived in the apartment.

"Sure we got the right place, Symons?"

Thorne holstered his weapon. He had to blame someone, and Lakeysia was his chosen fall girl.

"Come on, give the lady some credit. Miss Knight may be a psycho, but she ain't stupid. What? You think she'd make it easy for us and roll out the welcome mat?"

The lieutenant buttoned his jacket. "I'll circulate a photo to the press. Issue another statement. Tell our friendly reporters the killer's still at large. I'm sure someone can find her."

He turned and walked away.

"Yeah, Lenora's next sparring partner," Lakeysia said as he left.

The assault team officers exited with the Lieutenant, but Kyle stayed behind.

"Do I get a pardon now? For trusting Nicole? It would help if she trusted us too, but your friendly interview this morning might have ticked her off. Don't you think?"

"Sure, you can bring her round. Never been a girl you couldn't handle. Set a time and place yet?"

Lakeysia went through the apartment, checking cupboards as she spoke. Kyle followed her into the gym.

"Do you have a problem with me talking to her? You mind telling what you have against Nicole now you've crossed her off your suspect list? All I'm doing is looking out for the girl. She's in danger, in case you hadn't noticed. Is there something wrong with watching her back?"

"Bet you'd rather watch her front. Make sure you wear a rubber, Travis. Can't be too careful these days."

Kyle dropped his jaw, feigning innocence. But his reputation preceded him.

"What? You think I'm having dinner with her just to have a brief romance on the side?"

Lakeysia had a direct answer to her partner's question, but something caught her eye.

There was a white spot on Lenora's treadmill. She bent down to inspect it and saw a piece of newspaper trapped under the conveyor belt. Four feet away, a punching bag hung from the ceiling, its outside cover riddled with pinholes.

"So, Miss Tasoto invited you over to her house," Lakeysia said, dragging the paper into the open with her Biro tip. "That's interesting. Is she on the menu?"

Kyle grinned, hands in his suit pockets. "You know, Symons. You can be a real…"

"Pain in the ass?"

She showed him the newspaper scrap. It featured a picture of the Tasoto girl's head, torn along the neck.

"There's an old saying. It goes, the friend of my enemy is my enemy. Or something. Don't quote me on that. Always get it mixed up."

"Would you get to the point? Today, if you can."

Lakeysia sealed the news scrap in an evidence bag.

"Miss Tasoto's friends are all on our wacko's list. Lenora was her friend, too. Until your girl stole her ideas, betrayed her confidence. Nicole's no angel, so don't feel you need to be hers. And if you decide to play Cupid, ride her for all she's worth. Because when you wake up tomorrow morning, you might find yourself in heaven."

# CHAPTER TEN

## *Lady Ninja*

Kyle put on his best suit for the evening trip to Nicole's mansion. He would have brought some wine along, but his hostess had insisted on providing the drinks. He rang the front doorbell and waited for the mistress of the house to let him in. Someone had already replaced the damaged oak paneling after last night's police raid. Swift service was one advantage of being wealthy.

Nicole answered the door wearing a pale blue evening gown. The color matched her eyes perfectly, and the soft material was thin and revealing. Nicole's undershirt was brilliant white with fancy patterns embroidered into the cotton. Like her gold necklace and earrings, it was studded with sparkling sapphires.

"Am I dressed suitably, Detective?" she asked.

Kyle blushed, realizing he'd been staring a little too hard. "Yes. You look wonderful."

"Your friends certainly seem to think so."

Nicole was referring to the officers stationed out front. The police guard had been doubled after the recent murders. All four men were married, and two were over forty, but that didn't discourage them from admiring a beautiful woman.

"We should go inside," he said.

The girl presented Kyle with a bottle of wine once she'd closed the door. She had chosen a twenty-year-old, deep red vintage. People would normally reserve such a fine beverage for high society occasions.

"A token of my appreciation. A thank you for looking out for me. I realize I've not been completely honest. After what happened with my father, Kenji, and Sarah, I was scared that you might believe I had something to do with it. Then she killed Rebecca and Charlie and I..."

"Hey," Kyle said, relieving Nicole of the bottle. "I had no doubts about you. And Lakeysia was only doing her job by covering the possibilities. But that's all behind us. I'm here to make sure you're okay."

She hung Kyle's coat on a hook and escorted him across the main hall.

"And you'd like some background on Lenora. She was all over the news. Just looking at her face made me feel sick. The report said something about a reward for information."

"There's some incentive for you, then. A little extra money."

Kyle's intention had been to make her smile, but he immediately regretted his choice of words. She laughed it off, but thinking about her inheritance clearly upset the girl. Kyle knew she would trade the estate and all her wealth for the lives the killer had taken.

"I'm sorry. I realize you had differences with your

father, but I wasn't suggesting that you should be happy to get your hands on his money."

"It's okay. You aren't the only one who said things they shouldn't have. Would you like to see my father's true legacy? Come upstairs, and I'll show you. Leave the wine on the table. This won't take long."

Kyle followed Nicole to the master bedroom. The mansion's halls were silent and empty, but he was glad to spend some time with his hostess. She was a fascinating and extraordinarily talented woman who'd accomplished more in eighteen years than most people would in their lifetime. She'd shared portions of her life story, but there was so much he still wished to learn.

Nicole took his hand, leading him towards the four-poster bed. "Lie down," she said suggestively. "Relax. And close your eyes."

Surprised by Nicole's direct approach, Kyle did as she asked. He was beginning to understand what she meant by her father's legacy. She groped inside his suit, hands massaging his chest. Her touch was soft, warm, and gentle.

"No peeking now. You wanted to know what my father left me. Here it is."

She slid her thumb between Kyle's lips, pried open his mouth, and inserted something cold, metallic and square shaped between his teeth. It was the barrel of a .45 caliber pistol.

Kyle jerked back, opened his eyes, and grabbed his own weapon in defense. Then he saw the cable running from the grip, the lilac trigger, and the red button on the pistol's handle. It was just a game controller, a harmless replica of the real thing.

"Expecting something else?"

"Think that was funny?" Kyle yelled, shoving Nicole

away. "Jesus! I could have shot you! Don't pull a stupid stunt like that again."

She staggered back, laughing at her practical joke.

"Bang, bang. You're dead, Detective." The girl couldn't stop smiling. "Why are you getting yourself all worked up? It's only a game."

Kyle waved his weapon. "Well, this shoots real bullets. And this isn't the time to be joking around."

Nicole ran a finger along her collection of DVD-ROM cases. "This was my father's gift. He saved me when he took me away from the orphanage. Toshigi gave me the opportunity of a lifetime, allowed me to fulfill my dream. Together, we built Dragonsoft from nothing. Now Lenora wants to tear down our empire. Well, I'm not about to let her."

Nicole was doing her tough girl act again. Kyle was worried her headstrong attitude could get her killed.

"This isn't one of your damn video games. Lenora's a killer. You leave her to me. All right?"

"I'm not the harmless young lady you perceive me as," she said. "I'm quite capable of dealing with Lenora. I'll prove it to you."

She selected a game disc, placed it on a console tray, and booted up the system.

"First, let's see how well you handle guns."

Nicole tossed Kyle a controller, took another for herself, and sat beside her guest.

"This is the only decent idea that bitch ever thought of. It's called *Murder on the Golden Gate*, about a cop hunting a killer in San Francisco. Not very original, but I'm sure you'll get a kick out of it."

"Is this the idea you stole from her?"

It was hard to accuse a beautiful girl of theft, but Kyle

had to know the truth.

"I see you've been talking to Detective Symons."

Nicole waited for the Dragonsoft logo to disappear and pushed the start button.

"The original concept was mine," she said. "Lenora only developed the idea. Back then, rail shooters were outdated, considered a relic of the past."

"Rail shooters?" Kyle wished she'd drop the video game lingo.

A grated male voice announced, "Stage One," then the game began.

The main menu faded to a picture of wooden planks and poles, not unlike the piers at the Marina. Nicole fired at targets: masked men and thugs who appeared on screen. Kyle needed a few seconds to get used to handling a toy gun, and his character took several hits before he finally shot an opponent.

"I see you're a rookie with games," Nicole teased. "Rail shooters are modeled after the old arcade machines, where the player moves along a fixed path. My idea was to make things more dynamic, give freedom to move laterally within the screen. Backward and forward, taking cover behind obstacles. The illusion of 3D, but still a set route. Lenora designed the enemy AI, artificial intelligence, to behave more realistically. The stupid bitch thought that entitled her to half the credit."

As Nicole talked about her former friend, she focused intently on the screen, blasting one bad guy after the next. She was lethal with her toy pistol. Every shot she fired struck its target in the head for bonus points. Opponents sprinted for cover, but never made it.

Kyle watched the expert at play. "There are people who claim murderers get their inspiration from games. Do you think there's any truth to that?"

Nicole smiled. Obviously, she found his comment amusing.

"Games don't create killers, Detective," she said, blowing a tough guy away with another pinpoint accurate shot. "Society does that all by itself. I understand the difference between digital gunmen and innocent civilians. See?"

To show her point, she took out a criminal hiding behind a human shield.

"Does Lenora know the difference?" Kyle asked. "She murdered the maid, no problem. These light guns, they're pretty close to the genuine article. Same weight, same grip. A lot less conspicuous practicing shooting at home than at a firing range."

"Stage cleared," grated the console voice.

Nicole blew imaginary smoke off her pistol, then switched off the game.

"You've fired guns for real. You know it's not the same thing. Not only is their recoil and actual tension, but it takes hatred to kill somebody. Even a psycho bitch like Lenora. It gets to you, doesn't it? Taking human lives."

Nicole dropped her light gun, swung her legs up onto Kyle's lap, and leaned back on her duvet. She lifted her skirt slightly to expose her shins.

"Where would you rather be? Safe in my bedroom, or out patrolling the streets? And who would you choose as your partner? Me or Lakeysia?"

"You," Kyle replied, edging closer. "In a heartbeat."

He moved his hand up Nicole's knee and squeezed her bare thigh. With no forewarning, she grabbed Kyle's wrist and twisted his forearm. Nicole clamped her legs around his chest, holding him against the duvet cover. A firm, inescapable hold. The girl was much stronger than she looked.

"Relationships require commitment from both parties," she said. "And I haven't decided yet. Know why I'm so successful? Because I never let myself be dominated by men. People think they can take advantage of a young woman like me. I enjoy being independent. Is this how you arrest someone, Detective?"

She applied extra torque, bending Kyle's arm behind his back. He wanted to yelp in pain, but that would be embarrassing. The girl smiled and opened her legs to release him.

"Call me Kyle," he said, shaking off the discomfort. "What was that shit?"

"Another of my hobbies. We should eat something. Put our games on hold. I hope you like sushi."

* * *

Kyle helped himself to another glass of wine while Nicole served dinner. She'd changed into a traditional kimono, a pale green satin dress typically worn by geisha girls. In true Japanese style, the hostess cooked her guest a meal in front of him. Bowls of soup, steamed rice and sushi rested on a knee-high dining table. The atmosphere inside her dojo was romantic. Incensed candles burned in silver holders and Oriental music played in the background.

As Nicole prepared the main meal, Kyle studied a portrait, one of several she'd painted in her youth. The theme was Feudal Japan. There wasn't a single picture that didn't feature a colorful drawing of some pagoda, training ground or ancient temple. Her view of the old world was violent and bloody. Buildings burned while hooded ninjas and samurai battled in courtyards.

One figure made a recurring appearance: a female dressed in bright green, the same shade as Nicole's kimono. She wore a face mask, but her smoothly curved body, wide hips and breasts gave away her gender. The woman was as tall as the male warriors and no less deadly. Someone was always shown dying by her hand. The ninja's weapons included samurai swords, daggers and throwing stars.

"This lady seems to feature prominently in your work."

Nicole poured sauce over her chicken teriyaki and placed the platter with the other food.

"Lady? That's hardly the word to describe her."

Kyle sat down opposite Nicole. "So, who is the girl in green?"

"Jade Dragon," she said, tucking into the meal. "She's a Kunoichi, a female ninja. Me and the other Cyber Maidens created her. Jade was the star of our best-selling video game."

He struggled with the chopsticks. Somehow he lifted a sushi cube twice, but lost his grip both times.

"Here, allow me."

She licked her own sticks clean and used them to insert the food into Kyle's mouth.

"How did that taste? Would you like some more?"

She bent forward and collected another cube between her teeth. Kyle leaned across the table, meeting her halfway. Simultaneously, he and Nicole chewed the morsel until their lips touched.

Their initial contact blossomed into a full-blown kiss. She was so close he saw the girl's naked body beneath her kimono. The hostess retreated with a seductive smile, swallowed her half of sushi, and poured him a third glass of wine.

Kyle coughed, still taking everything in. He tried to focus on the investigation, but Nicole had stolen his thunder.

"You mentioned Cyber Maidens."

The girl sighed, as if talking about her past was an unwanted distraction. "You can ask your partner when she's feeling in a good mood, assuming there are such moments. I told her my life story this afternoon."

"You'll have to excuse Lakeysia. She can be heavy-handed. I ought to know."

"Jade would decapitate the arrogant bitch and be done with it."

Nicole spoke so bluntly Kyle dropped his chopsticks.

"But don't worry," she said. "I'm a little more civilized."

Her disarming smile put him at ease. She obviously intended her comment as black humor, but it fell rather flat.

"Sounds like somebody pissed this woman off."

"Want to know the story?" Nicole stopped eating and leaned back to recount her tale. "As a child, Jade watched her parents die. A ninja grand master took her under his care. She grew up swearing revenge. When she reached adulthood, she hunted down the murderers one by one. That was the object of the game, to assassinate all those who'd wronged her. Jade had a quirk. Before she killed a target, she looked them in the eye, and showed them her face."

"Why do that?"

"To let them know an eighteen-year-old girl had beaten them. That she was stronger, smarter, and more ruthless than they were."

As Kyle finished his wine, Nicole tidied up the plates and carried them into a neighboring room.

"Sounds like the present day killer's a fan of hers," he

said.

While the character intrigued him, the connections between this Jade Dragon and the real life murderess were too strong to dismiss.

"Lenora always was a copycat," Nicole shouted. "Whatever path I followed, so did she."

She returned with a photograph and passed it to Kyle. The picture showed two girls in their early teens. Both of them wore karate uniforms and stood in a ready stance. The Asian's belt was black, and the redhead's brown. The photo was so outdated he didn't immediately recognize the young Japanese girl.

"You were close friends with her."

"Once upon a time, but that's all in the past."

Nicole tossed the photograph aside.

"You're a karate student. I should have guessed."

"Lenora was the student." She turned around and unfastened her kimono sash. "I was the master. Would you like to see some of my moves, Kyle?"

She slipped off her gown and kicked it across the room. Beads of sweat trickled down her bare back, glistening orange in the candlelight. She rubbed the liquid into her smooth brown skin and spun about to face Kyle.

She was the sexiest girl he'd ever laid eyes on. The Oriental vixen stood on a karate mat five feet from him. Her beauty was one hundred percent natural. Nicole was in wonderful shape, muscles toned through regular workouts in her dojo. She pushed her long, dark hair behind her shoulders to expose her breasts. Virtual criminals weren't the only competition she could blow away.

Nicole adopted the same stance as in the photo. She placed one foot forward, bent her knees, and stretched her rear leg.

"Let's see what you can do," she said, rotating her arms to protect her upper body.

Unable to resist the allure of this woman, Kyle set down his glass, unbuttoned his shirt collar, and discarded his tie. If Nicole wanted to play rough, he was more than ready.

He stepped onto the mat and clenched his fists. Nicole circled around her opponent, eyes focused on his face. She moved elegantly across the floor, distracting him with her naked body.

"Do you know what a woman's most dangerous weapon is?"

"Lakeysia already told me the answer to that," Kyle said, glancing downward. "I wouldn't mind having yours in my arsenal."

"Can't wait to get your hands on me? I'm yours for the taking, assuming you can reach me."

Before he could even try, Nicole stamped on his foot, punched him in the stomach, and knocked him down with a ferocious high kick.

"Why do you think Dragonsoft's marketers wanted me to expand Jade's breast size? Because most guys will buy a piece of junk if it has a busty woman on the front cover. The bigger they are, the better."

"There's more to it than that."

Kyle sat up, only for Nicole to force him back down with her foot.

"Of course there is. Having her completely naked with a nice ass helps, too."

He wasn't sure where she was going with this, but he didn't want her to stop. "Don't worry. You qualify on all three counts."

"That's why the killer's got the cops running around in circles. Men can't see women as threats, only sex objects. I told you I'm not as innocent as I look. Girls have to protect themselves. Lenora better not screw with me, or she'll get more than she bargained for."

Kyle grabbed Nicole's thigh. This time, she didn't resist.

"What about me? If I were to screw with you, would the same apply to me?"

"You can tell me in the morning."

She removed Kyle's shoes, unfastened his belt, and lowered his trousers. "To survive in the business world, I have to make the most of any opportunities that present themselves. And never look back."

His mobile phone rang. He switched it off without looking at the screen, then took off his jacket and holster. Nicole stacked the clothes in a neat pile.

"I take what I want," she said. "How about you?"

Nicole sat on his waist, reached between her legs, and pulled his boxer shorts down to his knees.

"You deserve everything you have," Kyle said. "Don't ever be afraid I won't treat you seriously."

"And just how serious are you?"

She unbuttoned his shirt, then pressed her body against his exposed chest. He rubbed her back, moving his fingers up her spine. When Kyle reached Nicole's shoulders, he brought his hands round the front to feel her nipples.

"The wine was an appetizer," she said, panting. "This is for saving my life."

She steadied Kyle's head and gave him a long, satisfying kiss. The candles cast shadows of the two lovers across the karate mat. They were fully committed, and neither of them held anything back. Nicole was his greatest ever catch: a strong-willed, intelligent, yet enticing woman not afraid of danger. She knew how to make a man happy.

Kyle could spend the rest of his days in the sexy games

designer's arms. If she asked him to travel with her to the far side of the world, he wouldn't hesitate to buy tickets. The romantic evening hadn't been a disappointment.

Kyle had finally found the woman of his dreams. It was, without doubt, the happiest moment he had ever experienced.

*　*　*

Jade combed her blonde hair while she waited for the images to upload to her hard drive. Her recent file purge had left plenty of space for her kinky snapshots. As a routine precaution, she'd wiped incriminating data from her computer in case the police discovered her hideaway. The killer considered that scenario unlikely. If the cops were all as dumb as Kyle Travis, then there was nothing to worry about.

Digital cameras had one crucial advantage over older film models. They were completely silent. The user could take a picture discretely, even from the same room. It was essential to Jade's plan that she didn't tip the policeman off when she'd photographed him making love.

That wasn't a big problem. Given Travis' infatuation, he probably wouldn't have noticed the camera had it been in plain view. As Jade had expected, he'd fallen for her. A ladykiller like him could never resist the wiles of a temptress, especially one as seductive as Nicole.

The killer had already thought up a suitable end for the womanizing detective. When the time was right, he'd die in Jade's arms while she administered the ultimate climax. She would be the last girl Travis ever kissed.

An on-screen message reported the file transfer was complete. Jade tucked her natural hair inside her wig, checked her disguise in the vanity mirror, and sat down at the computer desk.

She clicked through the compromising portfolio. Thanks to the camera's high-powered zoom and high resolution, the images were of professional quality. It required stealthy maneuvering to get the angle right, but the romantic pair were clearly identifiable. Travis wouldn't be able to deny he'd made love to Nicole Tasoto.

The pictures were explicit, showing the cop drunk and naked. Several pictured him fondling Nicole's breasts or squeezing her buttocks. Others showed the two lovers at the height of passion, embracing on the karate mat. One photograph captured a kiss with perfect timing.

Newspapers and cable networks would pay a lot of money for evidence a detective was having a steamy affair with Toshigi Tasoto's daughter, but the killer had other plans for her pornographic album. She would play with Travis and drive him to the edge of insanity before she killed him.

The camera's memory stick was full, containing a hundred images in total. Jade selected the best of the bunch and sent the files to her color printer. She changed into her biker's leathers while the hard copies were being deposited in the tray.

Another bonus of modern cameras was how they eliminated the need for developing and fixing prints in a darkroom. Jade didn't have the equipment or time for film processing, and involving a third party would have been an unnecessary risk. The digital age made it easy to produce glossy photos on home computers, and more difficult to trace the pictures back to their source.

Jade sealed the photographs inside a brown envelope. She used her computer to print a single line of black text on the front side, the name of someone certain to be interested in Travis' off-duty activities. The murderess was careful to wear gloves when handling the paper. The package contained no fingerprints, handwriting samples, or any other clues of potential value to the police.

Jade would deliver her bombshell on the way back. First, she wanted to catch up with two old friends.

# CHAPTER ELEVEN

## *Star of the Show*

After dark, the bars and nightclubs along Broadway became havens for party-goers and lonely men seeking an escort for the evening. Pink neon signs plastered the marquees, advertising happy hours, private viewing rooms and so-called dance shows.

Tourist guides cautioned women against walking through the red-light district alone at night, but Jade wasn't about to let the local riff-raff scare her away. Anyone stupid enough to attack her would be lucky to escape with their life. There were quite a few deserted alleys to dump a corpse where it wouldn't be found until morning.

Jade parked her motorcycle opposite *The Exotic Pearl*. Despite its posh name, the "gentleman's club" was no classier than any other strip joint in the area. The night was still young, and there were five hours to go before the dancers finished their routines. Patrons queued along the street, eager to get a glimpse of the girls inside. Most were in their early twenties, with the odd teenage boy hoping to crash the adults only party.

A single bouncer stood outside the front door, a heavyweight of a man wearing the official club jacket and tie. He carried a radio in his side pocket, but the big black guy could handle trouble by himself. One rude customer limped away, holding his bruised jaw. The doorman had dissuaded him from jumping the queue with a right hook to the face. Combined with brass knuckles, it was a brutal but effective tactic that quickly resolved the situation.

Jade tried a more subtle approach. She removed her leather jumpsuit and helmet. A group of tattooed female bikers stared at her, not used to seeing a motorcyclist in an evening dress. It was the same bright green outfit she had worn for Toshigi's farewell speech, a formal gown that made men drool at the mouth.

The killer smiled at her gawping admirers as she sprayed perfume on her neck. She put on her high heel shoes and a pair of dark glasses, slung a purse over her shoulder, and crossed the street.

"Sorry, miss," the bouncer said, obstructing Jade's path. "The queue starts over there. Rules are rules."

He pointed at the end of the line, some forty people behind.

Jade tilted up her glasses so the doorman could see her green eyes. "And you can't make an exception?" she asked, moving closer.

"No exceptions. You go to the back."

The bouncer's resistance broke as she pressed up against him. She stood on tiptoes and wafted her perfume scent up his nose.

"That's too bad," she said seductively. "Because I have

something to offer. Something I think you'd like very much."

Jade ran her silk-gloved hand up the man's trouser leg. He remained still, feet rooted to the spot. His breathing became heavier as she felt his groin area. She held a folded hundred-dollar bill in the doorman's face and kissed him on the cheek. Wolf whistles came from the men behind her. Nobody seemed too bothered a woman was using her sex appeal to get ahead.

"So what do you say?"

The doorman grabbed the money from her hand. "Enjoy the show," he said with a gold-toothed grin.

"Oh, believe me. I will."

Jade replaced her glasses and stepped into the club. The brute never presented a real obstacle. Brawn was no match for brains, skill, and technique. She could have busted the guy's balls or floored him with a single punch, but seduction and bribery allowed her to keep a low profile. The bouncer had gotten a close look at her face, but he wasn't smart enough to remember the details. He'd only recall the color of her wig and what brand of perfume she used.

The air surrounding the dance floor was warm and smoky. Waitresses in silvery bikini tops and miniskirts served leery-eyed customers around the stage. Many girls were young and good looking, but all the men were busy watching "Lady Cleopatra".

That was her stage name. Jade knew the bronze skinned stripper as Hannah Davies, her former colleague at Dragonsoft. She used to be the Cyber Maidens' graphic designer, but had since left the video game world behind. She now seemed content to promote her other artistic assets.

Hannah reached the pinnacle of her act. The Pharaoh impersonator discarded her scepter, headdress, robes, and finally, her underwear. She strutted across the stage, completely nude except for an ankh-clasped belt inscribed with mock Egyptian hieroglyphs.

The stripper climbed up the vertical pole and spun around, much to the delight of the cheering crowd of men. After her dance, she paused by each table to treat individual customers to kisses. Some showed their appreciation by sliding dollar bills under Hannah's belt. She had no objection to them feeling her body.

"Wasn't she delightful, guys?" a middle-aged male presenter said over the loudspeaker. "Let's hear it for... Lady Cleopatra!"

Patrons rose from their seats, whistling and applauding. Hannah made a last lap of the stage and collected her clothes. She blew kisses to the crowd, bowed, and walked out of the spotlight, where she disappeared into the employees' private dressing room.

"Next up, ladies and gents, is the Hawaiian beauty exclusive to the Exotic Pearl. She's sweet, she's sexy, our very own... Honolula!"

The stripper act followed her cue. This woman was a tanned dancer sporting a straw coat, skirt, and hat. The clubbers ordered extra beer rounds and settled down for more action.

Jade chose an empty booth over in the corner. It was the most secluded seating area she could find, as far away as possible from the loud dance music and multicolored stage lights. She lowered the table's lantern shade, reducing its bright yellow glow to a faint glimmer. The assassin wanted her discussion with Hannah to be private.

She called a waitress to her table. "Two blue margaritas," she told the woman, showing her choice on a drinks menu. "And pass on a message to the girl who was on stage just now, Lady Cleopatra. She and I are old friends."

The employee gave her a strange look, but soon shrugged it off. "If you're asking for an autograph, talk to the manager. Anything personal you do outside the club."

Jade slipped the waitress a hundred dollars.

"Let's keep this between us. Our business is rather… private. I just want to have a drink with her, then I'll leave."

"Who should I say wants the pleasure of her company?"

The killer crossed her legs and relaxed in the seat. "Lenora. Miss Davies will know who I am."

The server accepted the generous tip, whispered some instructions to another serving girl, and walked backstage. A minute later, the woman delivered two cocktails to Jade's table.

Jade licked the salt from her margarita glass, watching Honolula remove her coat and wiggle her body for the crowd. The act from Hawaii was attractive and her dancing good, but she was hardly in Hannah's league. Much as the assassin despised her, the former Cyber Maiden was definitely the star of the show. If only Toshigi had hired Hannah as a motion capture model instead of employing her mediocre skills as a character artist. Then she might have been a valuable member of Jade's design team. As things stood, she was a failure.

Hannah exited the dressing room's side door. She'd changed into casual clothes (in her case, a prom queen dress and cowboy hat), and taken off her Cleopatra wig. The real woman wasn't that different from her stripper alter ego: a buxom mantrap who probably moonlighted as a prostitute on nights she didn't work.

Looking round, Hannah spotted Jade in the corner. She walked to the booth clutching her skirt, as if modeling on a

Parisian catwalk. She brushed peanut shavings off her seat, sat down, and viewed her face in a hand mirror. After repainting her nails with glittery gold varnish, she finally acknowledged Jade's presence.

"What brings you to my club?"

Hannah put on an annoying posh accent, phrasing the question as if she owned the place. Perhaps it was a way to convince herself she was someone important.

"We were never on the best of terms," she said, putting her mirror away. "One assumes this isn't a social visit. I like your blonde wig. It gives you a certain element of attractiveness. Even so, I understand why you'd prefer to sit in the shade."

Jade couldn't resist shattering the stuck up cow's ego. "When did you become the expert on beauty? Nice to see you've found a new job. I don't imagine too many companies want to recruit a brainless bimbo. Do you enjoy dragging our sex's reputation through the gutter?"

Hannah took the disparaging comment with a pinch of her margarita's salt.

"Time is a precious commodity," she said, licking her finger. "I've been courteous enough to sit at your table, but if you're going to insult me, I'll have security eject you onto the street. Then you can go back to designing video games for pocket change. So, let me ask you nicely once more. Why have you come here?"

"I wanted to say goodbye," said Jade with a charming smile. "After tonight, I doubt we'll see each other again."

The killer lifted her dress under the cover of the table. She'd prepared a cocktail of her own, a healthy dose of household cleaning fluid. Four test tubes were taped to the front of her panties. If security had frisked Jade on the way in, they'd have been reluctant to feel there.

"Did you hear about Toshigi?" asked Hannah.

"I was there for the annual meeting. In fact, I spoke with Mister Tasoto just before he died."

"I thought you worked for Digital Dawn Studios these days. Dragonsoft's arch rivals. Surprised you were even on the guest list, considering all the bad blood between you. I was always curious why you never sued his ass."

"I wasn't officially invited. But you know me. I'm a clever girl. I have methods, ways to get what I want."

Jade untaped a test tube, concealing it behind her wrist. She rested her elbows on the tabletop, leaned forward, and discretely added the poison to Hannah's drink. The margarita turned a darker shade of blue as the liquids mixed, but Hannah wouldn't notice the difference.

"And what is it you want from me?" the stripper asked. "This diversion has been really fascinating, but unless there's something important…"

"I was hoping you'd humor me. We never had much fun together at Dragonsoft."

Hannah yawned, raising her glass. "I might even laugh if I knew the joke."

Jade dropped the empty tube in her handbag and rested her cheeks between her knuckles.

"You're going to play the super heroine, Princess Astra."

The killer pulled a plastic tiara from inside her gown and tossed it on the table. It was a worthless replica she'd bought at a fancy dress store, an artificial silver crown with colored glass in place of real jewels.

"Sorry Lenora, but I don't play games anymore. You've got me confused with Iris and Nicole. Try asking one of those losers to be your superhero."

An evil smile crossed Jade's face as she watched Hannah finish her margarita. The stripper slammed her cocktail on the table and clutched her throat, choking on the poisonous bleach. The dying girl staggered to her feet.

"What did you... Hel... Help... me."

Jade swiveled round the booth and clamped her hand on Hannah's shoulder, forcing her back down.

"No," the assassin whispered. "You're not Princess Astra. How do I know? Well, for one thing, she's immune to lethal toxins."

The killer uncorked a second test tube and refilled the glass with bleach. The intoxicated girl was powerless to act. She looked round desperately for someone to assist her, but the waitresses were all busy serving other tables, and Honolula had the full, undivided attention of every man present.

"And Astra relies on her own abilities to escape precarious situations instead of ignorant jerks who couldn't care less. Look at those sex craved maniacs over there, staring at their dream girl while you sit here and choke to death. I guess you're not so important to them after all. It sounds as if you need to clear your throat. Would you like another drink?"

Jade slammed Hannah's head against the table. She tilted it back, squeezed the girl's nose, and poured the bleach into her mouth. Hannah struggled and coughed, but couldn't prevent herself from swallowing the bulk of the poison.

The assassin raised her dark glasses and looked deep into her victim's eyes. "Remember your old friend now?"

The girl said something, but violent coughs drowned out her words. Jade ripped Hannah's dress, threw off her cowboy hat, and loosened her bra strap. She placed the tiara around the stripper's head and released her shoulder.

"It was nice seeing you again. It's time for your last

performance."

Hannah dragged herself up and stumbled towards the dance floor, gasping for air. She wobbled unsteadily from side to side, showing symptoms of dizziness. Her dress and bra fell off, leaving her naked apart from the tiara. The stripper knocked over an empty chair, tripped, and tumbled backwards into a booth. The drunken men around the table laughed and cheered, massaging her body.

Hannah brushed them away, broke free, and climbed onstage. The audience applauded as she careered into a pole, hands clawing at the reflective metal. Only her colleagues realized she was in serious trouble. Waitresses rushed for help while Honolula ran to her dying companion's side.

There was nothing anyone could do. The poison had already entered Hannah's system. She coughed in sporadic bursts then lay still, blue stained tongue protruding from her mouth.

The men fell silent. As news of her death spread, Jade left through a fire door at the rear of the club. She heard Honolula scream, and a flurry of activity from *The Exotic Pearl*'s security staff.

The building would be locked down until the police arrived, but Jade didn't plan on being among those detained for questioning. The killer changed back into her biker leathers and stored the remaining test tubes in her motorcycle pannier. Poison was always handy to have, especially the untraceable household variety.

* * *

Hannah Davies had been dead less than ten minutes when the press got wind of her murder. Vultures flocked to *The Exotic Pearl* in droves. The Jade Dragon killings were now the leading national story, and everybody wanted a bite. Radio announcers and news anchors reported live from Broadway, halting traffic in both directions. Some well-connected analysts had already made the connection with Dragonsoft. Professional gamers, psychologists, and other unqualified 'experts' voiced their opinions on air.

"Roll up, roll up," said Lakeysia, driving through the crowd. "The circus is in town."

She honked her horn, hoping to clear a path. It had the opposite effect, drawing the parasites to her like iron to a magnet. Cameras and microphones suddenly pointed in her direction. Inquisitive reporters thumped on her car windows, asking a series of stock questions.

Lakeysia had difficulty telling the voices apart.

"Is Miss Davies' death connected to Toshigi Tasoto?" one pushy lady asked. Others soon followed her lead.

"Care to speculate on the killer's motives? Is it true you believe she's a woman?"

"Have you made any progress? What's your advice to the public?"

"Is Lenora Knight still the prime focus of your investigation?"

Lakeysia blasted her horn again, keeping it pressed until the reporters shut up. She parked her car opposite the club entrance and got out, ready with a no-nonsense response.

"Detective Symons, Homicide. Ditto what every other tired, worn out cop says. No comment."

She fought her way to the *Exotic Pearl*, identified herself to the cops outside, and left the media spotlight behind her.

To her dismay, the interior was just as chaotic. Detectives were busy questioning several dozen hostile witnesses. Most clubbers were drunk or high on drugs, and so had no desire to cooperate. It needed four burly officers to keep the angry mob away from the dance floor, while Matthews and his forensics team took pictures.

"What's the lowdown on the latest casualty?" Lakeysia asked, stepping through the police cordon.

The doctor studied Hannah's tongue, collecting bleach residue with a cotton swab. "According to her driver's license, her name was Hannah Davies, a resident of South Beach. The locals knew her as Lady Cleopatra. She was a dancer here at the club."

"You mean a stripper, don't you, doc? Dancing's what normal girls do, usually with their clothes on. So, how did our Pharaoh queen bite the dust?"

Matthews held the swab up to the light, rotating it to inspect the soaked cotton.

"Cleaning fluid. That's what the deceased swallowed. A large quantity of domestic bleach. Foul taste. No way she would have digested it unknowingly. My guess is the killer slipped some into her drink, then forced the rest down her throat."

"She mustn't have cared for the local poison too much."

Lakeysia took the Cyber Maiden photo from her pocket and compared it to Hannah's face.

"Yep," she said. "Miss Davies was a talented games designer in a former life. Now history will remember her as the girl who died at a strip club on Broadway."

She called the precinct on her mobile.

"Detective Symons. Put me through to Frances Moore, Homicide."

"Care to fill me in?" a male voice boomed from behind.

Lieutenant Thorne had arrived to 'assist' with her investigation. With all the shouting, she hadn't heard him come in.

"Lenora's going after the Cyber Maidens. This isn't just

about Nicole Tasoto. Her former colleagues are targets too."

"That seems to blow your revenge theory out of the water."

In his own smarmy way, Thorne was asking if she had a credible alternative. Before she could think of an answer, Frances responded to her call.

"What do you need, Detective Symons?"

"I want you to find out the last known address of one Iris Levier." Lakeysia spelled out the girl's family name. "Make it snappy. Call me back the moment you got something."

She hung up and joined Thorne by Hannah's body. "The killer left us a message."

The lieutenant looked to Matthews for an answer. The doctor shook his head, puzzled.

"Just this tiara," the forensics man said. "No notes, coded messages, or anything like that."

"She's through with leaving notes. Now she lets the stiffs do the talking for her."

The blank looks demanded further elaboration, so Lakeysia continued her psychoanalysis.

"We're not safe at home, at work, or in a public place. This lady does her thing in the open, bends the rules. She could have killed this girl in private with nobody watching, but that would be too easy. Burning, electrocution, and now poison. She likes variation, a challenge. This is Lenora's finale game, her masterpiece."

"Where's Travis?" the lieutenant asked.

Lakeysia had a good idea exactly where her partner was and what he was doing, but she covered for him.

"He's following your instructions to the letter, pressing the Tasoto girl for information. Tried calling his cell, but got no answer. I imagine he was in the middle of something important."

A uniformed policewoman escorted a witness to the stage. Some big African guy with a fake gold tooth.

"Mike," he introduced himself. "I work at the front door. I spoke to her, the killer."

Lakeysia took out her notebook and pen. "Can you describe her?"

"Green dress. Blonde. Green eyes too, I think." The bouncer frowned in deep thought. "Five foot nine tall, maybe six. Could have been six one. I don't recall the details exactly. It was dark, difficult to see too much."

"Do you remember what size her tits were?"

"Yeah," the employee said with a moronic grin.

This guy was so dumb he believed the question had been serious. Lakeysia had put her notebook away before she asked, but he hadn't gotten the hint.

"You ever hear the saying that the female's deadlier than the male?"

From the man's actions, it was doubtful he had. So Lakeysia spelled out her opinion plainly.

"When guys see an attractive girl, all they want to do is get in her pants. Feel her up, go back to her place. They don't give a shit why she's chatting up an ugly brute instead of a wealthy banker with tons of money. The thought she might actually be smarter than them never enters their mind. Because the moment they lay eyes on her big, juicy melons, all common sense goes flying out the nearest window."

Lakeysia nodded to the policewoman who'd brought in the witness. The officer was having a hard time hiding her smile. After she'd escorted the confused man away, Frances called back.

"I found the address you wanted," the secretary said. "Miss Levier changed her name after marriage. She's now known as Iris Vega. Her residence is at unit three six two, Paradise Grove. It's an apartment complex on the corner of Ellis and Hyde."

"In the Tenderloin district. I'm familiar with the area, a real nice section of town. Send a black and white, but all they do is stake out the place. Nothing else. They spot anything unusual, they stay put and wait for me. No silly heroics. Got that? I want no more keystone corpses."

"I'm coming with you, Symons," Thorne said, chasing after her. "Suppose the stakeout team hears screams from inside. What happens then?"

"That would be Iris Vega dying, in which case they're too late to do any good."

# CHAPTER TWELVE

## *Officer Down*

Randall's midnight cruise had turned sour. The attorney left his female guests on the upper deck and retreated to his private cabin. He bolted the door and shut the portholes. The lawyer knew all the girls on board from previous engagements, but with Jade on her murder rampage, he took extra precautions.

The mysterious woman first approached him two months ago. In the dead of night, the assassin sneaked into his bedroom and held a sword against his throat. Randall didn't realize this until water dripped from her chin onto his face, stirring him from his sleep.

It was dark, and the intruder wore a black wetsuit and tinted goggles, but he guessed she was female from the body shape.

"Good morning, Randall." She spoke calmly, as if her behavior were perfectly normal. "I'm Suzanne. We haven't met before, but I have a business proposal you'll be interested in. I suggest you pay close attention. It's a matter of life and death."

Her voice seemed familiar. But he'd dealt with many girls, so it could just be coincidence.

"You don't mind if I dry my sword, do you?"

It wasn't really a question. The woman rubbed the flat of her blade against Randall's neck. She had only to flick her wrist, and he'd perish in his bed, but it was obvious she hadn't come to kill him. Not yet.

"I presume you've kept me alive because you have a favor to ask," he said.

The scuba girl twisted her katana, and its razor-sharp edge cut into his skin. He felt blood trickle across his neck, but remained focused on the woman's face.

"A favor to demand. I need certain tools from you. An untraceable handgun, silencer, and enough plastic explosives to reduce a car to scrap metal. Before you play innocent, I know you have contacts in the arms trade, men who owe you their lives and freedom. As you owe yours to me. Agree to help, and I'll leave your body in one piece."

Randall nodded, careful not to slit his throat on her sword.

"There is a supplier I can reach out to, but he won't be cheap."

The girl found that amusing. "You'll get your money back," she said, suppressing a chuckle. "With interest. You can trust me. We're partners now."

"Trust you?"

Randall considered himself an expert at analyzing people. The mysterious woman had kept her face hidden behind a mask, but her words implied they both had something to gain.

He wanted to know what she was planning. While he wasn't in a courtroom, the current situation was similar to cross-examining a witness. It was all about making the right arguments.

"Holding a knife to someone's throat doesn't exactly encourage trust. And if you and I are to be partners, our arrangement should be beneficial to both of us. You strike me as being smart, capable, someone prepared to dirty her hands."

So far, she hadn't turned hostile. And that encouraged him to continue.

"You selected me for a reason. My guess is that you intend to eliminate one of my many enemies. If I refused your request, then you'd kill me. But you've shared this information, hoping it will compel me to cooperate. Am I right?"

Randall kept a straight face. He listened to the woman exhale, gauging if her breathing was steady. For ten long seconds, she remained silent. Then the scuba girl lifted her sword from his throat.

"You're even smarter than I'd hoped. We have a common interest, a certain Japanese businessman with a mansion in Pacific Heights."

"Very well. We have a deal."

He replied without hesitation. If the woman was serious, he had everything to gain from Toshigi's death.

He felt no guilt about the decision. His associate would have done the same in his position. Randall offered to shake his partner's hand, but the girl kept hold of her sword hilt.

"All I need now is the name and contact details for your supplier," she said.

That was how their partnership started. To distance himself from the messy affair, the lawyer referred the woman to a former client with connections to the Russian mafia. She could be involved with terrorists, and Randall didn't want government agents tracing this back to him.

Two days later, police discovered the supplier's body at the marina docks. Someone had put three bullets in his chest and sprayed graffiti on his car windscreen. The killing bore all the signs of a gangland hit, but it was clearly a setup. His partner had staged the arms dealer's death to cover her tracks.

A package arrived in the mail later that week, verifying his suspicions. It was the cash the assassin have him to purchase the weapons. A note clipped to a stack of bills read: *Your money back, as promised. We're in this together now. Suzanne.*

Going to the police would reveal his involvement, so Randall recorded all the phone conversations he had with her. He also kept records in his safe, insurance to protect him from a similar fate. Eight weeks after their first meeting, his documentation was still full of holes, but at least he had a name: Lenora Knight.

Randall finished his brandy and tuned into the late night news. The killer had struck again. This time, her victim was Hannah Davies, a Dragonsoft employee who he remembered fondly from his private parties. She'd attended many social events, both during and after her employment at the company. Randall's friends had enjoyed her striptease dances, but she would entertain them no more.

Lenora had every reason to hate Toshigi and Nicole, but Hannah had done nothing to hurt her. The killer was tying up loose ends, which meant Randall would be on her hit list, too.

It was risky contacting her, but he'd much rather go to prison than suffer like the others. After they caught this psycho woman, he could always buy his way out or make a plea bargain with the police.

He dialed his partner's number and left a message on her answering machine.

"Hello, Jade, or should that be Lenora? You know who this is. Things are getting out of control. This was supposed to be a one-off deal, but now you're turning it into a personal bloodbath. Before you consider putting me to the sword, you should be aware I've made contingency arrangements. I have no desire to make enemies with you, Ms. Knight. You've done me a favor, and I'm very grateful, but try anything and you will regret your decision."

Randall switched off his cellphone and prayed his warning would be enough.

*  *  *

*Paradise Grove* was anything but. The ugly, graffiti smeared apartment complex was in the Tenderloin district, an area of San Francisco with no parks, gardens or even trees. Union Square and City Hall were both under five blocks away, but very few tourists ventured into this region, especially after sunset.

Recent urban renewal projects had done little to ease the poor living standards faced by residents. Homeless tramps begged for spare change outside takeaways and cheap hotels. Those fortunate enough to have somewhere to live were trapped in a vicious cycle of poverty.

Jade parked down a side street and chained her motorcycle to a drainpipe. Vehicle theft was rife in this part of town, and she didn't feel like becoming a victim. A gang loitered on the front steps of *Paradise Grove*, smoking cannabis in public. There were five thugs altogether, a mixture of skinheads and Mohawk cuts. Only one took any interest: a dark tanned guy wearing a studded leather jacket and bandana.

"Where you going, dude?" he asked, grabbing Jade's shoulder.

Because of her powerful build and height, the criminal had mistaken her for a man. She opted to keep her gender secret. There wasn't a single woman in the gang, and she didn't need extra attention.

"Personal business," Jade said in a hoarse, masculine-like voice. "Somebody messed with the wrong people in Japantown. Sure you want to get involved?"

A quick flash of her katana discouraged the kid from pursuing the matter any further. Jade kept the sword sheathed in a scabbard on her back in case of unexpected trouble. A wise decision in retrospect.

Not wanting to add his name to a Yakuza hit list, the bandana guy patted her on the shoulder and backed off.

"Hey, man. You don't have a problem with us, we don't got a problem with you. Everything's chill."

The killer swung open an iron-barred gate and entered the lobby. Maintenance was a low priority. Everywhere Jade looked, paint peeled off walls and flies buzzed around lamp stands. The plants above the front door were all withered, the vending machines busted, and both restrooms displayed dirty *Out of Order* signs.

The manager slept in his chair, snoring away without a care in the world. He was a blond-haired, bearded man with a bloated belly and puncture marks down his forearm. In the trashcan behind his desk, Jade saw scores of empty vials and syringes. A heroin addict, which made it easy to check his records.

Tracking down Hannah had been straightforward. Lady Cleopatra was the star attraction at *The Exotic Pearl*.

Her topless body appeared in every nightclub guide, men's magazine and adult classified section.

Iris was much harder to find. She was married, and no longer used her maiden name. It took four phone calls to her relatives before a careless uncle provided the information she wanted: the identity of her target's spouse, Roger Vega.

The assassin pushed a half-eaten, moldy chicken sandwich off the register and looked up the husband in the book. After she'd memorized the apartment number, Jade restored everything back to how it was and took the stairs to the third floor.

Unit 362 was at the far end of a long corridor sprayed with amateur artwork. Fluorescent gang tags obliterated the doors and windows, but nobody was brave or stupid enough to remove them. Despite wearing two layers of clothing, Jade had to rush to keep warm. The radiators were rusted heaps of junk, and many water pipes had burst, revealing lime scale that had accumulated over decades.

Jade checked she was alone, then broke down the front door. A single kick shattered the locking mechanism. With a wood splitting crack, the wreckage swung inwards and jammed on a safety chain.

The killer reached through the narrow gap and unhooked the bolt. She gained entry before Roger even got off his sofa.

The resident couch potato was a greasy-haired, six-foot tall, overweight lout in a replica American football jersey. Jade had interrupted his favorite sports talk show, and now he was out for blood.

The angry male marched towards her and rolled up his sleeves. Either the strongman hadn't noticed the katana, or he wasn't afraid of intruders. Or perhaps he was too stupid to consider the consequences of confronting an armed assailant.

"Whoever you are," he roared, "I'm going to rip you apart."

Not worried by tough talk, Jade back-heeled the door closed and removed her helmet. The sight of her long, blonde hair stunned Roger into silence. Clearly, he wasn't used to picking on women his own size.

"But I'm just a girl," she said, raising her hands. "Hardly a fair fight, is it?"

Jade struck Roger's neck, flicking her wrist to maximize the impact. He reeled backward and clutched his crushed windpipe.

The assassin stalked her prey without mercy, executing several spinning kicks to his face. Her opponent punched back in self-defense, but his telegraphed, clumsy swings were easy to block.

"I'm not some wimpy housewife you can muscle around. How does it feel to be a victim for a change?"

Roger was horribly out of shape and soon grew tired. Jade dodged a feeble kick and poked the sweating man in the eye. He blinked and slumped against the wall, exhausted.

The murderess kicked him in the neck, lifting her foot high while balancing on her other leg. She forced the man's head back, digging her boot in so hard he couldn't breathe. He squirmed, unable to break free.

"What happened to the tough guy? Your television's so loud. No wonder the neighbors can't hear us. Even if they could, they're too scared to call the cops. Nobody's coming to help you."

Roger grabbed her ankle and attempted to twist it, but his hands slipped on her leggings. He wiggled his body, a puny effort to escape the chokehold.

"Which is good, because Iris will be back shortly. She

and I have some things to catch up on, and I don't need any distractions. Girl talk. It doesn't concern you."

Jade increased the tension in her leg, and applied so much force Roger's neck snapped in two. His knuckles thumped into the wall, and the dead man's knees collapsed under the weight of his body. The killer released her foot, tossing back her hair as the corpse slid to the ground.

The busted lock rattled as someone outside turned a key. Iris, being the dumb fool she was, pushed open the apartment door instead of fleeing in the opposite direction.

The world may have changed since the Cyber Maidens broke up, but she was the same purple haired gothic punk who didn't know when to quit. Marriage to an uncaring bastard had taught her nothing. Jade doubted she had a single good idea in her pea-brained head.

The wimpy girl dropped her grocery bag and cupped her hands around her mouth.

"Roger!"

Iris backed into the hallway, trying to make sense of what she saw: the broken lock, her murdered husband, the blonde in black leather.

"You can thank me later."

Jade drew her tranquilizer pistol. She allowed Iris time to turn and run before shooting a sedative tipped dart into her ankle.

The target fell flat on her stomach. She scraped the floor with her fingernails, attempting to crawl to safety.

Jade put away her gun, grabbed Iris' legs, and pulled the frail girl back into the apartment. The killer closed the door and wedged a chair underneath the handle. She had a private interview to conduct, and it was time to get started.

"You know, it's remarkably simple to convert common household items into torture tools."

Jade rummaged through the kitchen cupboards, making as much noise as possible. It was a small, one-bedroom apartment with little storage space, but potential murder weapons were easy to find.

"Bleach is a very effective poison. You can ask Hannah when you see her in the lava fields of hell. It won't be long before the Cyber Maidens are all together again. Well, at least the three incompetent ones will be."

Jade switched off the apartment lights and television, leaving her prey in total darkness. She heard heavy, almost constant breathing. The killer let her target sweat before shining a flashlight in her eyes.

She turned Iris on her side, pinned the girl's arms behind her back, and bound her wrists in thick, gray duct tape. After three revolutions, the murderess sliced the reel with her katana. Miss Vega never stopped screaming the whole time.

"You're not much of a heroine, are you?" Jade said mockingly, wrapping more tape around her victim's ankles. "I thought the legendary Eve Niagra of *Girl Superspy* fame was supposed to be a clever and resourceful woman."

"Who are you?"

She blinked as the sedative took effect. Jade silenced her by sticking adhesive tape over her mouth and shone the beam on her own face.

"Hello, Iris. Remember me now? Trouble keeping your eyes open? Perhaps a little pain might help."

The killer unsheathed her katana and traced its tip across the girl's cheek. The terrified girl stared at the gleaming metal, unable to stop watching its path. Jade lifted the sword high, then plunged down, skewering her victim's chest.

The blow was designed to maim, not kill. Blood spilled

from under Iris' jacket. The duct tape muffled the groans.

"Did that hurt? Let's fix you up."

The killer wiped her blade clean, then walked into the kitchen, movement shown by the flashlight beam.

Iris rolled sideways and tried to free her limbs. Inadvertently, she put weight on her wound, leading to more high-pitched shrieks and faint cries for help.

Jade switched on a stove burner and heated her katana in the flame until its tip glowed red. She rejoined her captive, holding the fiery end so close the sweat on Iris' forehead evaporated.

The killer placed the sword on the injury to seal it. She laughed, ignoring the girl's subdued wails as her blood boiled.

"But then, Eve wasn't the greatest of characters. I let you develop your own project, and what happens? The biggest sales flop in Dragonsoft history. You should have used my ideas. I was the brain behind every success the company ever had. I'm the reason their games topped the charts for weeks on end. And who gets all the credit? Toshigi, and people like you."

Jade lifted Iris' shirt to expose her chest and burned the letters *EN* into her skin. The girl nearly blacked out, but Jade spread her eyelids apart, forcing her to soldier on.

"Surely you didn't think I was going to write it with a felt-tip pen? It has to look authentic. A secret agent with initials branded on her body. What kind of stupid design idea is that? Oh yes, yours."

The murderess cooled her katana in the kitchen sink and returned with a roll of cellophane.

"A dumb character, a boring title, and a terrible designer. No wonder the game bombed. Well, the world won't have to suffer through another one of your mind numbing adventures. Good night."

Jade peeled off a sheet of film and pressed it down on Iris' face, staring into her eyes. The plastic closed around her skin, forming a clear mask.

The girl shook her arms and legs, squirming as she suffocated. Her nose ring cut her cheek, and blood spread over the inside of the cellophane.

Iris' violent convulsions became weaker by the second. Jade didn't stop smiling until the girl's air supply ran out.

* * *

Lakeysia saw flashing lights as she approached the ghetto otherwise known as *Paradise Grove*. To her relief, the patrol cops had heeded her instructions and remained in their vehicles. Lieutenant Thorne pulled up alongside her, adding to the substantial presence. The detectives and their backup were the only people about. The local gang members had fled, not too keen on having a shootout with four police officers.

"Listen up," the boss said. "The suspect we're hunting, Lenora Knight a.k.a. Jade Dragon can be considered armed, dangerous, and queen psycho bitch of the universe. This girl enjoys collecting feathers in her cap, especially those of the SFPD blue variety. So if you make a positive ID on the target, you have my permission to shoot on sight. I'll vouch for you and take any flak we get from the Captain about procedure. I'd rather have to explain why we stopped a murderer than why she killed a cop."

Thorne took point. He ducked behind lampposts and parked cars as he closed in on the apartment building. The two uniformed officers followed his lead, treading almost exactly the same path.

A dog barked further down the street. Lakeysia turned to face the unseen animal, but the sidewalks were quiet. The barking continued for a few seconds, then abruptly stopped. That sounded like a squeal of pain, but she couldn't be sure.

"Lieutenant, we should cover the exterior, in case she doubles back and makes a pass at us. That's how this sicko's mind works. She uses Iris Vega as bait, then reels in the big fish."

As usual, he thought he knew best. "Symons, we have the element of surprise, so let's use it. Four's better than two. Now get a move on."

"Lenora knows we're onto her ass. This girl ain't stupid. I'm telling you. She's waiting for us. Whether in that fleapit or out on the streets, I don't know, but she's waiting. I say we put a team of two out front, another round the back. Then we sit tight, and call in reinforcements."

"And what about Miss Vega? Does she factor into your plan? Are we supposed to just let her bleed to death?"

"I had Frances make a few calls, but nobody picked up. Which means Iris is lucky enough not to have been home, or she's already dead. My money's on answer B."

Lakeysia dismissed Thorne's concerns without putting much thought into it. Her attention was on the road.

"Fine," he said. "You stay here and play street sweeper. That's what you want, you got it."

Thorne led the uniformed officers into the apartment building. Unlike the veteran detective, the patrol cops didn't have the guts to stand up to a superior, and they obeyed his orders without question.

Lakeysia climbed the front steps and backed slowly against the wall. From there, she had a good view of the crossroads and the street beyond the northern hill. Whichever direction the assailant came from, she wouldn't be able to mask her approach.

When the murderous biker struck, her attack was brutal and swift. The killer rode out from behind a truck and switched on her motorcycle headlamp.

Lakeysia shielded her eyes, blinded by the intense light. She aimed at the blurry figure in black. As she squeezed the trigger, her muscles seized up, paralyzed by a tranquilizer dart.

Jade had hit her in the wrist. It was a shot worthy of a world champion markswoman, taken from two hundred feet without the aid of a laser guide or scope.

The biker turned off her motorcycle headlight and sped up towards *Paradise Grove*, swerving from side to side. She kept to the shadows, and the only way to determine her position was to listen for the engine.

The detective fired three shots, missing every time. Her pistol felt heavy in her hand, and she couldn't hold on.

Lakeysia fell to her knees as Jade rode up the steps, braked, and drew her katana. Summoning her strength, the cop flung herself forward so her body impeded the sword swing.

It was a bold move that saved her life. Instead of cutting off her head, Jade slashed Lakeysia's waist. The serrated blade went under her bulletproof vest, penetrating deep into her skin.

The killer's momentum carried her down the front steps. Thorne raced outside, the patrol officers close behind. While the lieutenant dashed to help, the police fired at the fleeing motorcyclist. She rode with the headlight off, making herself a hard target. Jade used the parked cars and vans to her advantage, made a sharp turn, and vanished from sight.

"Officer down!" Thorne shouted into his radio. "Corner of Ellis and Hyde. Send an ambulance. Don't quit on me,

Symons. You hear me? Show me some fight! Someone get hold of Kyle Travis. I want him right here, right now."

Thorne applied pressure to the wound, but he could only slow down the flow of blood, not stop it completely.

The lieutenant's face faded among the streetlights as tiredness set in. Lakeysia heard sirens, but never saw the ambulance.

# CHAPTER THIRTEEN

## *The Red-Haired Assassin*

Kyle Travis woke up in the land of the rising sun. A new day had dawned, and the Earth's star shone through the paneled wall of Nicole's dojo. His Oriental hostess lay beside him on the karate mat, her naked body gleaming like gold in the morning light. Before he opened his eyes, he was afraid his romantic evening would be a wild dream. Their date was indeed a fantasy, but one that they both experienced.

Nicole was already awake. She leaned on her elbow and rubbed her knee against his chest. "So, how do I rate next to the others?"

"Others? You think there's anybody else besides you?"

Kyle scratched his neck. A patch below his ear felt sore. Some bug had probably bitten it during the night.

He yawned, stretching his arms and legs. Nicole grabbed his wrists, rolled on top of him, and pinned him to the mat. He hadn't yet come round, and so wasn't strong enough to fend off the girl's advances.

"A man as handsome as you must have had a few conquests under his belt," the girl said, kissing Kyle's chest.

"The same goes for you too, I imagine."

Kyle flinched as Nicole's lips touched his bruise, the spot where she'd kicked him the evening before. He grappled with her, but she held him down with ease and tightened her grip.

"Games are all about competition, Kyle. I like to finish on top."

"That doesn't bother me. So long as we're on the same team."

Nicole kissed him one more time and rolled onto her back. She lifted her legs, bending them backwards so her toes touched her chin.

"Aren't you supposed to be working?" she asked.

"My assignment is to watch you."

Kyle checked his cellphone messages. The lieutenant had phoned three times, but he'd switched on silent mode so they wouldn't be disturbed.

"Best see what the boss wants."

Kyle dialed Thorne's number and waited for him to pick up.

"Travis. What's up?"

"Your partner's in intensive care. That's what's up. If you answered your phone, you'd already know."

Thorne shouted so loud Nicole overheard him. Kyle motioned her to keep quiet. He didn't want Thorne jumping to conclusions.

"Lakeysia? Is she all right?"

Kyle got dressed as quickly as he could, suddenly a lot more concerned.

"Your lady killer sliced open her stomach. Hit and run. She also made space for two more in the morgue while you were busy bedding Miss Tasoto. The victims were Hannah Davies and Iris Vega, born Levier. Pass on my condolences to your girlfriend."

"It wasn't like that. Nicole asked me to keep an eye on her."

"And she was naked at the time? If by some chance you care about your partner, Symons is over at Adamson General. Ward nineteen F. The doctors told me she'd live, but they didn't have a definite answer on how long."

Kyle snapped his cellphone closed. "She got to Lakeysia," he said, securing his holster. "I wasn't there for her, and I should have been."

"You were protecting me, making sure I was safe."

Nicole stepped closer, but Kyle moved away, threw on his suit, and left the dojo. The girl put on her kimono and chased after him, sash trailing along the garden.

"I thought you weren't on speaking terms," she said.

"Lakeysia's my partner. She may be a pain in the ass, but she's still a good cop."

Nicole ran in front of Kyle. "Why are you avoiding me? This is not just about Lakeysia. Is it? Answer me!"

Kyle had to break the bad news to her eventually, so he got it over with.

"Your old friends, Hannah and Iris. They were both killed last night. That leaves you and Lenora. I'm worried you might be next."

"She's killing the Cyber Maidens. Why?"

"We don't know." Kyle consoled her with a hug. "I have to get back to the station."

"I'm coming with you," she said. "Don't say it! You were about to tell me it's too dangerous."

"No, I think it's a great idea for you to tag along. That way, I keep my eye on you, and you can help me catch the bitch who did this."

* * *

Kyle and Nicole watched doctors perform emergency surgery through an observation window. The operating table was obscured behind a mass of intravenous tubes, drip stands and monitoring equipment. The attending physician had stitched and bandaged Lakeysia's chest, and there were resuscitation pads on standby in case she flat lined.

She was in critical condition and on a respirator, but for now, her vital signs remained stable. The medical personnel at Adamson General Hospital were among the world's best, but Kyle feared his partner was beyond saving.

"I'm going to find Lenora," he said, pressing his hands against the window. "Then I'll look into her eyes and blow her brains out. Let her try to stop bullets with that fancy sword of hers."

Nicole hugged him from behind. In the glass, he saw the reflection of a caring woman.

Kyle couldn't complain. She'd put aside her dislike for Lakeysia and accompanied him to the hospital to offer her get well wishes. He just wished the girl had chosen a different outfit. Nicole's black suit, trousers, and gloves were nice enough. For clothes worn at a funeral service.

"I appreciate you staying at my house last night," Nicole said. "It's good to know a man is prepared to risk his life for me. I realize you're upset about your partner, but there's no guarantee you could have done anything. If you'd been there, Lenora might have put you on that table."

"And maybe we'd have the bitch in custody. Lakeysia called me, needed me, and I didn't answer. I chose you over her, put your safety before hers. What does that say about me?"

Nicole rested her chin on Kyle's shoulder, hugging him tighter. "That you're a good man. Protect and serve. Isn't that what cops are supposed to do?"

"And go on a date? Does that make me a good man, Nicole?" Kyle swallowed his guilt and focused on finding the suspect. "You're the central link to the killings. I'd rather not ask you to do this, but..."

"Ask me to do what? Me, Hannah, and Iris were like sisters. The Cyber Maidens lived and worked together for over two years. Whatever I can do to help find Lenora, I will. If you're worried about me looking at dead bodies, it's nothing new to me. Maybe a week ago, but not now. I've seen what she's capable of, up close. What do you need?"

Nicole had already proved she could handle herself. Perhaps Kyle should stop patronizing the girl and treat her as his equal.

"You know Lenora better than anyone. She leaves clues with her victims, items related to your games. I won't force you, but it would be helpful if you'd come down to the precinct. To look at what we've found. Tell us if it means anything. This woman's tough and resourceful, but so are you."

Nicole watched Lakeysia's air pump rise and fall. "Even great criminals make one mistake, but she's used up her quota. Lenora won't fail a second time. Sure you want to get close to me, Kyle?"

Kyle answered her with a kiss. "Positive. You're my new partner now. If the killer wants you, she'll have to go through me."

* * *

Doctor Matthews stood between two open freezer units. The bodies of the most recent victims were on steel slabs, corpses covered with white sheets. Kyle didn't know which Cyber Maiden was on the right, nor did he care. All that mattered were the members still alive: the red-headed assassin he wanted to kill, and the Japanese girl he'd sworn to protect.

Travis felt uncomfortable bringing her to the morgue instead of questioning her upstairs. Showing her photographs of the dead girls would have sufficed, but she was adamant about seeing her ex-colleagues one last time.

"It won't be a pretty sight," Matthews said. "Relatives have already identified the victims. This isn't something you have to do."

Nicole wiped the frost from her face. "Can we please get on with it?"

Kyle clasped her hand as the doctor drew the sheet back. She dragged the detective towards the first victim's slab, clinging on tight. They paid their last respects together, heads bowed.

"Yes. That's Hannah. How did she die?"

"You can see the blue marks around her mouth." Matthews pointed to the girl's stained lips. "They're the result of poisoning."

Not wanting him to go into all the gruesome details, Kyle gave the short version.

"It was quick. She didn't suffer," he lied. "Could you show Miss Tasoto the headpiece?"

The doctor removed the bagged plastic tiara from a cabinet drawer. "We don't believe this belonged to the victim. It's not consistent with the other clothes she was wearing last night."

"Hannah took pride in her appearance," Nicole said. "She'd never wear jewelry that cheap. Lenora planted that thing. A circlet of power, like the one worn by Princess Astra. Another of our game characters. She was an extraterrestrial superheroine immune to radiation, disease, and…"

She sniffled, fighting back tears.

"And poisons. Lenora is basing her murders around our video games. Astra was the protagonist of *Beyond the Universe*. It was Hannah's favorite. What about Iris? Did she leave anything with her?"

Before anyone could stop her, Nicole lifted the second cover and exposed the victim. The corpse told the complete story: swollen wrists, torture marks, branded initials, pale face, open mouth.

"The killer tortured Miss Vega before suffocating her with cellophane."

Did Matthews have to relay the information in such a morbid tone? Gory details weren't needed right now.

"They burned those markings onto her skin while she was still alive. We don't know what the letters mean yet."

"Eve Niagra." Nicole coughed, covering her mouth. She looked as if she was about to throw up. "Bathroom?"

"Upstairs," said Matthews. "On the left side."

Miss Tasoto exited the room clutching her stomach. The forensics man covered up the bodies of Hannah and Iris, and pushed the slabs back into their storage units.

"Young, innocent, female. I've seen too many girls like these brought into the morgue. There's always an orphaned parent to comfort, or a devastated friend. The body train never stops."

"Another young woman's coming your way," Kyle said, "except this one's not so innocent. And I won't be sad to see her on a slab."

Kyle's mobile phone rang. The caller wasn't in his address book, and he didn't recognize the number. He left the morgue and answered with his standard greeting.

"Detective Kyle Travis, Homicide."

"Did you enjoy yourself last night?" the killer asked. "You were so absorbed in having sex with that geisha girl you didn't see me outside. But I saw you and Nicole. Was her karate mat comfortable? Which did you like the taste of most, her sushi or her nipples?"

"Bullshit! You weren't there."

He looked round, fearing the psycho was planning a surprise attack. Then he realized he was still in the police station.

"You're a risk taker. Was it worth sacrificing your partner to spend the night in a Japanese whore's dojo? I considered sending my kinky snapshots to the press, but I thought your boss would want to look at them first. Will he appreciate you chasing Nicole instead of me? I'll see you shortly, when I put a bullet in your girlfriend's brain."

The lunatic chuckled at her own psychotic ramblings.

"Or would you rather I kill your lieutenant? That way, you can keep your affair secret for a little longer. What's the matter? Can't decide? I'll take that as a yes, then."

The killer hung up. Suddenly, the station didn't feel so secure. Kyle drew his weapon and ran down the corridor.

"Nicole!" he shouted, banging on the women's restroom door. There was no answer. "You in there? Nicole!"

A female shadow fell across the wall nearby. Someone was coming downstairs. Kyle crouched behind a vending machine, waiting in silence as the woman approached.

Then she walked into view. It was Kari, the doctor's assistant. She gasped in horror, staring at Kyle's gun.

"Have you seen Nicole?" he asked. "The Japanese girl! Toshigi Tasoto's daughter."

The intern backed off, shaking her head.

"Stay inside."

He holstered his weapon and ran up the steps. Kyle checked the lobby and waiting rooms, but there was no sign of her. Then he remembered the killer's last words.

"Thorne."

Kyle sprinted to the elevator, but the doors closed before he reached them. He banged the call button in frustration, then took the stairwell instead. He climbed two steps at once, ran past the Homicide desks, and entered the lieutenant's office unannounced.

Christopher Thorne was very much alive. And alone.

"Nicole! Where is she?"

"Last time I saw Miss Tasoto, she was with you."

He gestured to an open manila envelope on his desk. There were no postmarks, only a single typed name: *Lt. Thorne*. Explicit photographs of Kyle and Nicole were spread out on top.

"Lieutenant, I can explain, but right now —"

Thorne banged his fist down on the photos. They scattered, and the wooden table shook so hard it moved an inch.

"In case you hadn't noticed, there's a serial killer on the loose!" He signaled a detective outside to close the door. "And people want to know what I'm doing about it. Whether we're any closer to catching this psychopath. Should I tell them my lead investigator was out pursuing his own leads? That he was more interested in screwing a key witness? Don't you think Miss Tasoto's a little too young for you?"

"The killer sent those photos. She called me, threatened Nicole. Threatened you too, sir. She wants to drive a wedge between us. This is all a game to her."

"Is it a game to you, Travis? This case is dominating the news. Police resources are at breaking point. That means you don't take time off for R and R unless I say so. Understood?"

"Nicole feels more comfortable with me around."

"You seem quite cozy yourself." Thorne grabbed a photo and waved it in Kyle's face. "I get the picture, all right. If internal affairs don't crucify you, the press will. Not that you care. Who was there to back your partner up last night?"

Kyle remained silent. He'd never seen the boss so furious.

"Me! Three guesses where you were. You're a God damn liability, Travis. I'm suspending you without pay. Leave your shield and your gun, get the hell out of my office, and go back to your girlfriend's place. When you're through feeling her ass, maybe you should ask her for a job."

The killer had struck again, manipulating Thorne to have him thrown off the case. And she wasn't finished yet.

"I'd watch it, Lieutenant." Kyle tossed his detective badge and weapon on the desk. "She said she'd kill you, and this woman doesn't make idle threats."

"What's she going to do? Walk into the station and do me in here? Let's say she has a suicide wish, and gets past all our detectives. How will you protect me? With your handsome looks and boyish charms?"

Thorne threw the photos in Kyle's face. Before he could follow up with another rant, the telephone rang.

The boss jabbed the loudspeaker button. "Yes?"

"Good morning," Jade said. "Lieutenant Thorne, isn't it? Are you any closer to catching me?"

The woman's voice made Kyle do a U-turn. "That's her. The killer."

A uniformed officer knocked on the door. Thorne stood up and waved her away. Once the woman turned her back, the Lieutenant resumed his conversation.

"Jade Dragon I presume. Or perhaps I should call you Lenora Knight, former Cyber Maiden and employee of Dragonsoft."

"Perhaps you should call me Meagan Wilson. Former officer and employee of the San Francisco Police Department. Now deceased."

The female cop entered Thorne's office, tossed her cellphone in the trashcan, and closed the door.

Except the woman wasn't a cop. She was a tall, Caucasian assassin wearing dark glasses and leather gloves, a scheming killer who'd used Meagan's uniform to infiltrate the precinct. Kyle didn't know if her red hair was real or another of Lenora's wigs, but he recognized the weapon in her hand. A tranquilizer pistol.

Jade pulled the cord that lowered the Venetian blinds. "I heard you were looking for me. Well, here I am."

Kyle dived to retrieve his gun from Thorne's desk. While he was in mid-air, the assassin aimed her own weapon and fired a dart into his neck.

As Kyle collapsed, she sprinted across and kicked his sidearm away. She collected a letter opener, grabbed the Lieutenant's suit collar, and held the blade to his throat. It happened too fast for her target to do anything. He watched in silence as the killer pinned a plastic sheriff's badge to his shirt.

"You remind me of Earl Pritchard, the bumbling sheriff

from *A Few Revolvers More*. One of my favorite titles, after *Jade Dragon,* of course."

She tilted Thorne's head all the way back and slit his throat from ear to ear, chuckling as blood spilled onto his suit.

The lieutenant toppled sideways, eyes rolling. The killer propped him up and lifting his feet on the desk. She steadied the prone corpse and balanced the letter opener on his forehead. It was like she considered the dead man a grotesque work of art, left on public display for others to view.

Kyle crawled towards his gun, but Jade got there before him. The killer stood on his arm, grabbed him by the hair, and pressed her tranquilizer pistol to his temple.

"I'll race you to Nicole," she said. "First one to reach the prize gets to take her home and have some fun. Give me a head start."

The red-haired assassin blew Kyle a kiss, smiled, and squeezed the trigger.

* * *

Soon after Kyle regained consciousness, he felt a vicious slap to the cheek. The office shimmered in and out of focus. Confronted by multiple, distorted images, he swooped at his attacker's wrist and reached for his holster.

Then he remembered Jade had disarmed him. His weapon was still on the floor by the Lieutenant's desk. The person he'd grabbed broke free. Her face was blurry, but unmistakably Asian.

"Travis! It's me."

"Nicole," Kyle said, releasing her. "You're safe."

"We haven't found Miss Tasoto. I'm sure she's fine."

Kyle's confusion turned to concern when he saw the girl's lab coat. He was talking to Kari.

Matthews had established a cordon around the desk. Outside in the main office, detectives watched through the window blinds, stunned at the breach in security. Nicole was unaccounted for, and so was the killer. Wet blood dripped down Thorne's neck, which suggested there was time to find them.

"You seal off the building?"

Kyle retrieved his badge and gun. He checked the pistol for signs of tampering, but found nothing unusual.

"We've posted officers at all the exits," Kari said. "Nobody's going in or out."

He wiped his eyes, talking on the move. "Not even cops?"

"Cops? Are you saying the killer's one of us?"

The absence of a direct response implied her answer was no. Kyle left the office to begin his search, knowing every second he wasted counted against him.

"Nicole!" he yelled, to astonishment from his fellow officers.

"Detective Travis," Kari said, following him. "Miss Tasoto came down to the morgue about ten minutes ago. When she couldn't find you, I think she went home."

"Home? Why the hell didn't you tell me before?"

Upon reflection, he realized the girl was only trying to help.

"Thanks. I'll check it out."

Kyle decided not to risk the slow-moving elevator. He sprinted down five flights of stairs, showed his ID to the officer on duty, and dashed into the parking area beneath the precinct building.

It was one of the safest garages in the city, with CCTV

cameras and abundant light sources. There were three levels, each with space for a hundred cars. Some spots were for official use, but the majority were unrestricted. Most vehicles belonged to cops, criminals or civilian workers. Other than government bureaucrats and lawyers, few visitors could afford a flashy sports car. That ought to make Nicole's silver corvette easy to locate.

With the precinct in lockdown, the area was unnervingly quiet. Kyle made a methodical sweep of the first sublevel. If Nicole hadn't left yet, the assassin was likely still around, too.

Jade had already murdered someone in a parking garage and incapacitated an armed police officer, so nothing was off limits. Wary of a potential ambush, he kept close to the outside wall, peering around concrete pillars and underneath parked cars as he proceeded.

The elevator doors opened with a ping, and a uniformed policewoman stepped out. Seeing she was a redhead, Kyle aimed his gun.

"Don't move!" he said. "Hands in the air. Slowly."

The girl turned her head, prompting him to fire a warning shot. After that, she did as he instructed. A set of keys dropped from the woman's trembling fingers. She wasn't wearing dark glasses or gloves, and her hair was shorter and slightly brighter than Jade's.

"Officer Carmen Narobi. You can check my badge."

Her voice was nothing like the killer's either. All the evidence suggested she was an actual policewoman, but Kyle knew Lenora's potential for deception and so kept "Carmen" in his sights.

"I said don't move," he said, edging closer.

Once Kyle got within twenty feet, he recognized the girl's face from a police social event and lowered his weapon.

"It's okay, Carmen. I'm sorry."

A car accelerated up the ramp, bathing them in light. Kyle turned, ready to fire, but relaxed when he saw a familiar silver corvette with an Asian girl behind the wheel.

"Nicole!"

She pulled to a stop beside him. "What's wrong? I thought you were in the morgue, but when I came back, you weren't there."

"Lenora's here, dressed as a cop. She killed the lieutenant, and now she's after you. Carmen! Clear it with the man on duty outside, then take her home. Set up a perimeter with the officers on stakeout. Nicole, lock all your doors and windows. Don't answer the phone unless it's me."

She buckled her seatbelt. "All right. What are you going to do?"

"Stay and find Lenora."

Kyle scanned the garage while Carmen got in the car's passenger seat.

"She's still here," he said. "You can count on it, and I won't let her use you as a bargaining chip. Now go."

Nicole reversed to the exit and drove up to street level. Once the corvette had left Kyle's sight, he resumed his search.

He completed his sweep of sublevel one and made his way to the stairwell. From outside the building, there was a loud metallic crash, followed by the constant beep of a car horn. He sprinted up the ramp, showed his badge to the gate guard, and ducked under the barrier.

The garage entrance was behind the precinct, on a quiet, downtown side street. Nicole's battered corvette was upended against a lamppost. Its front windscreen was smashed, and steam rose from beneath the buckled hood.

Pedestrians stood around the scene of the accident, staring at a twisted body on the pavement.

"Nicole!" Kyle waved his gun to clear the crowd. "Police! Step aside! Out of the way!"

At first, he was relieved to see it was Carmen—and not Nicole—who lay on the sidewalk. Then remorse took over as he checked the girl's pulse. She was dead, her broken neck propped against the curb. Jade had murdered another cop and abducted her next victim while Kyle was in the garage. After he'd stupidly let her out of his sight.

"Damn it!"

He stamped his foot in frustration. Then he spotted a whitish figurine on the corvette's passenger seat.

The object was a ceramic carving of a deity from classical mythology. Not being a student of ancient Greek culture, Kyle had to rely on the name inscribed on the statue's base. *Apollo*.

# CHAPTER FOURTEEN

## *Hope Sinks with Apollo*

The stranger had his back turned, but Kyle could tell he was a government agent from his black suit and equally dark glasses. Unlike his late predecessor, this guy kept the Venetian blinds raised. He wanted everyone in Homicide to know he was now in charge.

Under the agent's supervision, Matthews combed the office for evidence. A miserable faced brunette in an identical outfit stood outside the closed door, ensuring their privacy. The badge clipped to her shirt confirmed Kyle's suspicions. She and her boss were FBI.

Kyle sprinted over to Lakeysia's desk and rummaged through her belongings. He had no intention of sharing information with the feds. This was a personal battle between Jade and himself, and involving outsiders would only tip the balance in her favor.

The killer had made no demands since abducting Nicole,

but Kyle was certain a private meeting was on the cards. History was repeating itself with the kidnapping of a second Tasoto family member. He had gambled with Toshigi's life and lost, and he was determined not to make the same mistake with Nicole.

"Detective Travis."

Frances' sudden appearance gave Kyle a pulse boost. In his hurry to retrieve his partner's notes, he hadn't seen the secretary come in.

"There's a federal agent in Lieutenant Thorne's office."

"Not now, Frances. I'm pressed for time. It'll have to wait."

Kyle dumped a stack of papers on Lakeysia's chair and started on her desk drawers.

She wouldn't let it drop. "Agent Baker told me to inform him when you returned. He asked specifically for you by name. I'll tell them you're here."

Before he could protest, Frances walked off to speak with the FBI woman. Kyle checked his watch. It was almost four o'clock in the afternoon. In half an hour, the killer would have darkness on her side, and he wanted to get back on the road before then.

He found what he was looking for beneath an empty pizza box. He brushed spilled breadcrumbs off Lakeysia's notepad and scanned the top sheet. Prior to hospitalization, his partner had scribbled a series of words pertaining to her leads. Names, telephone numbers, and spider diagrams cluttered the page. Several obscure references had been crossed out, but they were still readable.

"Apollo. Randall Forbes."

Before he could study the note any more, Frances returned with the woman.

"Agent Baker's waiting," the black suited lady said,

omitting the customary pleasantries. "He'll see you now."

Kyle followed her glance, seeing the senior agent's face for the first time. Baker was an imposing, square shouldered man with curly blond hair and hawkish eyes. He popped a mint in his mouth and inclined his head, signaling Kyle to enter the office.

"Just a moment." He pulled Frances aside, lowering his voice so the FBI woman couldn't hear. "Randall Forbes. Does the name ring any bells?"

The assistant had a photographic memory and answered without a pause. "He was Mister Tasoto's attorney, a partner in his company. With the president dead, he inherits control. Detective Symons asked me to prepare a profile. She didn't tell you?"

"We were working different angles. I was assigned to somebody else. What other information did you come up with?"

"Mister Forbes owns five cars and residences throughout California. Several private interests as well. He has made many contacts in the underworld. During his career, he's represented known mobsters, corrupt officials, all people with powerful connections."

Baker joined his female companion. The two agents marched towards Kyle like officers about to arrest a suspect. He was running out of leeway.

"I need something that might give me a lead on Randall's location," he pressed. "What's Apollo?"

"A private yacht registered under his name. Forbes holds a berthing license at Fisherman's Wharf. He must have a small fortune to afford that."

Baker stepped between them, swallowing another mint.

"Detective Travis," he said ominously. "Nice to finally meet you. Agent Simon Baker, FBI."

Figuring he was about to be demoted, or worse, Kyle decided he had nothing to lose. Time to cut the feds out of a police investigation, for once.

"Plain old Mister Travis now. The lieutenant suspended me a minute before the killer paid him a visit. Talk to the secretary if you want details on where we stand. I'm off duty."

Kyle dropped his shield on Lakeysia's desk. He walked away, ignoring the stunned looks he received from the FBI agents. Luckily, nobody thought to ask for his weapon. Though he regretted delegating responsibility to Frances, Baker was a problem for another time. Right now, the only thing that mattered was finding Nicole.

***

Randall switched off *Apollo*'s engine and exited the control cabin. He'd given his crew their annual leave before traveling out to sea with Asuka. She was down below, preparing some entertainment while the pilot took care of navigation. The water surrounding Randall's yacht was black under the clear night sky. With no storms forecast, he figured this would be a calm, relaxing voyage.

Things were heating up. A police lieutenant was dead, and it was time for Randall to leave town before the assassin came for him. He'd arranged a private charter flight out of the country, but his plane wasn't due to depart for five hours, and he felt safer spending the interim on his yacht than at a deserted airfield.

He could have invited more girls to his farewell party, but there was always the possibility of Lenora sneaking into the group. One woman would keep him occupied, and an evening with Asuka was guaranteed to be memorable.

Randall steered his ship west of Alcatraz Island, slowing to a stop a mile off the coast of the famous "Rock." The lighthouse beam rotated, periodically shining on open topped boats ferrying tourists to the disused prison. The nighttime tour of the cell blocks was about to begin, but the attorney had other plans for the evening. He glanced at the Golden Gate Bridge before descending below.

Asuka had already stripped naked. The Asian girl stood behind a drinks cabinet in his personal quarters, preparing a glass of brandy for her host. She added a slice of lemon, stirred the beverage with a cocktail umbrella, and served it to Randall.

"Have a seat," she said, escorting him to the sofa.

She held the drink to Randall's lips and tipped it back.

"There. That will warm you up. After you're done, we can cool off in the shower. Relax. I've got a treat for you."

Asuka helped herself to the remaining brandy, then licked her mouth dry. Randall lay down on the couch, took off his shirt, and closed his eyes. He heard a loud bump before the girl sat on top of him.

Soft, damp hands massaged his bare chest. He reached towards her breasts. Before he touched them, she grabbed his wrists and flung his arms against the cushion. Asuka wasn't normally this dominant, but Randall enjoyed the change of pace. After a prolonged kiss, she pushed him away. The sofa creaked as she stood up.

"That was some treat," he said. "Where are you going?"

Glass shattered on the floor.

"Did you enjoy your blind date, Randall? It's been a while since you kissed me. I'd forgotten how disgusting it tasted."

He jerked upright and opened his eyes. It wasn't Asuka he'd been making love to, but "Suzanne."

The killer was in his cabin, dressed in the same tight, black wetsuit she'd worn two months ago. Her flippers and air tank were discarded near the door, but she'd kept on the dark visored mask over her eyes and nose. The assassin stepped over Asuka's body. She carried a bloody katana in one hand, and the girl's decapitated head in the other.

"It makes a change from her posing topless, doesn't it?"

She smiled sadistically, holding the head above Randall so blood dripped on his chest.

"It was very considerate of you to use your secluded love boat. Out here, nobody will disturb us."

Randall sprang off his sofa. He slipped on a pool of gore and tumbled into Asuka's headless corpse.

"Lenora," he said. "You have to understand. I never meant to hurt you, or any of the other girls. You were just..."

"Sex objects?"

The assassin crushed glass fragments under her foot, stalking her quarry across the cabin.

"Friends for you and Toshigi to play with? Your smooth talking doesn't impress me. You can be *my* toy tonight. How does it feel now our roles are reversed? Where are your all powerful associates when you need them?"

Randall ran to the drinks cabinet, grabbed a lamp, and yanked out the power cord.

"We had an agreement," he said, wielding his makeshift club.

The killer moved towards him, slashing the air with her katana. "So we did, but I enjoyed watching Toshigi squirm so much that I wanted to relive the experience."

"To hell with you!"

He threw the light at her face. The scuba woman blocked the missile with the flat of her sword, leaped, and shattered the light frame with a spinning kick. Randall had no room left to maneuver. She pointed her katana at his throat, forcing him back against the cabinet.

"Not exactly Leonardo the Fearless, are you?" she said, unzipping her wetsuit top.

The killer unfolded a cardboard buccaneer hat and placed it on Randall's head. It was soggy and fell off almost right away.

"Like you, the *Pirate of Trinidad* sailed high seas, stole other people's money and courted wenches. Unlike you, he didn't surrender his ship without a fight. And if you've played the game, you'll know…"

Sweat trickled down Randall's cheeks. He cowered against the wooden counter, terrified of the assassin's sword. She lifted her weapon and spun it round above her head.

Randall instinctively protected his face, but she aimed her attack somewhere else. The killer's katana sliced clean through his lower knee, chopping off his ankle and foot. He grabbed the bloody stump, wailing in agony as blood soaked his fingers.

"He also lost a leg," the woman said with chilling calmness.

She shoved Randall over and removed a block of clay-like material from inside her wetsuit.

"Look familiar?"

She held the brick before his eyes. Randall's strength was fading fast, but he concentrated long enough to read the identifying mark stamped on the side. *C-4.*

The same plastic explosive he'd asked his contact to acquire. The assassin planted her bomb under the desk and attached a detonator. It seemed she planned on using his own weapon against him.

"Suzanne" zipped up her scuba suit and collected her oxygen tank and flippers.

"Fancy going for a late night swim? The water's nice and cool."

The killer grabbed Randall in a bear hug and dragged him onto the main deck. She propped his chest against the yacht's guardrail, placed him in a chokehold, and directed his eyes towards the Alcatraz Island lighthouse. Its beam illuminated them, but the assassin could afford to expose herself. There were no other ships within three miles.

"Do you know why nobody escaped The Rock? It wasn't the cell blocks that stopped them. No, it was the icy waters of the bay. None of the prisoners who got out made it to shore alive. They all froze to death or drowned. Think you can do better?"

The assassin kicked Randall over the guardrail. He fell backwards into the ocean, landing with a tremendous splash. Freezing cold water closed across Randall's face, numbing his senses.

The Pacific currents dragged him away from his yacht. He flapped his arms, attempting to stay afloat, but his wounded leg made that an impossible feat. Randall could no longer feel his severed knee. Blood diffused outwards, adding a dark reddish tint to his vision.

The killer swam down to him. Slicing off Randall's limb and dumping him in the ocean apparently wasn't enough to satisfy her psychotic cravings. She wanted to watch him drown, to be with him until the very end.

The assassin locked her thighs around his waist. Salt stung his eyes as she pulled him deeper. "Suzanne" breathed through her mouthpiece, insulated from the cold by her wetsuit's thermal lining. Randall had neither air nor warmth. As water filled his lungs, the killer lifted her mask and discarded her breathing apparatus.

With all the blood in the sea, he couldn't tell the color of the killer's eyes, but he remembered them. He cursed himself for not realizing her identity sooner.

She smiled in triumph. Randall had made a terrible mistake and underestimated her ability. So had the police, but he would never be able to warn them.

* * *

Jade piloted *Apollo* back to Fisherman's wharf and weighed anchor. It was amusing how Randall had isolated himself at sea, believing he was safe. The killer had stored her diving equipment at her scuba school in advance, figuring the slimy attorney would retreat to his yacht once the tide turned against him.

Instead of accepting his losses and leaving town, the sleazy lawyer remained behind until the last possible minute. Jade wasn't sure of his motives. Maybe he wanted to assume control of Toshigi's company, screw Asuka one more time, or hand his useless information to the police. Whatever his reasons, he'd made himself an easy target.

While people thought it strange to go swimming in the bay at night, Jade's mask kept her identity secret from passers-by. Her photograph was all over the news, and she wanted her duel with Kyle Travis to remain personal. Randall had sailed two miles offshore, but she was a strong and accomplished swimmer. It was no real challenge to reach *Apollo*, climb the ladder, and sneak onboard. Taking care of her target was even easier.

The detective was waiting to ambush Jade when she returned to the wharf. She spotted his car parked half a block from the pier, beneath a broken streetlight. Darkness obscured the license plate, but smoke rising from the exhaust told her the engine was running.

Travis had blown whatever cover he'd hoped to establish. Despite being continually outsmarted, he still didn't take her seriously. The arrogant man was inviting death. Jade removed her flippers. She wanted to be agile when the inevitable confrontation came.

"Freeze!" he yelled from behind her. "Get your hands in the air and turn around."

The killer smiled and did as Travis commanded. It appeared he'd finally wised up and caught her by surprise. The parked car was a decoy used to distract her while he boarded *Apollo* and circled round to the ship's bow. He had a weapon aimed at her and the cabin's windshield to protect him.

"Drop the sword! Drop it now."

The killer tossed her katana aside. She had another trick up her sleeve, one she'd play at the right moment.

"Detective Travis," she said, acting compliant. "I recognize the voice."

"Yeah, you ought to."

He kept his distance from the window.

"Calling me at every God damn opportunity. Well, this time you're on the other end of a gun, not a cellphone. And I'm not putting it down so we can settle this with our fists. This isn't some dumb action movie. I don't believe in fair play, Lenora. I like having safety glass between us, and I'd love nothing more than to shoot a bullet between your eyes right now."

A bold proclamation, so Jade went for Travis' weak spot.

"But if you do that, you'll never find Nicole. You could always kiss her cold, dead lips at the morgue, but imagine the torment."

The cop's stare intensified. "Where is she?"

"Wouldn't you like to know?" the assassin said, stepping forward.

"Stay back! Take off your mask. I want to look into your eyes, bitch."

Jade pulled her goggles away from her face, stretching the elastic. "Are you sure about that, detective? You might not like what you see."

"Do it."

She dived behind a control panel and activated a remote trigger clipped to her wetsuit belt. Travis got off a shot. The bullet shattered the windshield, but flew harmlessly over her head.

A muffled explosion came from below as the C-4 exploded. The yacht pitched to starboard, throwing Kyle off balance. His pistol slid along the slippery bow and fell into the Pacific.

With her opponent unarmed, Jade sprinted towards the broken window, vaulted over the frame, and kicked Travis in the head. The cop toppled back, groaning in pain. He grabbed the guardrail to steady himself.

He threw a punch. The killer blocked the blow, thumped him in the chest, and knocked him down with a low, spinning kick. She raised her foot and brought it down heavily on Kyle's spine.

In retaliation, he snatched at her ankle. Such a move would normally be futile, but Jade lost her footing on the treacherously wet surface. Hoping to regain the advantage, she broke her fall with one hand and chopped Travis' throat with the other. The assassin swung her legs round, grabbed her opponent's neck in a scissor lock, and slammed his head repeatedly against the bow.

The yacht sank as water flooded through the breach in the hull. Jade sat on Kyle's back and forced his ear against the outer deck.

"Hear that? Hope sinks with Apollo."

She tossed the detective's radio into the sea. Deprived of backup, Travis foolishly took her on alone. He grabbed Jade's neck and choked her. She pulled his hands away and twisted his wrists. Her fierce grip rendered him powerless. There was no way for him to escape her clutches.

"What hope?" groaned Kyle, enduring the pain.

"The information that will help you find Nicole. It's down below, in Randall's safe. I left it unlocked, just for you. It wasn't very smart of him to use his birthday as the combination. But then, he got all his good ideas from Toshigi, and that bastard stole them from me. A familiar story. Are you tired of hearing it yet?"

Travis kicked at Jade's stomach, but he had little energy left, and his blows were pathetically weak.

"Is this another of your sadistic puzzles?"

"Difficult to solve, perhaps, but not sadistic. The others simply weren't up to the challenge. I'm all out of games characters for you to play, Detective. Suppose you'll have to be the generic hero who rescues his true love. I'd hurry if I were you. Nicole's a little stretched out."

She followed her obscure reference with a chuckle.

"How do I know you haven't killed Nicole already?"

Jade kissed Travis on his cheek. "You don't. That's all part of the game."

The killer released him and swan-dived into the ocean. From there, it was only a short swim under the piers to safety. The water was too cold for an unprotected swimmer to follow, and he couldn't radio for reinforcements.

If the police were already here, they'd have intervened

by now. Especially with a cop getting his ass kicked. That meant he was by himself. Faced with a choice between Jade and Nicole, it was obvious which woman the love smitten detective would pursue.

She could have eliminated him back on *Apollo*'s bow, but it was more fun to string his hopes along. Whether or not Travis found his dream girl, he'd be dead within twenty-four hours.

* * *

Kyle descended the steps to Randall's cabin. *Apollo* was heavier on one side than the other, and the staircase was at a forty-five degree angle. The water was already waist deep. White rapids swirled around the furniture. Bottles, documents and cushions floated across the room, caught in the currents. There was no sign of the flood abating, and the yacht could sink or capsize at any moment.

Spotting Randall's safe behind a slashed painting, Kyle waded towards it. As he passed the sofa, his foot got trapped under something long and heavy. The detective looked down to see the body of a naked, Oriental woman surrounded by a bloody haze.

"Nicole!"

He was scared the killer had decapitated her until he saw an unknown woman's head float between his legs. She must have been one of Forbes' girls. Kyle belched into his hand, pulled his foot free, and continued towards the safe.

Sparks flew from a severed lamp cable on Randall's desk, crackling as they touched the wood. At first, he paid little attention to them. Then he realized the rising water was about to come in contact with the bare wire. Once that happened, the entire cabin would become a deathtrap. He frantically searched for something to insulate him.

Kyle climbed onto the sofa, reaching safe ground moments before the power cord electrified the seawater. He bent his knees to avoid bumping his head and used a floating cushion as a steppingstone to reach the desk. He wrapped his jacket sleeve around his hand for protection and disconnected the cable. After he'd checked for other potential hazards, he dived back into the water.

The killer hadn't lied. She'd left the safe door ajar. There was a sealed, clear plastic folder on the middle shelf. Kyle removed the wallet, opened the clasp, and leafed through the contents.

Randall had been meticulous in recording his dealings with Lenora Knight. Everything was here: transcripts of telephone conversations, details of their secret pact to murder Toshigi, information on the arms dealer he'd put her in contact with, and a twelve page summary of the Cyber Maidens and Lenora's history with Dragonsoft.

The lawyer was nowhere to be found, but Kyle couldn't afford to waste time looking for a man who was probably already dead. He resealed the documents in the folder, waded to the exit, and evacuated the sinking yacht.

The killer's deadly game was reaching its climax, which meant one final murder. He prayed there was something in the files that would tell him where Lenora was holding Nicole.

# CHAPTER FIFTEEN

## *The Dragon's Lair*

Agent Baker's goon squad rolled into Fisherman's Wharf. He brought a small army of suited operatives, enough to fill five black sedans. The vehicles swerved, forming roadblocks around the pier where *Apollo* was berthed. The ship was sinking fast. Rising air bubbles popped on the ocean surface. The yacht's upper deck had fully submerged, leaving only the sails above water.

Kyle twirled his pistol and held it by the barrel, showing his intentions were peaceful. The FBI response team ignored his gesture and treated him as hostile. A dozen agents exited their cars and aimed handguns, using open doors as shields. The others readied the heavy artillery: shotguns, sniper rifles and riot cannons. The men and women under Baker's command all wore Kevlar vests. If a full-scale war erupted in San Francisco, they were ready.

At first, Kyle regretted not involving the FBI sooner. But

he felt better about his decision when Baker laid into him.

"Detective Travis," the lead agent said, stepping forward from the pack. "Dare I ask where the suspect is?"

He holstered his weapon and showed him the plastic document folder. "She got away. The bitch snatched Nicole right outside the precinct. We have to trace this number. Now."

"We? That's wishful thinking."

Baker had no interest in the files that he'd risked everything to recover. He seemed more bothered about establishing authority, no matter what the cost.

"There's no time to argue about jurisdiction," Kyle said. "Nicole's life is on the line."

A crowd of civilians gathered on the pier, snapping photos of the sinking yacht. Tourists pointed Baker out like he was an attraction, but the fed was too busy grilling his scapegoat to be concerned by negative publicity.

"Nicole, eh? So, things are personal between you and Miss Tasoto. That's why you ran off to play cowboy, to rescue the girl from your enemy and bring her back safely home to her ranch. Didn't work out I presume?"

"Listen, Baker."

"Agent Baker to you, Travis. And you listen. So far, three police officers have died. One in his own office right in front of you. Two more are in hospital, including your partner who, if I understand things correctly, went in without backup while you snuggled up to a suspect in a murder investigation. Yeah, I saw the pictures."

It was like dealing with Thorne all over again. The only hope was to placate him somehow.

"We're wasting time here. Let's combine our resources. Lenora's probably on her way to Nicole right now, while the two of us are having a slugging match."

Baker missed Kyle's point, assuming he was even listening.

"Ah, Lenora Knight, the suspect who's all over the news yet you can't seem to find. The body count is in double figures. A girl is responsible for all these deaths. One little girl."

"Don't underestimate her."

He turned to leave, but two agents obstructed his path.

"Like you did?" Baker said. "You had this Knight woman in custody, or at least that's what you claim. What happened? Did you trade her freedom for a cuddle and a kiss? Or maybe this is all some wild tale to save your sorry ass."

Kyle thrust the plastic folder into Baker's chest. "If you want to take over my investigation, fine by me," he said through clenched teeth. "I suggest you follow up on this lead."

He fingered a seven-digit number visible through the clear cover. Randall had circled it in thick red ink, highlighting its importance.

"A yacht just sank, as I'm sure you can tell. You'll need to send for a recovery team. Don't think they'll turn up anything of value, but I already got these notes from the guy's safe."

"And who might this guy be?"

Baker had dropped his confrontational tone at last. He opened the wallet and flicked through the papers.

"Randall Forbes," Kyle said. "Toshigi Tasoto's business partner. Apparently, he was involved with the killer, but was smart enough to keep files on her. Three digits, then a hyphen, followed by four more. What could that be?"

If Baker was amused, he didn't smile. Kyle punched in the numbers on his cellphone. After many unanswered rings, a man with a heavy South American accent picked up.

"Watts Inn. San Francisco International. Can I help you with something?"

"You already have."

The receptionist was understandably confused. "Say what? You want to make a reservation?"

"No. I'd rather do things in person."

Kyle hung up before the guy could ask any more questions, and related the address to Baker.

"Watts Inn, eh? How thoughtful of Miss Knight to leave incriminating evidence behind. With a forwarding number nicely highlighted."

Sarcasm heavy, but the FBI agent had the same doubts.

"I'm assuming she opened Forbes' safe for you," he said, "being the kind and generous soul she is. Did it occur to you she might be expecting company?"

"Yeah. It did. But Nicole's there. I know it."

Baker paused for a moment, then waved his agents back to their vehicles. "We're moving out," he told them.

"I'm going with you."

"Your feelings for the girl make you a handicap I don't need. Sit this one out at the precinct. Can't spare any room for extra baggage."

Kyle grabbed Baker's sleeve. "No problem. I brought my car. Nicole knows me, trusts me. She doesn't know you."

Baker stared at Kyle's hand until he let go. After some consideration, the fed gave into his wishes.

"I suppose you'll follow me anyway, so what the hell? You understand you're no longer heading up the investigation, and that if you screw up my operation, I'll have you hauled before a dozen disciplinary committees?"

"Yeah. I understand perfectly, Agent Baker."

Kyle added the name with an unsubtle touch of hostility. The FBI was in charge now, but he didn't have to like it.

"Good. Then let's go check into Watts Inn."

* * *

Hotels near San Francisco International were primarily for overnight stopovers, business travelers, and temporary housing of passengers with severe flight delays. No tourist would wish to stay so far from the city's attractions, or listen to whining airplane engines fifteen hours a day. There were two types of airport accommodation: affordable but respectable budget options, and bare-bones cesspools like *Watts Inn.*

Rooms went for less than fifty dollars a night. There was a reason they were so cheap. The decrepit building was a hellhole, a dirty brick eyesore with an overgrown parking lot, rusted fire escapes, and boarded-up windows.

It was the type of place Internet travel sites refused to list, a cockroach infested dump where people stayed when they didn't want to be found. In daylight hours, the bed-and-breakfast was a pit stop for drug dealers. Only hired assassins, murderers, and heavily armed police officers dared to visit the area after nightfall.

Baker's team approached the motel in assault formation. The nearest streetlights were on the pillared highway that connected to the city's south side. Against the night sky, the agents in pitch-black clothes, vests and ski masks were almost invisible.

The FBI unit specialized in covert raids and made very little noise as they advanced through the brambles and weeds. Kyle was behind them. With only strap-on body armor, he was rather vulnerable by comparison.

"I spoke with the manager," Baker said over the radio. "Some Latin American prick named Juan Enrique. He's got a female lodger registered at Watts Inn under the name of Lenora Tasoto. She paid a full month in advance. Does this guy ever watch the news? Or maybe Miss Knight offered him a bonus. You know what I mean, Travis?"

"What the hell are we waiting for? Nicole could be dying in there."

Baker had gone on ahead, eager to lead the charge. Now Kyle was supposed to wait for clearance.

"Not what," the FBI man said. "Who. My team. Your girlfriend might be dead already. Ever think of that? This woman parades police officers as trophies. So my unit conducts a sweep. If they give the all clear, then we move in. If not, then we remain out here. You don't have to like it, but that's the way it's going to be."

"You're right. I don't like it."

Kyle broke off contact. Despite their differences, he had no complaints about Baker's professionalism. The agents worked fast to secure the area. Fifty seconds after the operation started, they'd surrounded the building.

If the killer was inside, Baker had enough firepower for a weeklong siege. His troops converged outside the room the innkeeper had identified as Lenora's. The advance squad climbed to the second floor and took their positions out front, while another group split off to cover the rear. Snipers lay in the grass, rifles aimed at the windows.

The team leader removed a long-handled mirror from his belt. He used it to peer over the window ledge without exposing himself.

"Living area's clear," he reported. "No sign of the suspect."

Baker waved his agents forward.

"What about behind the wall?" he asked his second in command. "Any surprises waiting back there?"

The agent rotated his mirror pole. "Negative. Nothing there. What's on your mind?"

"The killer gave us this address. I'm thinking the room might not be empty. Prepare a full assault. Flash bangs, teargas, the works."

Kyle watched the feds arm themselves with automatic rifles and hand grenades. He joined Baker on the outside balcony as two men prepared to bust down the door.

"What about Nicole?"

"Don't worry, Detective Travis. We won't shoot your girlfriend, not on purpose. If she's being held prisoner, we'll do our best to get her out alive."

"Your best?"

Kyle got the impression she wasn't the priority.

"So, in your eyes, the girl is essentially collateral damage?"

"Yes, she is. My aim is to ensure the safety of my team, and take the suspect down before she harms any more innocent civilians. I'm not a reckless man. I'd be thrilled to see Miss Tasoto safe in your arms. But given the choice between letting this psycho go free, or sacrificing that girl's life, it's a straightforward decision."

A female agent handed Baker a carbine with a barrel-mounted light. It was a weapon that a special ops commando would use: a high-powered, automatic rifle with enough ammo to wipe out a terrorist cell. He was going after Lenora in true action hero style.

"On my mark, move in. Three, two, one. Go!"

The agents synchronized their assault. Their timing was near-on perfect. Operatives smashed windows and tossed in stun grenades. Soon after, the flash bangs exploded, and the motel room filled with teargas. Baker and his team charged through the breached front door. Their weapon lights pierced the smoke, sweeping the bedroom walls.

"Clear!" the leader shouted.

The agents continued their search, fanning out into the bathroom. "We got a hostage in here," a woman said. "She's still alive."

"Nicole!"

Kyle covered his mouth and stepped into the smoky motel room. Baker had issued his team with breathing filters, but there were none left over for the detective. Whether through misfortune or selfishness, he'd no protection from the teargas.

Kyle coughed, choking on the wispy fumes as his eyes filled with water. He tripped over exercise equipment, but felt his way to the bathroom. The smoke thinned out nearer the door, and he saw a web of torch beams ahead.

Everyone stared at Nicole. She hung from the shower rail, wearing nothing but her bra and panties. The girl's wrists were handcuffed above her head, with an industrial steel cable linking the chain to a concrete brick in the bathtub. The killer had secured similar blocks around her knees, practically doubling her body weight. Jade's reference to her victim being stretched out now made perfect sense.

The cables creaked as Nicole swung sideways. Scratches on the shower pole suggested it wasn't her first attempt to escape. Her underwear was drenched in sweat. By any standard, she was a physically able woman, but not strong enough to lift two slabs of concrete.

An FBI agent tried to cut the chains around her legs, but his bolt cutters kept slipping on the wet skin. Duct tape silenced her whimpers of pain. Kyle tore off the gag so

Nicole could speak.

"D... Detective," she gasped. "Be... behind... you."

He turned round to search the room. Thinking she was referring to the toilet, he lifted the cracked seat. Flies buzzed around the bowl, and thick, yellow sludge clogged the drainage pipe. Overcome by the sickly stench, Kyle dropped the lid down and moved to the medicine cabinet. The mirror was missing, and the shelves were empty.

"H... Higher. Look higher."

With her guidance, he found a handcuff key on top of the cupboard. It was another of the killer's sadistic games. She'd placed the means to escape within Nicole's sight, but not her reach.

Kyle grabbed it, stood on the bathtub rim, and unlocked the handcuffs. The foundation brick crashed into the bowl, dragging the loose industrial cable with it. He jumped down to catch Nicole before she fell.

"Th... Thank you."

Exhausted from her ordeal, the girl barely mustered the strength to embrace her rescuer.

"Get a medic in here!" Kyle said, comforting her with a cuddle. "It's all right. She can't hurt you now. You're safe."

* * *

Nicole sat on the bed, wrapped in Kyle's cloak. A field agent held an ice pack on her swollen ankles, but she still shifted with discomfort. The handcuffs had left abrasion marks on her wrists, and she had trouble holding her paper cup steady.

Baker had ordered a steaming pot of black coffee to aid with her recovery. Kyle recalled how the family maid had done the same when he first visited her house. He hoped it wasn't an ill omen, though Baker's private army ought to keep the killer away from *Watts Inn*.

The FBI had torn the bedroom apart. It appeared to be the killer's base of operations. Old newspaper clippings were pinned to the walls, forming a collage of Dragonsoft game reviews and stock market reports. Every picture of Toshigi had a thick, red cross drawn across his face. A DNA comparison with the hair sample from Twin Peaks confirmed it was Lenora's blood.

Agents carried away weighted barbell poles and boxes full of bladed implements. Then more crates with chemicals and DIY tools. In the hands of a serial murderer, common household items could be potential murder weapons.

Baker twisted the rope of a punching bag, then released it. Photos stapled to the cover spun past. Glossy images of Toshigi, Randall and the two dead Cyber Maidens.

"Busy doing your job? Perfect angle for a photo, captures the subjects perfectly."

He stopped the motion and pointed to the largest picture: Kyle and Nicole making love in her dojo.

"Come round yet, Miss Tasoto? Why don't you tell us what happened?"

She stared into her coffee, downbeat. "I was at the precinct with Kyle. I mean Detective Travis. Lenora had just killed that cop. Kyle thought she was still in the building, and that I'd be safer if I went home."

"You followed his advice? That was your first mistake."

He ignored Kyle's hard stare and continued with the questions.

"What happened to the officer assigned to you? The girl we found with her skull cracked on the sidewalk. You'll have to excuse me, but with all the dead police, I've forgotten her name."

Nicole sipped her coffee. "Carmen. She was called Carmen. Lenora rode in front of us on her motorcycle. I swerved, crashed into a lamppost. Next thing I knew, I was hanging from the shower rail in there. Carmen must have gone through the windscreen. I don't think she was wearing her seat belt."

Baker squeezed his chin, scratching his lips. "Why not run the bitch over there and then? Save us the trouble of hunting her down. Unless Randall Forbes wasn't her only partner. Now that makes more sense. You reckon so, Travis?"

"I would gladly pulverize that woman." Nicole squashed her empty cup and threw it in the trash. "Believe me. She was wearing a helmet. How was I supposed to know it was Lenora?"

Baker viewed the newspaper clippings.

"It seems to be a carefully planned vendetta against you and these Cyber Maiden friends of yours. Miss Knight must bear quite a grudge to collect all this."

"Hey!" Kyle was tiring of Baker's insinuations. "If you got something on your chest, come out and say it. We both know this woman's an animal."

"Animals respond to base instincts, but human predators require motivation, a reason to hate their prey. So your girlfriend stole some of Miss Knight's design ideas. Hardly the crime of the century. It's too petty a motive. Who'd go on a killing spree over video games? Depraved teenagers, perhaps, but Lenora seems much too clever for that. What does she really want?"

"She's freaking crazy. Who knows what's going through her head?"

Kyle helped the girl to her feet. "Even by FBI standards, Nicole's had a pretty rough day. So if you have no objections, I'd like to take her home."

"Oh, I don't mind one bit, Detective Travis," Baker said, handing over the photo. "So long as you stay out of my way, I couldn't care less what Miss Tasoto teaches you on the mat. Though if I were in your shoes, I'd find out what your girlfriend's secret is. It might help you prepare for when the psycho comes calling."

* * *

Nicole relaxed, sharing the last of her wine with Kyle. She'd recuperated on the way back from *Watts Inn*. Perhaps it was the absence of Baker's unfounded accusations, or simply that she was more relaxed in her dojo, but she seemed totally at ease.

It was still three hours before dawn, and the weather had taken a turn for the worse. Rain pattered against the roof, heavy enough to be constant. Occasionally, there was a rumble of distant thunder.

"You think Lenora's out there?" Nicole asked. "Watching the house? Waiting for an opportunity to strike?"

Kyle sipped his wine, listening to trees creak in the wind. "I hate to be pessimistic, but you're the only person left on her list. She murders your friends, your colleagues, then comes after you."

"You're on her list, too. That's why she kept me alive. She'll come for you first, then move on to me. Jade Dragon's final kill, her moment of ultimate victory."

Nicole lowered her head. Kyle shuffled across the mat and stroked her face.

"Hey. She won't get to you," he said. "Not if I can help it. You've had a rough ordeal. Perhaps you should go lie down. You need rest."

She finished her drink and tucked her hair behind her ears.

"You're right. I'm tired of playing this stupid waiting game. You finish your wine. I'd feel safer if we spent the night together."

Kyle paused, trying to determine whether there was a double meaning to Nicole's words.

"I'm quite happy to sleep on the mat. But that's up to you."

"My bed's a queen size. There's space for two. I'll go get changed."

Nicole kissed him, stepped into her private room, and closed the door. Kyle poured the final drops of wine from the bottle and drank them in one gulp.

Something nagged at the back of his mind. Baker was a jerk, but what he'd said about Lenora's lack of motivation made sense. Having her game design ideas stolen wouldn't drive a person to mass murder. Crazy or not, there had to be a deeper reason. He wondered if his lover had kept the truth from him, a dark secret buried in her past she wanted to forget.

"Kyle!" Nicole shrieked. "It's Lenora! She's—"

A high-pitched scream, then nothing. The detective dropped his wine glass, drew his gun, and ran into the next room.

Jade was waiting behind the door. The tall, blonde woman stood beside Nicole's bed, her leather jumpsuit bathed in green light. Kyle aimed his pistol, but she kicked it from his hand before he could fire.

"I feel sorry for Lakeysia."

Kyle went for her throat. She sidestepped out of the way and punched him in the face. The murderess lifted her leg and brought her boot heel down on his shoulder. There was so much power behind her attack she dislocated his joint. She pounced while he winced and wrestled him to the ground.

"Sorry that her partner thinks with his dick instead of his brain."

Her voice sounded different, softer, yet very familiar. The killer unzipped her jumpsuit, exposing her body to the light.

He had seen her underwear before, less than an hour ago at Watts Inn. The woman's face and neck were Caucasian pink, but the rest of her skin was Oriental brown. She wore tinted contact lenses, but Kyle would recognize Nicole's eyes anywhere.

He looked around Jade's room: her scale-carved bed, the computer she'd used to print the photographs, her colored lampshades. Baker had FBI agents posted outside, but the added security wouldn't help. The killer was already inside the house.

Lenora had been a scapegoat framed by the woman Kyle loved. Nicole was Jade Dragon, and now she had him cornered in her lair.

"Surprised, Detective?" she said with a gleeful smile. "My father had that same vacant expression in his eyes. He tried to tell you before he burned away, but you were too dumb to listen. You look exhausted."

Nicole elbowed Kyle in the face. She stood up, kicked him twice in the hip, and drew her tranquilizer pistol. For the second time, she shot a dart into Kyle's neck.

He had one final thought before he blacked out. The killer wasn't finished playing games just yet.

# CHAPTER SIXTEEN

## *Modus Operandi*

Nicole chained Travis' right leg to her lower bedpost, pulled the links taut, and snapped on a padlock. The restraints fastened around the detective's wrists and ankles were so tight his body stretched to its limit, with his back barely touching her duvet cover.

The killer had stripped the policeman of his weapon and clothes, leaving him vulnerable and naked. Without a gun, he was as helpless as the others. Even if he somehow escaped, he'd pose no threat. In a fight to the death, it would take Nicole four seconds to overpower him, and half as long to snap his neck.

She'd kept Travis alive because she wanted him to understand what it was like to be a prisoner in another person's bed. Now he was at her mercy, the murderess would subject him to the same torture she suffered as a child. Beneath his suave exterior, he was no different to

Toshigi or Randall. Kyle had pretended to be a protector, but his only interest was seducing her. All three men had taken advantage of a young woman, and none regarded her as their superior or even an equal.

Nicole was the heart and soul of Dragonsoft. It was her innovative game designs that had propelled her father's company to the top and funded his luxury empire. Everyone wanted a piece of his success, yet nobody showed the chief architect any respect. She received royalties on her games, but Toshigi and his sleazy attorney took most of the money. A small fish in their pond, but the other employees still accused her of being daddy's girl. Charlie, Rebecca, the Cyber Maidens—they all hated her. In the eyes of her coworkers, she was an attractive Japanese schoolgirl, not a pioneer.

Nicole sat on the bed, pulled the dart from her victim's neck, and tickled his face until he jerked awake. She chuckled as he wrestled with his chains.

"That's the third time I've got the better of you, Detective," she said, scratching his chest. "You can't stop falling for me. Seems I'm very good at this game."

Travis tried to conceal his confusion with steely determination, but Nicole knew he only remembered being knocked unconscious twice.

"Once in my bedroom," she reminded him. "Once at your office, and the time before that, you were too busy squeezing my ass to notice. I kissed you to sleep and added a little knockout powder to make sure. Did you enjoy your after sushi mint? I hated it. Every second. But thanks for the alibi."

Kyle had been so interested in feeling her body it never occurred to him *he* was being used. As expected, he accepted her invitation and came by himself. He'd left his partner to crack the case while he had dinner with the prime suspect.

Of course, Travis never questioned her innocence. From the day they met, she'd ensnared him in her web of seduction and lies. Even though he knew the killer was female, he was quite prepared to have sex with the woman who had the most to gain from Toshigi's death.

Nicole's scheme played out perfectly. She mixed crushed sleeping tablets into his food. Later that night, she stabbed a tranquilizer dart into his neck while they made love. Once he dozed off, the killer went to her bedroom to download the digital photos.

She'd mounted her camera on a tripod in advance and left the connecting door partially open. All she needed to do was lure Kyle into position, and the automatic timer took care of the rest. The beguiled idiot never suspected a thing. Nicole eliminated Hannah and Iris, put Lakeysia in the hospital, dropped off the incriminating pics at the precinct, and returned home with time to spare.

"You killed them?" Travis asked, still flabbergasted at Nicole's betrayal. "Why? Why are you doing this?"

"You're the master sleuth," she said, plucking the dart's wings. "You figure it out. Do I look the part, Detective?"

"What are you? My dream date?"

Nicole sat at her vanity table. She removed her blonde wig, placed it on a plaster bust, and straightened her natural black hair.

"I'm barely eighteen. Don't you think that's a bit of an age gap? No? Well, neither did Toshigi nor Randall. They had me in their beds at thirteen. It's all in my private photo album. Have a look. I'll be with you in a minute."

Nicole soaked a cloth in cleaning solvent, wrung it, and wiped the creamy pink paint from her face. As her Caucasian disguise dissolved, Kyle glanced around the room, seeing the paintings for the first time.

They were hand drawn, and showed key moments of her life. Her parents being murdered while she watched from hiding, the San Jose orphanage where she grew up, Toshigi adopting her, working with the Cyber Maidens at Dragonsoft, and hints at the sexual abuse she endured at the hands of her beloved father.

The artwork was the prize of Nicole's collection. She had painted them recently and kept their existence secret. Her childhood experiences were so traumatizing she could recreate vivid memories exactly as they happened. She used the latest computer graphics technology, so the detail level was so high a casual onlooker might mistake them for actual photographs.

"They abused you. I'm sorry."

Kyle stared at a picture of Nicole being sexually assaulted by Randall while her father watched from the bedside. She was a teenager, completely at their mercy.

"Yet you did nothing. Said nothing for five years. I don't understand. Why wait? Why not go to the authorities?"

"Because I was afraid! I was a child then. Weak and helpless. What could I have done? Who would have taken the word of a young girl against respected businessmen? My father had powerful friends, and I had nobody. Even vengeance has its limits. Besides, I had to do Jade Dragon's character justice."

Travis recounted Jade's tale. "As a child, she watched her parents die. The ninja sought revenge on those who'd wronged her, hunted them down one by one. Before she took their lives, she looked them in the eye, and showed them her face. To let them know they'd been murdered by an eighteen-year-old girl. Your character's history... is your own."

Nicole stored her contact lenses in their case. With the

disguise removed, she resembled the sweet young Japanese lady Travis once loved so dearly.

"You've got a wonderful memory, Kyle. Shame you don't have any intelligence to go with it."

She put the blonde wig bust beside her redheaded one.

"You really thought I was Lenora, didn't you?" she said, circling the bed. "I led you all on a wild goose chase, planted clues. I snipped a piece of that bitch's hair to leave at Charlie's office, cleaned out her apartment, set up the room at the inn. Smearing the newspaper articles in her blood was a nice touch, don't you think? I made complete fools of the SFPD and the great Detective Kyle Travis. You wouldn't even have gone after Lenora if your partner hadn't deciphered my code. How's Lakeysia doing, by the way?"

Nicole took down a painting and showed it to Kyle. The Cyber Maidens gathered round a screen, clutching control pads. The Asian woman in the background was about sixteen years old. She worked alone at a sloped table, sketching concept art. The drawing within was her green Kunoichi, Jade Dragon.

"I've proved I'm the greatest games designer who's ever lived," she said, "and not some pretty face at the office. The other girls never respected me. They always believed I only got the job because I was the president's daughter. My brilliant designs had nothing to do with it."

"What about the maid? Your secretary? Rebecca? The two rookie cops? Lakeysia? Thorne? What did they ever do to piss you off?"

Nicole rehung the picture. "Not much, but I had to get your attention. People die in this city every day. Who cares about a few murders here and there? They wouldn't even make the headlines. Eleven kills in three days. Now, that's a story that gets noticed. Yesterday, I was a name in small print on the back of some game boxes, but tomorrow, I'll be famous."

"I thought you wanted to frame Lenora. Won't she be the famous one? Are you going to kill me as well?"

Nicole climbed on her bed, stood over Kyle, and stripped to her underwear. She kicked her boots away, then stepped out of her jumpsuit.

"How often do you play games? Before the surprise ending, the hero always gets the girl. Or vice versa."

"What? You expect me to kiss you now?"

The fool actually believed he had a choice. The killer pulled down her panties, unfastened her bra strap, and tossed her underclothes aside. Completely naked, she sat on Kyle's waist and assumed a lovemaking position.

"I'll be doing the kissing," she said. "It's called rape. Not a very pleasant experience. You wondered why I hated my father so much. I thought I'd reconstruct the crime for you. Cheer up. You're about to have the best sex of your life. Me too."

Kyle spat in Nicole's face. "Relationships require commitment from both parties, and I haven't made up my mind. Your words, remember?"

She calmly wiped away the saliva. "That's no way to treat a lady, especially a damsel in distress. It was fun watching you save me, even if I was never in any real danger."

Travis had been so eager to play the knight in shining armor and dash to her rescue. The predictable "hero" did exactly as she expected.

It was easy to rig the hostage situation at the motel. After the encounter at the docks, Nicole ditched her scuba outfit and took two separate taxis to *Watts Inn*. Once there, she exercised with the barbells and punching bag until sweat dripped from her body. She needed the cops to believe she'd been held captive since midday, and her story would be far more plausible if she was exhausted when help arrived.

Nicole had selected a second-floor room so she could see the steps outside. When the FBI agents came, she ran into the bathroom, stood on the tub's rim, and chained the concrete blocks to her ankles. She cuffed her wrists behind her back, rested the handcuff chain on the hook, and jumped.

The bricks weighed her legs down, while the counterweight prevented Nicole's feet from touching the floor tiles. Her calculations had been accurate. She ended up suspended in mid-air, ready to be rescued. Travis took his time finding the key, but that was to be expected.

Despite the snap decision to increase the difficulty after killing Rebecca, it proved equally trivial to strangle the puny Officer Wilson. The footprint trail she'd left for Lakeysia inside the house misled even her.

Assassinating the maid in front of Travis was more satisfying, if only for the challenge of planning a murder in less than an hour. When Kyle telephoned ahead to announce his visit, Nicole staged Sarah's death to divert his suspicion. She'd bought a silenced nine-millimeter pistol from the arms dealer recommended by Randall, and knew the daily cleaning routine off by heart. With the supplier taken care of, there was no way to trace the weapon to her.

Nicole simply hid the gun under her gown and turned her back on Kyle when she was ready. To throw ballistics off the scent, she waited until the maid was in line with the French windows before she put a bullet in her temple.

The tricky part was making the cops believe the shot came from the garden, but there was enough C-4 to spare for two panes of glass. She remotely detonated the first block when she killed Sarah, and then blew up the second before she destroyed the vase. Kyle was too busy taking cover, so he never saw the gun in Nicole's hand.

With the stage set for Jade's appearance, Nicole reached into her gown pocket, dialed Toshigi's home number, and activated her mobile phone's playback function. Memorizing her recorded message beforehand made it easy to add verbal responses when prompted. Then all she had to do was deliberately put herself in the imaginary shooter's line of fire. She used her pretend anger as an excuse to press the answering machine's delete key, erasing any chance of voice analysis.

Desperate to woo Nicole with his heroic antics, Travis abandoned her and leaped through the window. Naturally, he discovered the footprints and shell casing she had planted near the statue, but she hid the actual evidence while he was chasing shadows.

Only three people knew about the secret drawer inside the samurai armor display case, and Nicole's father and maid wouldn't be sharing that information. While Travis hunted the phantom killer outside, Nicole retrieved the explosive residue and stored it in the compartment with her cellphone and gun. In retrospect, she should have worn gloves, but nobody thought to check her hands for powder burns.

"Since you're such a clever girl," Kyle said, interrupting her thoughts. "Why not let me go? You think you'll get away with killing me? Everyone back at the station knows I'm at your place. They'll connect you to my death."

Nicole smiled, unconcerned by Kyle's desperate pleas.

"If they ever find your remains. They will assume you ran off to Miami with some bimbo tucked under your arm. And if not..." She stretched forward so her breasts touched his body. "Spending a hot, steamy night in my dojo ought to convince them I'm innocent. Passion can melt a guy's brain. The method's tried, tested, and proven."

"Forget it, Nicole. Your boyfriend's not coming tonight."

Travis shut his eyes and lay prone on the bed. He'd suddenly grown a conscience. How pathetic.

"No hard on?" she said. "I can fix that. You think you're real tough, don't you? Some girls like to squeeze the juice from forbidden fruit, but I've always preferred nuts."

Nicole reached between her knees and grabbed Kyle's crotch. She squeezed his balls so tight they creaked with tension.

"I crack them open with my bare hands. Typical male. All talk. They say twisted testicles can cause a man unbearable pain, but us girls wouldn't know. We're the weaker, uneducated sex, aren't we? Let's hear you scream. Cry out, and I'll let go."

Travis winced in, but remained defiant. "Fu... y..." he croaked, unable to complete the words.

"Be patient. I'm getting to that."

Kyle arched his back and pulled away from Nicole. She kept his private parts in a vice hold. Her fingernails cut into her captive's flesh, drawing blood. Nicole's grip was so tight his skin turned red around the groin.

"I'll hand it to you. You're tougher than Lenora was. One broken kneecap was enough for her. She begged me for mercy before I finally shut her up with her own controller cord. In the time it took her to die, I completed the first level of *Jade Dragon*. That was despite the stupid bitch waving her arms in my eyes."

She squeezed harder. He groaned in pain, his resistance crumbling.

"Then I started my real campaign. You can't figure out how I pulled it off, can you? How I outsmarted Travis,

Lakeysia and Thorne. The dynamic trio. Most of the setups were easy. Sarah, the motel room, my father. Hannah and Iris. Any idiot with a fraction of my intelligence could come up with those, but killing your lieutenant at the police station. That was a classic. Want to know how I did it? Yes, I bet you do."

Nicole hadn't been certain Kyle would take her to the precinct a second time. But just in case, she'd stashed Meagan's uniform and her "Lenora" disguise in the alley opposite. The night she delivered the photos to Lieutenant Throne, she hid her trash bag behind a dumpster. Somewhere homeless people or refuse collectors wouldn't remove it.

After faking sickness upon seeing Iris' body, Nicole called Travis from the corridor outside the morgue. While he dashed to Thorne's office, she left the precinct and changed into the cop outfit.

The killer wore the patrolwoman's shirt and trousers over her black suit, taped her empty bag and high heels to her waist, and buttoned her blouse over the top. To complete her change of identity, Nicole applied paint to her face, then put on her red wig and dark glasses.

When she was ready, the fake Meagan walked back to the precinct. She used the elevator, headed straight for Homicide Division, and interrupted the Lieutenant's meeting with Travis. The assassin slit his throat, knocked Kyle unconscious, and made her getaway.

Before detectives found the body, she locked herself in a women's restroom stall. Now in privacy, she took off Meagan's uniform, and stashed it in the black bag along with her shoes, glasses, and wig. Nicole washed off her face cream, exited the cubicle, and stuffed the bag into a waste bin, pausing on the way out to put on her high heels. She smirked as she checked her appearance in a mirror. The redheaded murderess had become an innocent Japanese girl again, and Travis would never question her brief disappearance.

When the fool sent her home with Carmen, it provided the perfect opportunity to lead him further astray. Nicole waited for a break in traffic, pressed the button that disengaged Carmen's seat belt, and sped up into a lamppost.

The stunned officer flew through the front windshield and cracked her skull on the pavement. Somehow she survived, but nobody was around to see Nicole snap the woman's neck. She left the Apollo figurine for the police to find, then fled the accident scene before any nosy bystanders showed up.

Then the killer took a cable car to Fisherman's Wharf. It would be a few hours before Travis connected the clue to Randall. Ample time for a night swim in the bay.

Nicole released Kyle's groin. "You're stronger than I thought," she said, "but your tough guy act won't save Lakeysia. The poor woman is going to die in bed like her partner, all because you chose me over her."

"Don't count on it. She'll survive, and she's got you fingered. Even made a bet you were psycho. I should have listened. She's always been right about women."

Nicole repositioned herself on Kyle's waist. "Are you upset with me?" she asked, crossing her feet underneath his back.

"You might say I'm pissed off, yeah."

She picked up her bra, looped it over her prisoner's head, and gripped the two elastic straps.

"Then let me make it up to you. Ever hear of erotic asphyxiation? It's my first time, so you'll have to forgive me if I get carried away."

She crossed the bands and yanked the makeshift garotte

taut around Travis' neck. He jerked violently as Nicole cut off his air supply.

Chain links rattled against the bedposts, scraping and clinking as he flexed his muscles. The killer refused to let go. She crushed the detective's waist between her powerful legs until she felt his body stiffen.

"Come on," she panted, pulling the elastic tighter. "Is that all you've got?"

Deprived of his voice, Travis gurgled in response. Nicole stared into his eyes, smiling as she licked her lips. She bent down, kissed him, and sucked the saliva from his mouth.

"That's better," she said, coming up for air. "Enjoying yourself yet?"

She stretched the material to breaking point, but stopped short of going all the way. If she tightened the straps any more, Travis' neck would break, and she wanted this to last as long as possible.

On the verge of losing consciousness, the cop clenched his fists and exerted all his strength on the chains. The right post held, but the left shattered. The desperate man pulled his arm from the unwinding chain, grabbed the end, and flung it at Nicole's face. She ducked underneath, laughing as the flailing steel whooshed overhead. Kyle swung again, this time lashing her body.

Nicole passed one bra strap behind his neck, transferred it to the other side, and twisted both elastic pieces with one hand. With her other, she grabbed the swinging chain, snared her victim's forearm, and pulled her metal lasso tight.

Kyle wrestled and shook his limbs, but he had no fight left. Nicole had complete control over his arm. She directed his contorting fingers down her damp chest, ignoring his scratching. Travis realized his struggle was hopeless and lay still.

His stiff body sank into Nicole's bed sheets. Kyle's dipped head rolled against his shoulder. His breathing grew shallower and stopped altogether. Nicole held onto the elastic straps for two full minutes until she was certain he had nothing more to give.

# CHAPTER SEVENTEEN

## *The Final Boss*

Nicole paused for breath, unwrapped her bra from Kyle's neck, and eased off his limp body. She tossed her underwear into a laundry basket, slipped into her kimono, and returned to the house.

After she'd brewed her bodyguards a pot of decaffeinated coffee with added milk, sugar and crushed sleeping pills, the murderess ran a bath. She stripped naked and soaked herself in freezing cold water. Her skin was still sweaty from the workout at *Watts Inn*, and she wanted to relax before making her next move.

When enough time had elapsed, Nicole rinsed her hair, drained the bathwater, and took a peek through the window. The FBI agents were all asleep in their cars. One white-haired man had collapsed against his young female partner. His head rested on her bosom, and he'd be in for a rude shock if she woke up first.

The killer smiled to herself and went back to the dojo. She changed into her biker's outfit, unfastened Travis' chains, and rolled him onto a polythene sheet she'd laid out beside her bed.

There was little chance of anyone finding the body. To hamper future identification, she sliced off his fingers and thumbs with her katana, pulled out his teeth, and disfigured his face with corrosive acid. She wrapped the clear plastic around the corpse, taped the sections together with duct tape, and sealed the ends.

The killer dragged her victim into the garden. She lifted a pre-cut section of turf, grabbed Toshigi's statue by its arms, and shoved the stone figure aside. Nicole had dug a grave in her own backyard. Dozens of brain dead cops had walked within inches of her hidden burial site and suspected nothing.

Travis' remains weren't the first she'd buried in the hole. Lenora's scarred face was visible through another polythene sheet, her lifeless pupils reflecting the moonlight. A bruised depression around her neck showed where Nicole had strangled her with the controller cord. Deceased for two weeks, the redhead's body was decomposing. Earthworms had found their way into her shroud. The slimy creatures slithered across the naked body, scattering dried blood flakes from fingerless knuckles.

Nicole flipped the corpse into the burial pit. He landed with a squelch, sinking into the soft mud. As she replaced the statue and turf, she reflected on the irony. The charmer would share his final resting place with a beautiful woman, while Toshigi danced on Lenora's grave.

The killer could view the rotten bodies whenever she liked, but the cops were doomed to hunt their missing suspect forever. The only person who truly suspected her was Detective Symons, and she would die later tonight.

Nicole returned to the dojo, made her bed, and glued the broken post back together, removing all traces of Travis' presence. She walked round to the front garage and got behind the wheel of the family minivan.

Her father's backup transportation was a shiny red luxury wagon fitted with a portable videophone, GPS guidance system and—most importantly—tinted windscreens. The SUV lacked the speed and acceleration of Nicole's corvette, but Toshigi's obsession with privacy was a distinct advantage. Since his death, the media had publicized her face, and she didn't want to attract attention.

The killer drove from Pacific Heights to the downtown parking space where she'd ditched her motorcycle the night before. Nicole opened the glove compartment, removed her syringe and poison, and taped them to her knee. She swapped vehicles, put on her crash helmet, and then headed for Adamson General Hospital. Since Travis was kind enough to show her, the assassin knew exactly where to find her target: ward 19F, in the intensive care section.

Nicole had intended to slice the bitch's head off outside Iris' apartment, but the detective's agility both surprised and thwarted her. It was too bad Lakeysia was incapacitated. She had more skill, intelligence and combat prowess than all the other victims combined, and would have made an excellent last opponent.

* * *

Nicole rode into the hospital parking lot, switched off her motorcycle engine, and thought up a plan. It was a busy building, but cops would be on alert, especially those around Lakeysia's ward.

The eastern sky was pale blue, and the first rays of

morning light shone on the emergency wing. It was the last hour of the night shift, the perfect time to strike. The police would be tired and ready to go home. All Nicole needed was some way to move about undetected.

Then the solution presented itself. A female surgeon walked to her parked car. She wore a thick cloak, with a stethoscope tube partially visible under her collar. The Asian woman was of average build, but her hospital uniform was approximately Nicole's size.

A signpost cast a long shadow over the killer's motorcycle, keeping her hidden. She waited for the doctor to unlock her car door, then crept up behind and wrapped one arm around the slender girl's throat. The surgeon reached into her purse while stamping at her attacker's toes. Her moves were amateur self-defense techniques, pitifully easy to dodge.

The woman pulled out a can of mace and sprayed it blindly over her shoulder. Liquid trickled harmlessly down Nicole's helmet visor. Another useless attempt to incapacitate her. The killer tightened her choke hold and lifted the surgeon off the ground. Her prisoner kicked at her ankles, wheezing as Nicole crushed her windpipe.

"I'm afraid you're the one who'll need surgery, doctor. Dead on arrival."

The murderess broke the surgeon's neck, dumped her body inside the car, and shut the door.

She replaced her leather outfit with the green hospital gown. Its sleeves stopped at Nicole's forearms, and the trousers were pressingly tight round her waist, but she couldn't afford to wait any longer.

Nicole transferred the syringe and test tube to a side pocket, placed the stethoscope around her collar, and rifled through the woman's cloak. When she'd found the other uniform sections, she tucked her hair inside the elastic rimmed cap, and secured the facemask over her mouth.

The disguise proved to be an excellent choice. Mistaken for a busy surgeon, Nicole had the freedom of the hospital. Nobody at the main entrance or reception desk challenged her.

The world-class medical facility was a recent addition to the San Francisco suburbs, with beds for two thousand patients, and hundreds of doctors and nurses on the payroll. Intensive care staff were busy saving other peoples' lives, and to security personnel, Nicole was just another employee at Adamson General. The face mask hid any discrepancies between her features and the ID card's picture. Her tight-fitting gown might have tipped off an observant guard, but the night watchmen walked around half asleep.

All the white walled passages looked alike. Thankfully, there were plenty of signs throughout the labyrinthine maze of operating theaters, offices and storerooms. Nicole followed the clearly marked directions to ward 19F. The baggy eyed cop outside Lakeysia's room yawned, itched his chin, and frequently glanced at his watch. He seemed more bothered about counting down the remaining seconds than watching for trouble.

Nicole slipped on a pair of clear surgical gloves, stabbed the hypodermic into her tube's cork, and filled the syringe with household bleach. She concealed the weapon behind her back and followed three masked surgeons towards Lakeysia's ward.

After they'd passed the cop, the assassin broke away from the pack, charged her target, and thrust the needle into his neck. She pressed the plunger hard, injecting the poisonous blue liquid into his bloodstream. Before her victim could cry out, she clamped her hand over his mouth. She hooked her knee over his pistol, preventing him from drawing it from the holster. The policeman stared after the surgeons, but they never looked back.

Nicole twisted the handle and pushed the cop into Lakeysia's room. He collapsed to the floor, convulsing as the poison took effect. The man clutched his throat and belched up blue saliva. As he died, the killer closed the door, pulled out her syringe, and refilled it with bleach.

Lakeysia's eyes were open. The detective was still on a respirator, but appeared to be in a more stable condition. Since her previous visit, most blood drips had been taken away, and heart rate indicators recorded a slow, steady beat.

The monitoring system was fully automated. No doctors were on duty in the neighboring observation room, and Nicole had the target all to herself. She lowered her mask, sat down on the bed, and held the syringe needle against the policewoman's neck.

"How are you doing, Lakeysia?"

Her pulse rate rose, becoming erratic. The killer could sense the woman's fear. She breathed rapidly, water vapor condensing inside her respirator.

Nicole squeezed the ventilator tube and watched Lakeysia's eyes widen as she suffocated. "Are you having trouble breathing, Detective Symons? Some fresh air should help clear your throat."

She released her grip, pulled the oxygen mask away from the patient's mouth, and set it against her chest.

"Remember me?" she asked.

Lakeysia coughed in her face. "Of course. How could I forget a psycho as ugly as you?"

Nicole clamped her hand round Lakeysia's neck and squeezed her windpipe. The heart rate monitor beeped faster, showing a series of sharp spikes.

"Not so quick footed now, are you?" She pressed her syringe until her victim's skin turned white under the needle. "I'll give credit where it's due. You're intelligent for a cop. You even suspected me."

Nicole released her hand so the detective could speak freely. Lakeysia grinned before she replied.

"Any woman who wants to sleep with Kyle Travis has to be one hell of a crazy bitch. That's pretty conclusive in my book."

"I did more than sleep with him. Do you know what happens when you choke a man during intercourse? You should try it someday. It's quite exhilarating. Your partner's resting right now. Apparently, the stress was too much for him to bear. He died on the job, a true hero."

Lakeysia's head sunk into her pillow. "Want to volunteer to be the one who gets choked?"

"You don't like me, do you, Detective? But there is a mutual respect between us. We're equal in so many ways, yet on opposing sides. Without me and you, it wouldn't be much of a game at all. The others were minor characters. Grunts and mini bosses, but you're far more important. The final boss, all that stands between me and victory."

"Nice to be appreciated," said Lakeysia. "But I'd suggest you check your wiring, webmistress. Think you got your memory circuits crossed?"

The unfunny cop smiled at her lousy humor.

"That or it's loose somewhere. So you know. Point one, I don't subscribe to the serial killer fan club. Point two, respect. A black girl who goes round pretending she's white won't get much where I'm from. Point three, we ain't at all equal. I'm a police officer, and you're a sick wacko. And the rest of your lingo was pure gibberish, honey. Do I look like some great adversary to you?"

"No."

Nicole suppressed a chuckle. She flicked her syringe and shook it so the contents sloshed inside.

"You look like a dirty bitch who should wash her mouth out. Don't have soap and water, so cleaning fluid will have to do."

She squeezed Lakeysia's cheeks to force her lips apart, held the syringe between the gap, and tapped the plunger. Bleach trickled slowly down the needle. A droplet formed on the tip, growing larger until it fell onto the patient's tongue.

"Do you support the death penalty?" Nicole asked. "Purely out of interest."

"Not if the judge is a raving lunatic," Lakeysia said, coughing violently.

The killer grabbed the detective's chin and stared into her eyes. "In your case, I'm judge, jury and executioner, but you haven't answered my question."

"What does it matter? I'll be long dead and cremated by the time they put your ass in the gas chamber."

"Ah, but they won't. Thanks to your brilliant detective work, everyone thinks Lenora's guilty. They'll find her body when it's convenient, and then Jade Dragon will become a modern day legend. The greatest murderer in history, the woman nobody could catch."

She paused, letting her victory sink in. For someone about to die, the detective seemed very relaxed.

"Oh, by the way," the killer said. "Randall had a little boating accident last night. Which means I gain sole control over my father's company and all those profits. As video game haters will tell you, there's nothing like controversy to increase sales."

Nicole rotated her syringe, smiled, and pressed her thumb against the plunger in readiness.

"I've won and you've lost. I want that to be your dying thought."

Lakeysia grabbed the needle, keeping the hypodermic at bay. It was the first sign of resistance since their skirmish outside Paradise Grove.

"So, you decided to go down fighting. Do you have any last requests?"

The detective forced the syringe aside, and her renewed strength caught Nicole off guard.

"Played a few games myself when I was your age," Lakeysia said. "Until I realized they were for kids. I always thought they were kinda crappy. Why shoot blocky yellow alien spaceships when I got a flesh and blood psycho in my sights?"

She threw back her bed cover, exposing a telephone. Its receiver was off the hook. The wire coiled under the detective's body, through the bedspread, and into a wall socket. 911, the number she'd called, flashed on the display screen. The smart bitch had exaggerated her injuries while she stalled for time.

"Did anyone ever tell you that you talk too much, Nicole? Psychos can never resist telling people how clever they are, and here I was thinking you were smarter than the average wacko. See? No gun. Don't think the feds trusted me to take your ass alive. Could be the first smart thing I saw them do."

A powerful searchlight beam passed over the window, illuminating the ward in brilliant white. An FBI helicopter hovered in the glare, its rotor noise quietened to a faint hum by the double glazed glass.

Two sharpshooters armed with carbine rifles sat in the chopper's cargo bay, targeting Nicole with laser sights. A third man behind them trained a sniper rifle on her head.

More agents stormed into the room, covering the only exit. The four-person team was decked out with Special Forces weaponry, full body armor, and visored riot helmets.

Their leader stepped forward and aimed his pistol at Nicole's back. "Agent Baker, FBI," he identified himself. "Nice, detailed confession. Thanks to Symons' call, we got it all on tape. Put the weapon on the floor."

He totally flipped out when she didn't move immediately.

"Did you hear me, bitch? Drop the syringe now!"

Nicole maintained her position, grabbed Lakeysia's hair, and tightened her hold on the needle.

"You want to save your friend? I suggest you lose your guns." She nodded towards the dead cop. "Bleach doesn't mix very well with blood."

Baker stepped over the body and pressed his gun into Nicole's neck.

"He's not one of my men. I never seen this lady, and I'm not best pals with Detective Travis. So I don't care about your hostages, only you. This is the way it plays out. The woman lives, I'm a hero. She dies, and I'm still a hero. As for you, I can either slam you in jail or nail your coffin. Which would you prefer?"

"Feds aren't the smartest people on the planet," Lakeysia said. "But he's right on this one. He doesn't care if I die, so you got no leverage. Way I see it, there are three endings to your game."

"And they are?"

"You kill me, he kills you. Or you can drop the needle and get convicted on multiple murder charges. They put you on death row. You meet some new cellmates. Then we don't mind if you snap your friends' necks. Saves us paying for gas and electricity. And since you know that karate shit, you might avoid getting the shiv. Wouldn't bet on it, but you got a chance."

Baker wasn't listening to Lakeysia's monologue. "Drop the needle!" he screamed. "Now!"

"What's the third ending?" asked Nicole.

"They declare you criminally insane, which I'm confident they will. Then you get to discuss games design with a bunch of fellow lunatics."

"I won't ask again. Drop the needle."

The agent had exhausted his tired and limited vocabulary. She placed the syringe on the bed, pretending to comply.

"Someone has to tell my story, so it might as well be Detective Symons. She's the smartest person here besides me. Do you play games, Mister Baker?"

"It's Agent Baker," he said, reaching for his handcuffs. "And no, I don't indulge the whims of mass murderers."

"That's too bad."

Nicole eyed the syringe. She lifted her heels and studied the FBI agents' shadows on the wall.

"Because if you did, you'd know that they always end with the final boss exploding in a hail of bullets. Followed by a setup for a sequel."

Lakeysia spotted the evil glint in Nicole's eye.

"Shoot her!" she yelled.

Nicole leaped sideways, spun, and kicked the gun from Baker's hand. As his eyes tracked the flying weapon, she grabbed her syringe, rammed the needle into his unprotected thigh, and injected all the remaining bleach.

Baker staggered back, clutching the glass tube. His agonized screams brought a swift end to the standoff. Agents opened fire, ripping the duvet to shreds.

Nicole dived for the gun. A rifle round passed through

her knee, and a second through her shoulder. She rolled under the bed, ignoring the intense pain as she pulled the sheet across the gap.

The assassin grabbed the corner pole and dragged herself from cover. She blasted three FBI agents' kneecaps before they could return fire.

Baker's team kept their rifle triggers pressed, indiscriminately spraying the room with bullets. Holes perforated the walls and ceiling. Equipment exploded in sparks and monitor screens shattered. Somehow, Lakeysia survived the surrounding carnage.

The assassin plucked the empty syringe from Baker's lifeless body, staggered to the bedside, and raised the needle. All the windowpanes disintegrated as the chopper squad let rip. The FBI sniper shot Nicole in the back, narrowly missing her heart. The bullet emerged from her chest, clipping off a lock of hair. Yet again, Lady Luck was on the detective's side.

The killer fell forward onto the bed. Barely conscious, she screamed in rage, and stabbed at Lakeysia's eye. More bullets flew into her, and a stray round broke the syringe in two.

The bedridden cop shut her eyes to protect them from falling glass. Minor traces of bleach landed on her face, but the wounds were superficial. Nicole collapsed, smearing the patient's gown with blood. In her weakened state, she could only think of one explanation for Lakeysia's victory.

"You must be using a cheat code," she said. "What is it? Invincibility? Or are you that good? You win, Detective. Game over."

Blackness spread like an encroaching cloud, enveloping Nicole's vision. The killer felt cold steel slap around her wrists.

"Don't move!" an unseen man yelled. The officer forced her legs apart and frisked her body. "Nicole Tasoto, you're under arrest for the murders of Toshigi Tasoto, Randall Forbes, Hannah Davies, Iris..."

The murderess smiled as he rolled off her victims' names. The agent insisted on doing everything formally, though the list wasn't in chronological order.

A lesser woman would have died from multiple gunshot wounds, but Nicole hung on until she heard him mention her most prized scalps: Thorne, Wilson, and Travis. The arresting officer saved those for last. When he finally got around to reading her Miranda rights, she blacked out.

# CHAPTER EIGHTEEN

## *After Green Comes Amber*

The Captain told Lakeysia the good news after doctors declared her fit to leave Adamson General. Once she'd passed a medical examination, the detective was to succeed Thorne as Lieutenant of Downtown Homicide Division.

She wasn't in the mood to celebrate her success. Too much blood had spilled over the past week for her to forget Nicole's victims, and her own partner was among the dead. Just like her fiancee, Travis had fallen prey to a deceptively beautiful assassin, an actress so skilled she'd convinced everyone of her innocence.

It was the last day of the year. Lakeysia was to be honored at a special awards dinner, where she would receive a commendation from the mayor personally. The City Hall bureaucrats considered her a hero despite the excessive body count. Was this a case of them building her up, only to knock her down later?

Before joining the festivities, the lieutenant elect asked her driver to take a detour to the Tasoto residence. The mansion had become something of a tourist haunt since Nicole's killing spree. Cyber Maiden diehards, anti-video game protesters and tabloid reporters had all made camp outside the iron gates.

She couldn't understand why people were so obsessed with criminals and their lifestyles. While the three murdered officers received small obituaries in the local newspaper, a psychotic killer got treated like a celebrity. Lakeysia chalked it off to humanity's dark nature. The one constant in this miserable world.

Crowds had thinned with the approach of New Year, and police were rounding up the few remaining drunks and stragglers. Forensics had already come and gone, and the house and grounds were strangely empty. An officer remained on guard while Matthews and his assistant concluded their investigation.

Lakeysia met up with them in the rear garden, at the site where they'd found the bodies of John and Jane Doe buried beneath the statue. Another grim discovery in this case, and hopefully the last.

"Detective Symons." The forensics man shook her hand, though his expression remained solemn. "I see you're out of hospital."

She peered into the empty grave. Even the crime scene markers had been removed.

"Keen sense of observation you got there, Matthews. No wonder we call you every time a stiff turns up. So this is where she left him, huh? Next to Cyber Maiden number three."

"Are you certain the victims are Kyle and Miss Knight? It's hard to make an identification without a facial comparison, fingerprints or dental records. We found no personal effects or clothes."

Lakeysia pulled a twenty-dollar bill from her wallet and carefully unfolded it.

"Well, the six ladies who looked at the man's remains seemed pretty sure it was Travis. Don't ask me, doc. It's the first time I seen the guy's you know what. As for the girl, how many missing red haired body builders can there be?"

"Your partner. He was a good man. I'm sorry."

Matthews bowed his head out of respect.

"Bastard owes me twenty bucks that I'll never collect, but it's only money, ain't it?" Lakeysia dropped the banknote in the hole. "Yeah, Travis was a good man. He just chose the wrong girl to sleep with. First Mei Tan and now this bitch. Oriental women can be real killers. Sure you still want to marry her?"

She glanced at Kari with a smile. Matthews took his assistant's hand. The couple hugged each other.

"Yes, I'm sure. I'm thinking of retiring, taking Kari away from all this. I don't want her to live out her life in a morgue."

"We all gotta go there eventually, I suppose. But maybe you should take a break. Right now, I have a ton of other problems to deal with. Twenty eager cops under my command and a killer who refuses to die."

"Nicole Tasoto's locked up securely, isn't she?" the doctor asked.

"Oh yeah. Psycho lady has a comfy, padded cell all to herself."

"So, what's the problem?"

Lakeysia thought the answer was glaringly obvious. It must be that optimism thing, again. She'd never understood it.

"The problem is, the bitch ain't dead. And you can bet your life she's got a plan."

***

Nurse Cynthia Faulkner buzzed out the last visitor, and then made her regular, half-hourly check in with the main office. The slightly built, tangerine haired woman was the appointed night receptionist for New Year's Eve. It was her sole responsibility to monitor the patients, and send for help if required.

The Bellman Psychiatric Institute's maximum security zone was a titanium lined, concrete fortress with space for fifty inmates. Only those declared certifiably insane were admitted, and these rooms held people considered both dangerous and crazy. Compulsive murderers who'd killed family members without remorse weren't so unusual in this place.

Low risk prisoners had access to exercise yards, dining halls and communal bedrooms with windows. The glass was armored, barred and alarmed, but still let in daylight. The more violent inmates were locked in padded solitary confinement rooms twenty-four hours a day. Armed guards issued meals through security drawers and kept them under constant surveillance.

The other night duty staff considered the containment wings escape proof and regularly scoffed at Cynthia's job. They wasted away their early mornings playing poker and the console game *Jade Dragon*, which had become popular in recent days following the arrest of Nicole Tasoto.

The newest high risk patient intrigued Cynthia. The disgraced games designer was one of only three female inmates confined to the restricted area. She was unique, since the other women were suicidal sociopaths who posed no threat to anyone but themselves.

To see Bellman's detainees, a visitor first needed a thorough background check and pre-approved clearance from a judge. Nobody outside the institute, including the police lieutenant who had incarcerated her, had been issued a pass for Nicole. For the time being, only medical personnel were allowed inside her cell, and even then, an escort was required.

There was one fatal flaw in the system: Cynthia. The hospital staff (especially those obnoxious guards) saw the twenty-eight-year-old nurse as a token employee. She slaved away on a derisory wage to support her son through college, while her superiors treated her as a social outcast. They continually snickered behind her back and promoted less qualified candidates for management duties.

Cynthia blamed herself for marrying an abusive, poorly educated dockworker and getting trapped in a dead-end marriage, but her husband earned more money than she did. Even though he spent half those wages on booze and drugs, their child would have no future without his support.

She had considered abandoning Trevor for a more pleasant partner, but lacked the nerve to file for divorce. Her spouse was almost two feet taller, weighed over three hundred pounds, and had no problem hitting a woman. The nurse had applied facial cream to hide her latest household dispute, but makeup couldn't heal her mental scars.

Nicole was her opposite: an intelligent girl that refused to be physically intimidated. The murderess had many qualities to admire. Despite her horrific crimes, Cynthia had a lot of sympathy. From what she'd read on the Internet, most of the victims had deserved her wrath.

As midnight arrived on the west coast, the nurse went

ahead with her plan. She ejected the surveillance tapes for the main corridor and room thirteen, left the reception booth, and pulled out her master security pass.

She had far more intelligence than her supervisor acknowledged. When he logged on to his system that morning, Cynthia had turned her monitor screen and observed his reflection. With his password, she'd created a skeleton key that gave her access to the entire facility.

She heard loud cheers and laughter from the security office. The guards pulled crackers and clinked beer bottles to usher in the New Year. They were too immersed in joking, singing rowdy songs, and watching television to bother with a lowly nurse.

Unopposed, she made her way to Nicole's cell, tiptoeing along the deserted hallway. When she reached room thirteen, she unlocked the door, prepared for her unauthorized interview, and stepped past the point of no return.

Nicole was awake, as if expecting a new year's visitor. Or perhaps she'd lost track of time, with no means to tell night from day. Apart from the prisoner, the cell was completely white: walls, floor, ceiling, bed and the drainage funnel that served as Nicole's lavatory.

Glowing cushions illuminated the cubical chamber. The halogen lamps were shielded and flush with the padding. Nicole had been bandaged and secured in a straight jacket. Smooth, unbreakable plastic clasps fastened the soft but tough material. Should she escape, committing suicide would not be easy.

"Happy new year, Nicole," Cynthia said, kneeling beside the bed.

The inmate smiled at her visitor. "I'd prefer it if you called me Jade. I have nothing to hide anymore. You're not a doctor. I haven't seen you visit me. What's your name?"

"Nurse Faulkner. I just want to talk. That's all."

She kept her distance, too fearful to approach. The killer's eyes moved from side to side. She scanned the room as if expecting a trap, then focused on her visitor.

"Do you think it was smart switching off the camera? Coming in here all by yourself?"

She had an all-knowing look in her eyes. Cynthia blinked, shuffling further away. A psychotic smile from the murderess. Perhaps visiting her alone hadn't been a good idea.

"A redhead. Meagan and Lenora had red hair. So did Carmen. You know about them, don't you? Of course you do, otherwise we wouldn't be talking. Would you like some advice on how to murder the bastards who've made your life a misery?"

"Just one," Cynthia said hesitantly. "Only one."

"After you've killed the first, you won't be able to stop. Believe me. I know. Beat a game on easy mode, and there's a higher difficulty level to try. It's the same with murder. You always want to improve your performance. Release me, then we can talk about your problem. Prove you have some guts, otherwise this is pointless. I don't make deals with wimps."

Nicole was ice cool, casually discussing death the way a sane person would mention the weather or sports results. Cynthia's knees wobbled as she reached for the strait jacket's strap. At the very last moment, the nurse withdrew her hand.

"You can't kill me," she said. "You need me to get out of here."

"Possibly, but friends are scarce. You're wise to be cautious. Had you let me go, I'd probably have strangled you to death with my sleeve. Nobody would have known."

A logical thinker would leave immediately at the suggestion, but Cynthia had no other options.

"You shut off the camera to keep our meeting secret," the inmate said. "The control's outside for security reasons, so you'd need a second person to close the door after you. And you came here alone. You almost gave me a free ticket out of here. But you're smarter than that. How refreshing. A positive sign."

Cynthia pulled a photograph from her uniform, a copy she'd made from Nicole's file. It showed a painting found at the prisoner's house. The picture was of a lady in green ninja garb. She was standing over a decapitated body, holding a black woman's severed head.

"My image of the ideal world," Nicole said. "That's the last one I drew. Do you like my work?"

Cynthia nodded tamely. "Can you..." she stuttered, then composed herself. "Can you help me kill my husband?"

"Sure. It's straightforward. Buy yourself a gun and shoot him point blank in the head. If you're having trouble killing a man, pretend it's a game. I find it easier when I do that."

"No. You don't understand. If I go to prison, how will I take care of my son?"

Nicole grinned mischievously. "The police won't arrest you if they believe his death was suicide, or self defense. You're obviously a smart woman, nurse. You'll think of a way."

"Please, would you call me Amber? Amber Scorpion. I came up with the name. Do you like it?"

Cynthia presented another photo to Nicole. It was a computer modification of the former picture. The ninja was now colored orange instead of green, and she'd superimposed a man's face over the severed head.

"That's Trevor, my husband. There are other people I need to take care of. The patronizing doctors here at the institute, for instance. And an old boyfriend who abandoned me for a cheerleader slut."

"One step at a time, Amber," Nicole said. "There are some things you have to learn first. Being able to break someone's neck is a very useful skill. And so is finding a scapegoat. Work on your face, too. Guys love sexy women. They'll even die for them. For now, celebrate the New Year. Go play *Jade Dragon*, and we'll talk in the morning."

The protégé smiled at her master. "I was planning on buying that game for my son. But first, I'm going to run Trevor a bath. He's in for a shock, though. I've told him how dangerous it is to blow his hair dry before getting out of the water, but he won't listen to a little girl like me. He'll have to learn the hard way. Not as messy as shooting him, and easier to explain."

Cynthia left Nicole's cell.

"Good night, Jade," she said. "I'll come visit you again sometime."

Then she closed the door. The prisoner's maniacal laughter ended abruptly as the soundproof seal clicked in place.

# ABOUT THE AUTHOR AND PUBLISHER

Andy Phillips was born in Oldham, England. He holds a PhD in Applied Mathematics and a BSc Joint Honours Maths/Physics degree. In a varied career, he has worked as a scientific researcher in the USA, a police intelligence analyst, a data analyst, and a higher education teacher.

From a very young age, he became fascinated with strong female characters — whether good, evil, or somewhere in between — that appeared in action, science fiction, and thriller movies. His favourite era is 1990s direct-to-video, back when VHS tapes and rental stores were still a thing. Determined to tell stories of his own, he wrote five freeware interactive fiction games, and later founded the publishing imprint *Action Girl Books*.

His novels deliver fast-paced tales of action, suspense, and danger, including multi-faceted plots, high-intensity scenes, and cinematic storytelling. He thrives on creating strong heroines and complex villainesses, often pitted against each other. Drawing inspiration from books, TV, and film, he hopes to inspire others to be creative, too.

# LICENSED IMAGES USED ON COVER

Depositphotos: 41978567
iStock: 2160073964